"Should I start another song, or should we...?"

Start another song, he wanted to say, but didn't.

He had the orchard to build.

He had Gran and Amanda to support and, despite her reluctance to return to Slippery Rock, their other sister, Mara.

He wasn't about to mess up the plans he had for a night with Savannah Walters, no matter how tempted he was to continue caressing her curves.

Reluctantly, Collin loosened Savannah's hands from his neck and stepped back.

"Thanks for the dance. I'll see you around," he said and quickly left the bar, calling himself all kinds of a coward for doing so.

It shouldn't matter who she was. It should only matter that she was a willing woman, he was a willing man and it had been nearly a full year since he'd...

But it did matter.

Savannah Walters was not the kind of woman to mess around with.

Dear Reader,

I hope you enjoy this first book in my new Slippery Rock series, *Famous in a Small Town*. Slippery Rock is a place that was born out of my past—I grew up in a small town near Truman Lake in Missouri. There are many man-made lakes in Missouri—most were made to help farmers and ranchers with irrigation, and most have been turned into tourist attractions. Despite the growth of these towns, they still have that mom-and-pop feel, with town squares and main streets, and where people still wave at one another as they pass by in their cars.

Famous in a Small Town is special to me because of the setting, but also because I wanted to write about a family like mine. My husband and I adopted our daughter through the foster care system, and while she doesn't have the attachment issues that Savannah does, we've faced other hurdles, and those hurdles drew us closer together. An adoption quote that's very special goes: "Family isn't always blood. It's the people in your life who want you in theirs; the ones who accept you for who you are. The ones who would do anything to see you smile and who love you no matter what." That is the kind of family that both Savannah and Collin find...and it is the kind of love and family that I hope all of you find, too.

Have a great read!

Kristina Knight

KRISTINA KNIGHT

—

Famous in a Small Town

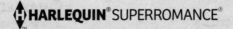

HARLEQUIN® SUPERROMANCE®

Recycling programs
for this product may
not exist in your area.

ISBN-13: 978-0-373-64027-0

Famous in a Small Town

Printed in U.S.A.

www.Harlequin.com

Kristina Knight decided she wanted to be a writer, like her favorite soap opera heroine, Felicia Gallant, one cold day when she was home sick from school. She took a detour into radio and television journalism but never forgot her first love of romance novels, or her favorite character from her favorite soap. In 2012 she got The Call from an editor who wanted to buy her book. Kristina lives in Ohio with her handsome husband, incredibly cute daughter and two dogs.

Books by Kristina Knight

HARLEQUIN SUPERROMANCE

The Daughter He Wanted
First Love Again
Protecting the Quarterback

A Slippery Rock Novel

Famous in a Small Town

For my Brainstormers: Connie, Jill, Jenna, Sloan, Katelynn, Shay. You inspire so much laughter, you offer such unreserved friendship, and I appreciate you all to the moon and back. xoxo ~ K

Acknowledgment

Special thanks to Julie Kyer, who answered question after question about reactive attachment disorder (RAD), the foster care system, family counseling and adoptive family dynamics. It takes a special kind of person to be a social worker, and Julie is one of those special people. I am forever thankful for her friendship, and for her willingness to be an advocate for children everywhere.

CHAPTER ONE

DECISION TIME.

Savannah Walters sat staring at the faded red stop sign at a crossroads—one would lead her into complete anonymity and the other back to a place where everyone knew who she was.

Anonymity beckoned, slick and sweet. A simple left-hand turn onto the southbound lane of a rural highway in southwestern Missouri. She would roll the windows down in her old Honda, smell the freshly mowed highway grass and maybe pass a tractor or twelve before she hit the next town, a town with a bigger road leading to an interstate that would lead her...anywhere.

She hit the turn signal even though there were no other cars on this stretch of blacktop and listened to the *click-click-click* of it for a long moment. All she had to do was make the turn. This was her chance. A bigger chance than the one she'd taken when she'd elected to go to Nashville. A bigger chance than the one she'd taken to get onto the reality talent show that had made the

Nashville move possible. No one would ever have to know she was *that* Savannah Walters again.

Hell, if she wanted, she could change her name completely and maybe cut off the signature micro-braids she'd spent three days installing, then no one would even make a tiny connection between her and about-to-fall-from-grace, one-hit-wonder Savannah Walters. She could be anything and anyone she wanted. The thought made her giddy. If she could, she would choose to be smart, strong and capable, rather than the dumb, weak and dependent person she'd been since she'd landed in Slippery Rock, Missouri, at the age of seven.

Her second-chance self would have a name like Nancy Smith because there had to be a million Nancy Smiths in the world. Nancy Smith would only sing in the shower or in the car with her windows rolled up. She would work as a bank teller and wear normal clothes without a single rhinestone, and maybe once she was settled she'd go to dental hygienist school. She would eventually buy a small house in a quiet neighborhood, and maybe she would meet a nice guy—not in a bar—and have a real relationship for the first time in her twenty-seven years.

Savannah's heart a beat a little faster. Nancy Smith wouldn't care what people thought of her. She would be stronger than that. Stronger than

Savannah Walters, who had been afraid of what people thought of her for...most of her life.

Nancy Smith would not be afraid, but she also wouldn't be reckless. There would be no judgmental dinner conversations, no too-high expectations and no comparisons to a brother who always did the right thing. She would be the opposite of Savanna Walters of Slippery Rock.

There would also be no midnight walks along the lakeshore with that boy—man, now—who couldn't help being practically perfect; it was simply his way. No whispered conversations through their bedroom windows on hot summer nights. No smell of Mama Hazel's coffee cake on lazy Sunday mornings and no comforting hugs or encouraging words from the only father she had ever known.

No disappointed looks when the three people who had saved her so very long ago learned that she, once again, had made every possible wrong decision.

God, she wanted to turn left. Take the easy road. They wouldn't really miss her. It might even be easier for them if she just kept driving out of their lives. Choosing to adopt her didn't mean they had to be stuck with her screwed-up self for the rest of their lives.

The turn signal kept clicking. Savannah checked the rearview, but there were still no other vehicles on the narrow country road, and so she continued to weigh her options. This might be the last chance she had to make a right decision, and it needed to be right not only for her but also for the people around her.

She hadn't had a choice about coming to Slippery Rock before, but it was her choice whether or not she returned now.

Maybe if she stopped running away from Savannah Walters she would finally stop mucking up this life she'd been given. Savannah clicked off the turn signal and rested her forehead against the steering wheel. Maybe it was time to stop being afraid of who she might have been, and time to start figuring out who she wanted to be now. She couldn't do that by running away.

It was worth a shot.

Before she could talk herself out of it, Savannah turned right. She rolled the window down and caught the faint scent of new grass. Tall trees lined both sides of the road. Maybe oak; she'd never bothered to learn the names of trees or the grasses along the road, or the vegetables whose baby stems were just beginning to show through the pencil-straight rows of tilled soil. Naming everything from the crops to the trees seemed too personal. She'd been waiting for her new family to send her away, to decide they didn't want her, either. Now she wished she'd paid at least a little attention to Bennett and Levi, her adoptive father and brother, while they'd talked at all those family dinners.

The city limits sign, with its welcome message from the local chapters of fraternal organizations, churches and veteran's groups came into view just as the engine coughed once, twice, and the car rolled to a stop.

Savannah clicked the key to the off position and then back on. Pressed the gas a couple of times and tried again. Nothing. Not even the clicking sound of a dead battery. She glared at the illuminated red check-engine light that had been on since she'd bought the car with her tip money from the Slope, where she'd chosen to clean up and wait tables instead of take a scholarship at a nearby college. Because she convinced herself she wasn't good enough for college. Of course, if she'd done the college thing, she'd have never tried the talent show and wouldn't have had a song on country radio.

Wouldn't be running from scandal now.

The blinking engine light she'd ignored for nearly four years mocked her. One more checkmark in the Savannah the Screwup column.

If she'd only turned left, the stupid car would have run without so much as a twinge, she was positive about that. Lord, sometimes doing the right thing just sucked.

Anyone else would arrive back in her hometown driving an Escalade and find a parade in her honor. Savannah had a broken-down Honda with more than two hundred thousand miles on it. And she'd have to call her parents just to make it into town.

She thunked her head against the steering wheel a few times, but that didn't make the check-engine light flicker off or the car miraculously start back up. The last thing she wanted to do was to call her parents. Maybe some of that car talk—Bennett helped Levi build his first car from parts found at the local salvage yard—at the dinner table had sunk in by osmosis or something.

Heaving out a sigh, Savannah popped the hood of her car and then stepped onto the pavement. The light wind was brisk—she should have remembered early May in Missouri was touch-and-go weather-wise—so she grabbed her neon-yellow hoodie from the passenger seat and shoved her arms through the sleeves.

At the front of the car, she pulled on the cherry-red hood but it didn't budge. She tugged on it again and then bent to see the hook still caught in the hood latch. She hit the hood, trying to jar the hook loose, but no matter what she did the hook remained safely in the latch. There must be a mechanism in there somewhere that released it. Savannah bent to look between the narrow spaces of the grille, but didn't see anything that looked like it might release the latch.

Crap, crap, crap.

Turning, she crossed her arms over her chest and leaned against the hood.

There were two options: walk the five or so miles to her childhood home or call the house so someone could come pick her up.

A responsible person would probably walk it, but Savannah had already done the responsible thing by not turning left and look where that had gotten her: stranded on the side of the road at six thirty in the evening. She sighed.

Call home. Like she'd done a hundred times in the past. Well, better now than in the middle of the night.

She grabbed her phone from her bag on the passenger seat and scrolled until she found the word *home*, clicked the button and stopped. The sound of an engine caught her ear. Maybe she wouldn't have to make that call, after all.

A dusty, blue truck rolled to a stop behind the old Honda and a broad-shouldered man sat behind the wheel, looking at her for a long minute. Savannah stiffened under his scrutiny. It was unlikely she had ever spoken to whoever was behind the wheel. When she'd lived in Slippery Rock she'd only had a handful of friends, and most of them had hung out with her just hoping to get to her brother. She tilted her head to the side, still studying the big truck. Not a single one of them would be caught dead in a big farm truck like the one taking up space behind her little car.

Dread crept down her spine.

It was likely, however, that whoever was behind the wheel knew her brother. Or her father. For all she knew, he was now making the call she should've swallowed her pride to make as soon as the engine gave out, instead of pretending she knew anything about general car repair. Or maintenance. Her knowledge of the car began and ended with how to put gas in the tank.

Well, this wasn't going to get better if she didn't get the man out of the truck. Savannah swallowed and offered a halfhearted wave.

"Hey," she began as the man opened the door of his truck and stepped down to the pavement.

Dusty boots to match the dusty truck, along with the frayed end of a pair of faded jeans appeared below the open door. Then he slammed it shut and the rest of him came into view.

Well-worn jeans covered a pair of nicely shaped legs. A red T-shirt with a grease stain near the hem hinted at a nice set of abs, and the tight sleeves highlighted a set of biceps that made her mouth go a little dry. Which was just silly. Savannah didn't go for athletes.

She liked gangly guys who knew how to work their instruments, and not the double-entendre instrument. Their guitars or drums or, a couple of times, keyboards.

He started toward her and it was as if her body went on point. Savannah stood a little straighter, every muscle seemed to clench and a warm heat sizzled to life deep in her belly.

Apparently gangly musician wasn't her only type.

Finally her gaze arrived at the man's face and her mouth went from dry to Sahara. This wasn't a stranger. And he wasn't a friend.

"Savannah Walters. I heard you were living it up in Nashville." Collin Tyler, her brother's best friend, shook his head at her. His voice was deeper than she remembered, and she thought he might even be taller. He was definitely rangier, and there was no way his arms had been that built in high school.

Not that she was looking, now or then.

Savannah ordered her gaze to fix on the truck behind Collin.

"Collin Tyler," she said, thankful that her voice was working despite her raging thirst. "Still a Good Samaritan, I see."

He shrugged, and the motion brought her focus right back to his body. Damn it.

"What seems to be the problem?" he asked,

walking over to the car. His hands slipped between the hood and the grille and before she could warn him it was stuck, he had it unlatched and resting on the thin rod that held the hood aloft. Collin put his hands on the grille and leaned in as if he might spot the problem. Probably, he could. He fiddled with a couple of wires. "What are you doing driving this old thing still? Figured you have traded up by now."

"I love this car."

Collin shook his head and scoffed. "Nobody loves a 1997 Honda hatchback, Van," he said, using the nickname that Levi had christened her within five minutes of her arrival at Walters Ranch.

"I worked hard for this car. I love this car," Savannah said, probably a little too stridently. But she did love the car. Even if she wanted something newer and trendier and…road-worthy. This car had taken her out of Missouri to Los Angeles then Nashville. And back again.

"Slinging beers at the Slope isn't exactly working hard." He fiddled with a few more wires but, to Savannah, everything looked fine.

"And watching apple trees grow is hard work?" Savannah knew there was more to Collin's family orchard than watching trees grow, but she couldn't just stand there while he insulted her car. She might know it was decrepit, but allowing someone to disparage it just felt wrong. They'd been down a lot of roads together.

"Actually it's apples and pears and peaches now. And in addition to watching them grow I like to prune from time to time, fertilize, and every now and again we actually pick the fruit, too." He motioned her to the driver's seat. "Why don't you try turning it over now?"

Savannah slid behind the wheel and turned the key. "Nothing," she called out. As if he couldn't tell the engine hadn't come back to life. "Idiot," she mumbled. She returned to the front of the car. "Is there still a tow truck in town?"

"Bud still has one, but he closes at five."

She checked her watch. Nearly seven. Calling Bud would have to wait until morning. Collin eyed her for a long moment as if weighing his options, and then went around to the driver's side, sliding behind the wheel. Savannah watched as he turned the key.

"Did you know your check-engine light's on?"

"Yes, I was aware."

"What's wrong with it?"

"Nothing, it's been on like that since I bought the car," she said, deliberately baiting him. She didn't know why. Collin Tyler was one of the nicest guys she'd ever known, even if he'd barely said ten words to her during her entire life. Outside of this conversation, anyway.

Collin sighed. "I meant what's wrong with the engine," he said, and she thought she detected a bit of annoyance in his voice. Good, he was annoying her, too. He could just get right back in his dirty, old truck with his dirty shirt and dirty jeans and she'd call the ranch and get on with her humiliating re-entry to life in Slippery Rock, Missouri.

Couldn't be any more humiliating than the way she'd left Nashville; the only thing missing from her exit had been the proverbial "A" she was positive a few people would have liked to sew onto her clothes.

"How would I know what's wrong with the car?"

"You never had it checked?" He leaned out of the car and, despite the waning sunshine, she could clearly see the incredulous look in his clear, blue gaze. "You've had this car at least four years, Savannah."

"They never said anything about it when I had the oil changed. Which I do religiously, every three thousand miles, just like the manual says."

"Did you even ask them? Did you take it to the dealership?"

"Of course not, I was in LA and then Nashville. I wasn't driving it back to Slippery Rock to have the oil changed. I took it to one of those 'thirty minutes or it's free' places."

Collin sent her a pitying look. Savannah stood straighter. Of course, she should have had the check-engine light checked but after a while, it became a kind of game. See just how far she could go before something happened. And then she'd mostly forgotten about it, chalking it up to a defective sensor or an overactive light or… something.

"Not the dealership here. A general Honda dealership where they could run diagnostics."

"Oh." She hadn't thought another dealership would look at her third-hand Honda. God, she was an idiot. "It's never done anything like this before. If it had, I would have taken the light more seriously."

He sighed and the sound had an interesting effect on her. All the heat that had been building up inside her morphed into a burning desire to smack the long-suffering look right off his face. Up until she'd made the right turn instead of the left, Savannah hadn't had a violent bone in her body. Interesting.

"A check-engine light, all on its own, is serious."

"As I discovered when the car stopped working. For now, could we save the lecture? I'm sure I'll do something equally stupid at some point, and then I'll happily listen to you drone on and—"

"Did you check any of your other gauges?" he interrupted.

Savannah blinked. "No."

"Because the battery seems to be fine, the coolant isn't off the charts, but the gas seems completely nonexistent."

She peered over Collin's shoulder. Sure enough, the red gas gauge pointed straight down, hanging at least an inch under the letter E.

She really was an idiot. Savannah closed her eyes, and would have thunked her head against the roof of the car had Collin not still been sitting in her seat.

"I didn't think to check that," she said, her voice quiet.

"I've got a full can in the truck—never know when you're going to need gas on the farm." He climbed out of the car and pushed past Savannah.

"Of course you do," she said to the air.

Collin Tyler, Good Samaritan, would never let his vehicle run out of gas. He would never ignore a check-engine light, and if his vehicle did run out of gas or stop working for some reason, he would have a solution.

Savannah Walters, Screwup, would forget to check her tank when she left Memphis, and would run out of gas five miles from her destination.

He returned with the portable can, opened the

tank and began filling it through a large yellow funnel.

"This old can only holds a couple of gallons, but it'll get you into town. You should fill up as soon as possible." And there he went with the free advice. He just couldn't help himself. And here she was wanting to stomp her feet or sink into the ground.

Running out of gas. It was a teenage mistake, not something a twenty-seven-year-old should do.

Collin finished filling the tank, closed the hatch and nodded. "See if she'll fire this time," he said.

Savannah slid behind the wheel and said a *please, please, please* before cranking the key. When the engine roared to life, she sank back against the beige seat.

Collin tossed the gas can into the bed of the truck and then crossed back to the front of the Honda, closing the hood. He tapped twice on the roof of the car. "Gas up on your way out to the ranch, Savannah, and get that check-engine thing looked at. Better to be safe than sorry."

He offered a quick wave and in a moment was behind the wheel of his truck. He pulled around her, honked his horn once and drove toward the setting sun.

Better to be safe than sorry.

Savannah closed her door and then pressed back into the seat.

She glanced into the rearview and smirked. "Well, Savannah, not making that left really is turning out to be a great decision." She put the car in Drive and continued through to the town.

The last rays of sunlight sank into the earth as she turned off the main road and onto the gravel lane that led to her childhood home.

She'd stopped in town to fill the gas tank. There'd been no sign of Collin or his big truck, thankfully, and the kid working the register in the station had barely looked up from his magazine long enough to take the twenty she'd pushed across the counter. Then she took the long way to the ranch, so that it was now after eight. For as long as she could remember, Bennett and Mama Hazel retired to their master suite by eight, and they were both up before dawn.

She stopped for a moment under an old maple tree. The porch light was on, glimmering in the twilight, as it had been every night for as long as she could remember. The last one in for the night was supposed to turn it off, and she wondered if Levi was the straggler tonight or if their parents had changed that eight o'clock bedtime habit.

Her brother, older by nine months and a full school year, rarely stayed out late. Or at least he hadn't when they were kids. She had no idea what he did as an adult. He'd been gone, to college and then playing in the NFL, while she'd finished school and waited tables at the Slope. She'd left for the reality show just before the injury that had taken him out of football forever.

Didn't matter. She would park, grab her overnight bag from the backseat and worry about the rest of her luggage tomorrow. Assuming she stayed past tomorrow. Savannah was still unsure just what she wanted to do. Go or stay. Wait out the scandal she knew was coming or run as fast and as far from it as she could.

Her father's beat-up F-150 sat under a tall tree at the side of the house, along with a newer model that had Levi written all over it—from the flat-black paint job to the chromed bumpers and roll bar. Mama Hazel's familiar station wagon was gone, probably traded in for the navy sedan that sat under the carport. Savannah couldn't remember the last time Mama Hazel drove herself anywhere, but she liked to have a car handy "just in case."

Huh. All the cars were accounted for, so who'd left the light on?

She took a deep breath as she pulled the old Honda in behind Bennett's truck.

Savannah climbed the steps of the familiar farmhouse with her overnight bag slung over her shoulder. Her hand shook as she reached for the white-enamel doorknob and she willed it to still. This was her home. The place she was safe.

How many times had she been told that as a child? Never, not a single time, had she wanted those words to be true more than she did now. There was a storm coming, one that could shatter her, and she had a feeling she would need the strength of these old walls if she were to withstand it. Maybe, just maybe, if she hid here long enough the storm would never come.

Her agent had said as much. If she left quietly, if she stayed away, maybe nothing would come of her indiscretion.

Savannah swallowed hard and twisted the knob. The door swung in, opening to the small entryway with its familiar hardwood floors and the same brass hat rack in the corner that she remembered from her childhood. Stairs, with that familiar navy blue carpet runner, rose a few feet in front of her, dividing the living area from the dining room and kitchen. A lamp remained on near Mama Hazel's rocking chair, the book she was reading lying pages-down on the seat, and in the low light she could see the pictures of Levi and her lining the wall. Levi's trophies were on the mantel. She crossed the room, ran her fingers over a new frame and caught her breath.

They'd framed the write-up in the *Slippery Rock Gazette* of her third-place finish in the talent show. She hadn't even called them after, had just said yes to the trip to Nashville and taken off. Under the frame was a copy of a music magazine with her smiling face on the cover. It ran the week her first single hit the top twenty before beginning its slow descent back down the charts.

"Van." The softly spoken word startled her, and she turned. Levi stood in the gloominess, coffee cup in hand. He wore his usual jeans and T-shirt, his dark-skinned arms looking like the trunks of a couple of the trees she'd passed on the highway. He still kept his hair cropped close to his head, and even in the darkness, she thought his deep brown eyes had just a hint of amber.

It was the same amber her eyes had. When they were kids, she liked to make up stories about how she'd been adopted by her birth family, and the people who'd had her before had been her kidnappers.

Of course, that had only been wishful thinking. The Walters family was wonderful, but they weren't hers. Her family had left her on the steps of a police station in Springfield with a note pinned to her chest.

Name: Savannah
Birthday in May
Seven years old

Eight freaking words on a note she couldn't erase from her memory.

"What are you doing here?"

Did he know? Levi always seemed to know when she was in trouble. She willed her thundering heart to slow. There was no way he could know what had happened this time. She'd been listening to the radio all day, and if the story had broken, she knew the DJs would be talking about it nonstop. So far, it seemed Genevieve was sticking to her word and keeping the whole sordid thing a secret. He couldn't know, she told herself.

"I, uh, needed a break from the tour," she said, deciding that was the safest answer. No one knew she'd been offered an extended touring gig with Genevieve's crew. An offer that had been summarily revoked later that night when Genevieve had ended the set early and found Savannah exiting her tour bus. "And I haven't been back here since the finale eighteen months ago."

Levi nodded. "You look good," he said. "Mama and Dad would have waited up if they'd known you were coming."

"I'll just surprise them at breakfast," she said. "What are you doing here, anyway? Shouldn't you have a house of your own by now?"

"I do. Used the foundation of the cabin," he said, motioning to the general area where the first Walters cabin had stood more than one hundred years before. Her father had torn down the walls when she was eleven, after she'd nearly been struck by a falling rafter inside. "They're finishing up the plumbing and then the floors, and I'll move in."

"You always loved that old place." She reached for something more to say but wasn't sure where to start. She never talked to Levi about why he'd walked away from his professional football contract. Everyone knew about the injury, but from what she'd seen on those Sunday-morning sports talk shows, he could have made a comeback. She didn't ask then, and it seemed almost too late to ask now. Besides, he'd never asked why she was so hell-bent on a reality talent show when, before leaving Slippery Rock, she'd been petrified of singing in the Christmas pageant at church.

Levi watched her and she wondered what he saw. Wondered how she could make sure he and the rest of her family never saw how truly bad she could be. She would figure out how to live with the shame of sleeping with a married man, but she didn't want any of that shame to fall on them.

"The porch light's still on." She grabbed at the only conversation starter she could think of. "You expecting someone?"

Levi glanced over his shoulder and a small

smile played over his wide mouth. "That light's not for me. It's been on since you left for the talent show. I turned it off once and the next morning Mama just about stripped me bare with her words. I didn't know she even knew that kind of language." He sipped from the mug in his hands.

Savannah blinked. The light was on...for her? After all this time? Emotion clogged her throat. To keep her threatening tears from falling, she focused on breathing.

"You want coffee? Something to eat?"

She shook her head, unable to talk as she stared at the thick, mahogany door and the glimmer of porch light she could see through the side windows. The light was still on, more than two years after she'd left, for her? She drew in an unsteady breath.

"Well, I was headed up for the night. We're planting alfalfa in the western field before dawn, and I still have some computer work to do before I turn in. You remember the way upstairs?"

If anyone else had said the words, the emotions she was feeling would have dried up in an angry burst. But this was Levi, and those were the same five words he'd been saying to her since that night twenty years before when Hazel and Bennett had brought her home to Walters Ranch.

"I remember," she said, but the words were barely a whisper.

Levi nodded and turned toward the staircase. He paused at the door. "Last one in, remember?" he asked, and Savannah could only nod.

In a moment, he'd disappeared up the stairs, and she was alone in the familiar living room with Mama Hazel's rocker and the porch light shining through the windows.

Slowly, Savannah made her way to the front door. She looked out, seeing vague shapes in the darkness beyond the porch. It was barely nine o'clock at night, and if she were in Nashville, she would just be going out for the night. But this was small-town Missouri, where farmers hit the fields before dawn and went to bed soon after sundown. Her fingers rested lightly on the porch light switch.

The emotion she'd held back when Levi was still in the room tore through her like a planter tore the ground during spring seeding. Her fingers shook and she tried to blink back the tears.

They'd left the porch light on for more than two years. For her.

Savannah depressed the switch, and the light flicked off in an instant.

Maybe this time, she really was home.

CHAPTER TWO

COLLIN GLANCED AT the clock on the dash as he accelerated the truck on the highway. He should have kept driving when he realized it was Savannah Walters on the side of the road playing at being a damsel in distress. Ignoring the red check-engine light. Running her car out of gas.

He didn't need her kind of drama right now.

Although why she was still driving that old beater of a car when she had a fat record deal in Nashville was curious.

Curiosity—and a penchant for drama, he'd always been certain—killed the cat. And he had no intention of going down just now.

Collin pulled into a parking spot on main drag of town, just a couple of blocks from the marina and the lake. He'd left his window rolled down and could hear a few gulls calling out in the evening air.

James Calhoun, one of his best friends and a deputy sheriff, waited on the steps to the sheriff's office. He wore the county uniform of khaki pants and shirt, the dark utility belt holding his gun and other cop paraphernalia around his waist, and he'd pushed his aviator sunglasses to the top of his head.

Seeing Collin, he started down the walk.

"She's inside. A little scared, I think, but she's hiding the scared pretty far under the usual teenage attitude."

Collin stepped out of the truck and met James on the sidewalk. "Damages?"

"She swears she wasn't in on it, and I tend to believe her. From what I've been able to get from the others, she was walking by when the fire started in the parking lot, and ran over to try to help put it out."

Well, that was a new one. Usually when the sheriff's department called about his little sister, the call was to come bail her out for some minor offence or another. At least this time she'd been trying to do the right thing.

"Thanks for calling my cell instead of the house. The last thing Gran needs is more Amanda worries." He grabbed the bill of his ball cap from his back pocket and shoved it over his head.

"No worries. How's Gladys doing?"

"Physical therapy three times a week, simple exercises every day to build up her strength. The doctor says she'll be getting around without the walker before long." Collin wasn't so sure. He'd seen his grandmother's post–hip replacement progress for himself, but there was something not quite right about her. He'd caught her staring into the distance a few times as if she didn't quite understand what she was seeing, and he'd had to remind her of dates and events several times over the past few weeks.

"I kept her out of the main holding area, since she wasn't actually involved in starting the fire," James said, motioning Collin up the sidewalk. "I have to tell you, though, I'm pretty much alone in my belief in her innocence. She's been involved in too many other incidents lately. A few of the officers think all eight of those kids should have the book thrown at them."

"And you're stuck in the middle."

"Call me Switzerland." James opened the door to the office and they stepped inside. There was no hectic movement, no scanners chattering in the growing gloom. The Slippery Rock sheriff's office at seven thirty on a Friday night was as quiet as a church on Monday morning. The receptionist had gone home and the 9-1-1 center in the next county took care of most dispatch calls.

God, but he loved his small town. He just loved it a little more when his sister wasn't doing her best to become a criminal.

"You shouldn't have to play peacemaker between my little sister and your squad room."

"Stuck in the middle is no place I haven't been a time or two, and since the other kids cleared her, there's no reason to add another asterisk to her record." He put his hand on Collin's arm. "But, Col, you're gonna have to talk to her at some point about the mischief calls, the skipping curfew. She's headed down a dangerous road."

James flipped on the fluorescent lights as he led Collin behind the bulletproof glass protecting the reception area. Collin knew from a school field trip that the holding cells were in the basement along with a storm shelter, the deputy's cubicles in the back half of the first floor, and that their workout room shared space with the department's small armory on the second floor. He followed James through the maze of cubicles.

Collin sighed. "Yeah. I know." He just didn't know how to have the conversation that Amanda obviously needed. He wasn't her father or even a guardian.

Since Gladys's fall just before the holidays, Amanda had been on a tear. Skipping curfew, getting speeding tickets as if she were trying to make the *Guinness Book of World Records*. She'd even been caught defacing the fountain in the square by filling it with laundry detergent. Amanda needed parents and he didn't have a clue how to fill that role for her.

"She's not a bad kid."

"I know that, too." She was just messed up, the way they'd all been messed up by their parents. Samson and Maddie Tyler had been absentee parents for half of Collin's life, and nearly all of Amanda's. There would be the occasional birthday card, and one year they showed up at Christmas, but for the most part the people who were supposed to parent Collin, Amanda and their sister, Mara, had simply not.

"I can get you guys into family counseling, if you think it would help."

Sitting in a stuffy office talking about their lack of parental supervision sounded like the fifth circle of hell to Collin. But maybe it wasn't such a bad idea. Something had to have set Amanda off and, despite all his efforts to talk to his baby sister, he hadn't been able to figure out what it was.

"I'll think about it."

They rounded a corner and he saw Amanda sitting cross-legged in an old plastic chair. Her long blond hair was pulled up in a high ponytail and she wore her old Converse sneakers—with fresh scorch marks—along with ripped-up jeans and a sweatshirt with an image of the galaxy and the words You Are Here with an arrow on it.

Collin wanted to shake her. She was here, in a police station, when she could be home with her family. All she had to do was stop whatever crazy train she'd jumped on.

Amanda chewed on her bottom lip and wrapped and unwrapped the string from her hoodie around her finger. She was just a kid. A lost, hurt kid, and he was doing a crap job of making her feel safe.

"Collin's here," James said as they neared the cubicle.

Amanda straightened in her chair, put her feet on the floor and folded her arms over her chest. "I didn't do anything wrong. You didn't have to bother him."

"How else were you going to get home, kid? You're grounded from the car, remember?" James backed away, leaving them to sort this out without him.

Amanda eyed him for a long minute. "I've got two legs."

"You'd rather walk the ten miles back to the orchard than spend fifteen minutes in the truck with me, huh?" Collin asked, leaned a shoulder against the cubicle wall.

Amanda twisted her mouth to the side. "I didn't want you to be bothered."

And just like that, Collin wanted to shake her again. She wasn't a bother to him, she was his sister. But no matter what he did, he just seemed to mess things up between them. After speeding ticket number four, he'd taken her car keys. After the laundry soap incident, he'd banned her from being out after five.

He wasn't sure what he could take away from her for this latest stunt.

Hell, maybe he should give something back. After all, she'd helped to put out the fire the other teens had set. A fire that could have decimated the courthouse square or that might have killed or seriously injured someone.

Maybe even Amanda.

"You're not a bother, kid."

She mumbled something he didn't quite hear. He waited, but she didn't say anything else.

Collin shoved his hands into his pockets, unsure what to do next. He needed her to know she wasn't a nuisance to him. But her actions lately were a nuisance to him. A nuisance and a worry. He was doing his best to keep the orchard profitable, to keep Amanda comfortable, to ensure their grandmother's recovery. His job was to keep everything and everyone in their little circle together, and he felt as if he was losing his grip on every single aspect.

He hooked his thumb toward the front door. "How about we get out of here?"

Amanda shrugged but she stood quickly and slung her backpack over her shoulder. "I'm free to go?"

"Unless you're changing your story about the fire," James said. He stood near the wall.

"I just tried to help put it out. I didn't even know they were in that alley until I smelled the smoke." She shot James a look from the corner of her eye, and Collin fisted his hands. She knew more than she was letting on.

"That's good enough for me, then," James said, using his cop voice.

"If it's good enough for the law..." Collin teased, but he wasn't rewarded with one of Amanda's reluctant smiles. Her shoulders stiffened and her mouth turned down at the corners. "Just a joke, kiddo. You said you weren't involved in the setting, just the dousing. That's all that matters."

She mumbled something else under her breath and didn't meet his eyes.

"Amanda—" he began, but she interrupted.

"Can we just go home?"

"Sure."

Once they were in the truck and clear of the sheriff's office, Collin said, "You want to talk about it?"

"About what?"

"About why you were still in town when you know you (a) don't have a car, and (b) still have a curfew, and I'm going to add a C to it—why did you lie to James about your involvement?"

She pressed her lips together. "Fine, we'll start with the easy one. Why didn't you ride the bus home after school?"

Amanda crossed her arms over her chest, a move Collin was all too familiar with. He'd done the same too many times to count when he was a teenager, but their sister, Mara, had made the gesture a near art form. "I'm seventeen years old. The bus is vile," Amanda declared.

"So you were...what? Going to walk the ten miles out to the orchard and you just *happened* to come across a few pyromaniacs who were trying to set the courthouse on fire?"

"They were just testing the combustion rates of visco fuses and spolettes. After the fire marshal did his talk about fireworks safety leading up to the Memorial Day Kick Off the Summer celebration, they got the idea that they'd mess with the fuses for the big fireworks show. Trick the workers into thinking they'd bought a bunch of duds, and then scare the crap out of them when everything started going off at once."

Collin gripped the steering wheel harder. That could have gotten someone seriously hurt. "And you know this how?"

Amanda blew out a breath. "I was hiding out under the bleachers in the gym during health class, and I heard them planning it all out."

"You skipped class—"

"For the five millionth time, Mr. Acres is doing the unit on intercourse. I couldn't face another hour of bananas and condom demonstrations. I swear he gets off on lubing up the fruits." She shivered with disgust.

Collin blinked and squeezed the steering wheel. "We'll get back to that in a minute. You skipped class, you overheard them talking about this prank and you…what, wanted to join in?"

"No, I was going to show them that what they were planning wouldn't work. And then I was going to show them what *would* work, but Courtney Gains is an idiot and instead of setting up the fuses on something nonflammable and using slow-burning punks to light them, he used his dad's grill lighter and stuck all the fuses on top of his backpack."

Collin wasn't sure where to begin. The skipping of class or the destruction of public property that Amanda nearly took part in because she'd wanted to see it done correctly. He was so in over his head here.

"And what would you have done differently?"

"Replaced all the usual fuses with fast-burning but connected fuses. Instead of delaying the explosions, which could get someone hurt, everything would just go off at once and without the delay. Simple. Added benefit? It would be prettier than a usual 'light one rocket, wait five minutes, light another, wait another five minutes' show."

Collin made the turn from the highway onto the gravel road leading to the orchard.

"Why?" It was the only question he thought he could ask without getting pseudo-parent-y and…angry.

"Why what?"

"Why mess with the fireworks? Why not just let people have a fun night without a bunch of drama and craziness?"

Amanda pulled her lower lip between her teeth and then turned her head to look out the window. Moonlight hit the apple trees blooming pink and white in the fields surrounding them. The pear and peach trees behind the main house would bloom later in the spring. He wondered what she saw in the fields. Did she see the security he saw? Or did she see only trees?

"This is dangerous, Amanda. Can't you see that?"

"It was just a prank, and now it's nothing because the fuse has already been lit once. They'll be expecting it."

Collin pulled the truck to a stop at the side of the main house and blew out a breath. "Pranks hurt people, Amanda—"

"It was just going to be a joke, Collin, jeez."

"And speeding down Main Street was a joke?

What if some kid ran out into the street chasing his ball? Would that have been a joke?" Her face paled, but Amanda kept her mouth in that stubborn line. "What if the detergent trick had clogged the line and flooded someone's house? Or if the stupid bubbles had blocked part of the road? Just another funny?"

"None of those things happened. And you and Mara did worse."

"That isn't the point."

"Of course it isn't. The point is I screwed up. Again. I'm not the amazing, the wonderful, the never-get-caught Collin Tyler, football hero and member of the Sailor Five. I'm just Amanda. The forgettable," she said, grabbing her backpack and running from the truck. Amanda slammed the front door, making the spring wreath of tulips bounce against the wood.

Sailor Five. Damn it, anyway. He'd been part of a winning football team, along with James, Levi Walters, Aiden and Adam Buchanan. Yes, winning the state football championship was a big deal, and yes, the five of them, along with Mara, had pulled their share of pranks and gotten away with it. Was that what this was all about? Amanda felt she was, what, being overshadowed by something he did in high school? That was just silly. The Sailor Five was in the past. Tyler Orchard, their family, their friends, those were the things that were important.

He should follow her. Go upstairs and make her talk to him. He wasn't some infallible god. The last four months were evidence enough of that. But going after Amanda would just lead to another misunderstanding. He would let her cool down. They could talk again in the morning.

God, he was so out of his depth.

CHAPTER THREE

"How did you not know she was back in town?" Adam Buchanan narrowed his eyes at the dartboard six feet in front of him, cocked his arm and threw. The dart embedded itself into the paneled wall several inches to the right of its target.

"It's called having a life. You should try it sometime." Collin marked down the missed shot and then gathered the darts for the next round. He, Adam, Levi and James had been playing darts at the Slippery Slope every Wednesday night for the past few years. Ever since Levi had ripped up his knee tackling a wide receiver in the first game of his team's playoff matchup.

Adam snorted. "Since when did working 24/7 constitute having a life?"

"Adam." Levi kept his voice low but the authority behind it was unmistakable. This was the captain of their football team talking and it annoyed the bejesus out of Collin. He could fight his own battles. And this wasn't a battle; this was Adam being a jackass because he was bored. And Collin lying through his teeth to his three best friends because, damn it, since he'd run into Savannah Walters on the road outside of town, he'd been hard-pressed to keep her out of his head. That had been nearly a week ago. He should have forgotten about a ten-minute conversation and gas tank fill-up by now.

"Since working 24/7 got the orchard out of hock, that's when. Some of us don't have the luxury of working for Daddy."

"Just play darts." Levi put the red-winged darts in Collin's hand and gave the blue ones to James.

When they'd started playing, darts was a way to get Levi's uber-competitive mind off his ruined football career and onto something else. Now, eighteen months later, it was habit. One Collin had never thought about changing until tonight. He took aim, and his dart landed on the twenty triangle. James threw and hit fifteen.

He should have stayed home with Amanda. God knew his baby sister could use a little more attention thrown her way. He could have gone over the projections for harvest, finished that proposal for the organic chef's association. The orchard was on stable financial ground for the first time in years, and now was so not the time to slack off. This was the time to build something that would last more than a lifetime.

"I'm not the one mooning over a girl at the bar," Adam said, and took a long drink of his beer.

Collin aimed again and hit the ten. James hit another fifteen.

"She's not just any girl. That's a fine looking—" James started.

Levi cut him off. "Before you say something you might regret, J, that's my baby sister over there."

Screw darts. Collin tossed his last dart toward Adam's head. It landed harmlessly on the Formica tabletop. "I'm not mooning over anyth—"

"Sure you are, Col." Levi picked the dart off the table and pulled the others from the paneling around the board. "Let's start the next round." He took up position and began throwing, narrowing his eyes as he took aim just as he'd done when they'd been kids playing football. Levi had been the quarterback, Collin and James the receivers, and Adam and his twin Aiden the defensive specialists. After practices or game nights, they would sneak in here, and Merle, the owner and bartender, would let them stay as long as they didn't try to scam drinks from any of the patrons.

Collin looked around the dingy bar. The same neon strip was burned out of the beer sign behind the bar. Same cowhide-covered bar stools.

Merle wiped down the bar this evening, entertaining Savannah and her giggling gaggle of former high-school cheerleaders.

Three of whom Collin had dated.

Not that Savannah would care.

Not that he should care if Savannah did care.

One of the women at the bar said something, and Savannah threw her head back, mahogany hair cascading past her shoulders in a mass of waves, and laughed like she was at a freaking Kevin Hart show.

He wasn't mooning. He was distracted, maybe. It wasn't every day a woman walked into the Slope wearing a rhinestone party dress and high-heeled, over-the-knee boots. What the hell was Savannah thinking anyway?

"You're up."

Not that she didn't look good in the dress that cinched tightly around her waist. And she'd learned a few new makeup tricks since she'd left town. That had to be the reason her eyes were so luminous.

"Collin."

And her hair had always been the color of rich wood, but it hadn't always been that thick, had it?

"Coll."

A dart whizzed through his eye line, and Collin shook himself.

"What?"

"While you're busy not mooning over the lovely Savannah, you might want to throw. You're up," Adam said, grinning. He picked up the dart from the hardwood floor.

Collin stepped to the line, gauged where the darts fell, and threw his first. It landed just over the white line above Levi's dart. Damn it.

"When did she roll into town?" Adam asked. Couldn't he leave Savannah out of five minutes of conversation?

"Friday night. And don't ask me why she's back. She's done a good job of not talking about herself since she got here." Levi took aim, and his dart landed in the bull's-eye. "Guess that's game."

"I'll buy the next round before I leave, boys," James said, signaling the waitress. Juanita Alvarez had worked at the bar as long as Merle had.

"Don't you have a shift later?" Collin asked.

"Yep. On midnights for the next few weeks." James finished his water. "It's why Juanita's been serving me bottled water all night. And why I'm buying the last round, not drinking it."

"None for me. Early morning." Levi sat back in the booth, stretching his arms over the vinyl back. "I'll take a cup of coffee, though," he said as Juanita arrived at the table.

"Coke for me," Collin said. There was still

time to go over the books, but not if he had another drink.

"You guys are wusses," Adam said and then asked Juanita for another draft. "Time was we'd drink in here until Merle shut it down and still get up at the butt crack of dawn for work or… whatever."

"Time was we didn't all have responsibilities," James reminded his friend and then added, with a pointed gaze, "like a lovely wife and two great kids waiting at home."

Adam rolled his eyes at that. "Jenny gets the guys' night out thing, and the kids have school, which means an eight o'clock bedtime."

"If Jenny was my wife, I'd be taking advantage of kids' early bedtimes with an early bedtime of my own," James said, a sly smile on his face. Of all of them, James had changed the most since high school. Back then he'd been the geek—the football-playing geek, but still the geek. Now he had half the single women in Slippery Rock panting after him, wanting to be Mrs. Sheriff James Calhoun. That was, if James's father ever left his post as sheriff. "See you guys next week," he said, grabbing his water bottle from the table.

"James has the right idea. See you guys next week," Levi said. He picked up his ball cap from the table and slipped it over his head. He looked back. "No more trying to maim each other with darts," he said, waving a finger between Collin and Adam. "Never mind the coffee, Juanita," he called as he pushed through the doorway.

Adam lifted his hands as if he were innocent. "You gonna go talk to her?"

"You're an ass." Collin shook his head. "No, I'm not talking to Savannah Walters. We don't have anything to talk about."

"Who said you needed something to talk about?"

Collin blinked. Was he missing something here?

"She's back in town." Adam said the words slowly as if Collin might not understand simple English.

"And?"

"You're currently available."

"And?"

"She's currently available, at least if you go by the tabloids."

"Again, I say 'so'?"

Adam blew out a breath. "So, she's always been cute, but you heard James. That girl—" he motioned toward her with his hands "—has turned into one hot—"

"Don't. Say. It." He needed to get his brain off Savannah's assets.

"What?"

"Stop acting like you're my wingman for cripe's sake. I don't need help in the female department."

"I'm just saying—"

"Well, don't just say. I'm not hitting on Savannah. I'm not dating Savannah and I'm not sleeping with Savannah."

"You're not sleeping with anyone." Adam held up his hands. "Just trying to get you off this celibacy shtick you've been on since last summer."

"It's not a celibacy shtick, A. I'm running a business that, until recently, was on very shaky ground. I've got a seventeen-year-old sister to raise."

Savannah sipped from her glass again and Collin swallowed. It was more than not having time for recreational sex. Women hit on him all the time, but he didn't have time for the dating thing, and random hookups had never been his thing. Until tonight, anyway. Somehow, since Savannah had walked through the door, all he'd had on his mind was meaningless, hot sex.

Which was ridiculous. He wasn't a twenty-year-old kid any longer. He'd grown up. Had responsibilities. He didn't need a woman like Savannah Walters screwing any of that up.

Savannah sipped from the plastic cup made to look like a high-end wineglass. It was boxed wine. When she convinced Merle to add wine to his twenty brands of beer, and the staples of Jim Beam, Johnny Walker and Jose Cuervo, she'd intended for him to add wines from one of the regional vineyards. Only Merle, stubborn, beer-drinking, wine-hating Merle, would buy wine for his bar from the local grocery store, insisting that people came to the Slope for conversation and "real drinking." She supposed he was right, she was the only one drinking it. And she hated boxed wine.

She also hated that the women she was drinking with—the women who used to be barely civil to her—were pretending to be her best friends because she was a minor Nashville star. Or at least, she had been.

More than either of those things, she hated that spending another night cooped up at the ranch might have caused a meltdown that could have ended with her spilling everything to Bennett and Mama Hazel. So she'd made one phone call and two hours later here she was on a girls' night out with strangers she had to pretend were her friends.

She glanced to the left as Marcy Nagle started another story about her eight-year-old son, the football prodigy. God, she hated football more than she hated Slippery Rock.

Scratch that. She didn't hate the little town. She just felt…surrounded by it. Watched by it.

Collin was still there. In the corner booth that her brother, Levi and the sheriff's son had vacated a few minutes before.

Sitting with…who was that? His dad owned the cabinet shop in town and re-did Mama Hazel's pantry a few years ago. Buchanan. Aiden Buchanan. Aiden had been so much fun back in the day. Carefree. A little restless. Always up for a good time. He'd been the ringleader of Levi's motley group of football buddies. The five boys who put Slippery Rock, Missouri, on the map all those years ago. The Sailor Five.

Aiden turned his head and she caught a glimpse of the scar along his jaw and neck. Her mind flashed to a car accident when she'd been a sophomore and the tangled wreckage she, Levi and Bennett had come upon on a Sunday morning on their way to church.

That's not Aiden. It's his twin, Adam.

The boy whose car slid on black ice. He'd missed most of a year of school from his injuries and, although he'd recovered, had never regained full mobility of his left shoulder. Adam had gone from one of the stars of their football team to the equipment manager.

Adam Buchanan. The sweet boy who'd danced

with her at the homecoming dance. Unlike his table mate who had never paid any attention to the younger sister of his best friend.

Just like he hadn't noticed her tonight, despite the stage-worthy outfit and killer heels.

Damn it, why couldn't Collin have gotten fat or bald or something while she'd been following her dreams to Nashville? But he hadn't. Collin was as handsome as ever and every time she looked in his direction those stupid butterflies started dancing around in her stomach again. As if she was hung up on her brother's best friend.

Well, she wasn't.

She was an adult who had learned the hard way what kind of man to stay away from.

Savannah sighed. Collin would be the perfect guy to have a little rebound, short-term relationship with while she was in town. He would be a harmless distraction and…who was she kidding? If Collin were either harmless or just a distraction she wouldn't still be obsessing over him a week after he'd rescued her on the side of the road. She'd been thinking practically non-stop about the orchard owner for the past five days.

One more reason to stay far, far away from him. Adam, on the other hand, would be fun and sweet and totally, amazingly forgettable.

"Excuse me, ladies, I think I see something a little more interesting than football mom stories and boxed wine," she said, nodding toward the corner booth. "No offense."

A chorus of "Go, girl" rang out at the bar, and Savannah used the enthusiasm to bolster her confidence as she started across the long space between the bar and the booth. In the fantasy that just popped into her mind, Adam fell instantly under her spell, led her to the dance floor—which was currently uninhabited—and danced with her to a Dierks Bentley song while Collin sat alone in the booth, wondering what he'd done so wrong that the fabulous, beautiful Savannah Walters didn't want to dance with him.

Her palms went clammy.

Adam said something to Collin, and Collin squinted his eyes. Savannah smoothed her hands over her hair. She wasn't the tagalong kid trailing after her brother. She was a grown woman with a life to lead.

Okay, so her life was currently in shambles around her, but it didn't have to stay that way. She could fix it. Adam would be a bit of a morale booster.

Collin could suck a lemon between his perfect teeth while eating his heart out for not noticing her.

She swallowed and took a steadying breath.

Adam shrugged. Collin looked annoyed.

Savannah straightened her shoulders as she arrived at the corner booth. The room seemed too quiet, not that it had been all that loud to begin with. Other than her group of high school friends, only a handful of townies occupied the bar.

Thom Hall, owner of the best restaurant in town, and his wife sat at a side table, feeding the jukebox quarters. Felix Brown, owner of the marina, leaned his beefy forearms on the bar as he talked to Merle. A few young people she didn't recognize. No one was paying any attention to the table in the corner, so why did she suddenly feel as if a spotlight was shining down on her?

"I'm not interested in no-strings sex," Collin was saying, and the words seemed to vibrate around the table.

Savannah let a playful smile settle on her face. This was going to be simpler than she'd thought. Any time a man said he didn't need or want random sex, it was exactly what he needed. At least, in her experience.

Not that she was going to have sex with Collin. She was here for Adam.

Bland, boring Adam.

She should have stayed at the bar. But since she was here… "That's too bad. I hear no-strings sex is the best kind to have." The words rolled from her mouth like she'd practiced them. It was exactly what Savannah would have said to a regular bar guy. The words seemed idiotic here, though.

Collin looked at her, blinking his eyes as if he were an opossum coming out of its den.

"Savannah Walters. Look at you," Adam said, whistling a little bit.

"Hello, Adam. Hi, Collin," she said, slipping into the booth beside Adam, and still, she couldn't keep her eyes off Collin. His blond hair was cut short and he wore a faded ball cap that read Tyler Orchards with a tree of some sort embroidered on the front. "So, what are you boys up to tonight?"

"Shooting the breeze. Playing darts. Exciting Wednesday night in Slippery Rock," Adam said after a moment.

"Mmm." Savannah nodded as if Adam had said they were heading out to a red-carpet awards show. "It's good to see you again, Collin. You'll be happy to know I made it to a gas station in one piece."

Adam's gaze darted between her and his friend. Collin didn't say anything; he just stared at the glass in his hands.

"Who won?" Savannah picked up one of the

darts and twirled it in her fingers, then threw it neatly at the board where it hit bull's-eye.

"Nice throw," Adam said. Collin stared into the glass of Coke between his big hands.

"You learn a few things when you sling beers here."

Savannah focused on Adam. Clearly, Collin had zero interest in her and, if she was going to salvage this night, she needed to make sure Adam had at least a little interest.

"Levi and James." Adam looked from Collin to Savannah. "I'm just going to go," he said, looking uncomfortable for perhaps the first time in his life.

"I was hoping you'd dance with me," she said, using her best, most sultry voice.

Adam shook his head. "That's not a good idea."

"Why not?"

Thom Hall and his wife walked to the door, waving at Merle and the marina owner as they left.

Adam held up his left hand and a thin gold band glinted in the low, bar lighting. "My wife's understanding about the weekly dart throw, but she's not so good with other women. But it was good to see you, Savannah." He looked pointedly over her shoulder, and Savannah slid out of the booth, feeling like a fool. Of course Adam was married. All the good, solid, normal, forgettable guys were married. And she'd just made a complete fool of herself—again—in front of Collin.

"I'd forgotten you were married," she said, the words sounding lame to her ears. How could she have forgotten that Adam got married to the homecoming queen as soon as she graduated high school, and right after Aiden left town for California?

"No worries." Adam threw a quick hug around her shoulders. "It was good to see you, Savannah. I'll leave an extra tip for Juanita at the bar," he said as he started for the bar. "Losers always tip."

He stopped at the register, handed a few bills over to Merle and then exited the bar. Savannah realized her pretend friends were gone, too. Merle wiped down the bar, but ignored them, and Juanita had disappeared into the back room. Leaving her alone with Collin and a jukebox playing a song about a battered woman killing her husband. Savannah wanted to leave, but wasn't sure how to excuse herself.

"Looks like we have the place to ourselves," Savannah said.

"Slippery Rock closes down around ten, remember?"

"Surely not *every* place in town is closed down." She sat across the table from him.

Collin looked at her, really looked, for the first time since she'd come over to the table. Savannah swallowed again, but this time not in anticipation. He looked at her as if…as if he didn't like what he saw. His sharp blue gaze studied her face for a long moment and then traveled down her neck, hesitating slightly when it reached her breasts. The table hid her long legs, but still she curled them back toward the booth bottom.

"I'm not sure what kind of game you're playing, Savannah, but whatever it is, I'm not in the mood."

"I'm…I'm not playing games."

Except she was, and she hated it.

He smiled but the expression wasn't friendly. This smile didn't make butterflies flap in her belly. This smile turned those sweet, sweet butterflies into roving vultures intent on eating her alive.

"Sure you are."

Maybe direct was the better way to go where Collin was concerned. Maybe it was time she stopped playing games altogether.

"Okay, I am. But I'm a big girl and I know the rules." She ran her hand over Collin's, and the flash of heat at the contact seemed to spike the temperature around them. Despite the dim light, she saw his pupils dilate, his nostrils flare. He didn't pull his hand away. She brushed her fingertips over his once more. The heat didn't intensify but it didn't disappear, either. "Would you like to dance?"

CHAPTER FOUR

THIS WAS A MISTAKE. A big, huge, lose-the-game-in-overtime mistake.

Collin drew his hand away from Savannah's. "That isn't a good idea."

She tilted her head to the left and widened her eyes a little, but he knew she wasn't confused. "Why not?"

Because the last thing he wanted to do with Savannah Walters was dance. An image of their bodies moving in time to some beat he couldn't place formed in his mind. Okay, maybe it wasn't the *last* thing he wanted.

In his imagination, though, they were dancing without clothes and Savannah getting naked with him was very definitely off-limits.

The last thing Savannah Walters had ever wanted was to live in a small town.

Whereas he wanted small town. He liked living and working in a place where he knew everyone.

Then there was Amanda to consider. He was

her brother, not her father, but he was all the girl had and he needed to give her security. Taking Savannah back to the orchard, bringing home someone who wouldn't stick around, was a disaster waiting to happen.

Savannah slid from the booth and sashayed across the dimly lit bar, stopping next to the jukebox. She slipped a quarter through the slot, and Collin heard it ping down the chute. Then she tapped a couple of keys and music filled the empty bar.

When had everyone left?

Merle still stood behind the bar, but his attention was on the money from the till, not his patrons. Juanita was nowhere to be seen and everyone else had gone, including Savannah's old cheerleader friends.

Definitely not a good idea.

Collin slid from the booth and tossed a few dollars on the table. Adam may have left a few bills at the register, but Juanita lived on her tips. Besides, taking bills from his wallet gave Collin something to do with his hands.

A crooning male voice filled the bar, and Savannah began swaying to the music.

He couldn't move.

Collin ordered his feet to walk to the door and out into the warm spring night.

His feet ignored him and remained firmly planted on the worn hardwood floors of the Slope.

Savannah turned, crooked her finger at him and continued swaying in time to the music on the dance floor. She should look ridiculous. The way she'd looked when she'd worn her mother's too-high heels to the homecoming dance that time.

Only she didn't really look ridiculous. She looked…damn good.

Too good. Like she'd done this a million times in a million bars and with a million other men.

Collin was no prude, but he didn't want to fall under some spell Savannah had been perfecting during her time in Los Angeles and Nashville. If they were going to do this, it was going to be his way.

Not that they were going to do this. He was not, repeat *not*, taking Savannah Walters back to the orchard. That wasn't the kind of example his baby sister needed.

His feet moved him across the wide dance floor that was so seldom used Merle didn't bother keeping it waxed anymore. Savannah seemed to melt into his arms. She lay her head against his shoulder and linked her arms around his neck as he swayed them to the music.

Collin fastened his arms around her waist, feeling her heat through the thin material of her dress. Savannah sighed. The rhinestones beneath his hands were warm beneath his touch, adding to the burn he'd felt earlier when Savannah had brushed her hand over his. This was crazy.

He wasn't some impulsive kid any longer. He wasn't the same teenager that followed along with his friends' reckless plans. He had a job, a family to support.

God, but she smelled good, though. Some kind of flowery scent seemed to envelop them on the dance floor. It started at Savannah's hair, but it seemed to be everywhere. Like it was a part of the atmosphere. Her soft hands began playing with the longish hairs at the nape of his neck.

"Should I start another song or should we…" She let the words trail off.

Start another song, he wanted to say, but didn't.

He had the orchard to continue building.

He had Gran and Amanda to support and, despite her reluctance to return to Slippery Rock, their other sister, Mara.

He wasn't about to mess up the future plans he had for a night with Savannah Walters, no matter how tempted his hands were to continue caressing her curves.

Reluctantly, Collin loosened Savannah's hands from his neck and stepped back.

"Thanks for the dance. I'll see you around," he said and quickly left the bar, calling himself all kinds of a coward for doing so.

It shouldn't matter who she was. It should only matter that she was a willing woman, he was a willing man and it had been nearly a full year since he'd…

But it did matter.

Savannah Walters was not the kind of woman he needed to be messing around with.

SAVANNAH BLINKED. LOOKED around the empty bar.

He'd left.

She ran her hands up and down her arms, suddenly feeling as if all the warmth in the bar had gone out the door as Collin closed it behind him.

He'd really left.

She'd offered herself up to him and… *Damn it, what was it about the men in this town?*

Okay, that wasn't fair. Not all the men in Slippery Rock were cold, clinical, orchard owners.

From what she remembered, Collin wasn't cold or clinical. Maybe he just didn't like her. Somehow, that didn't make her feel better.

Savannah Walters was a grown woman who knew what she wanted, and what she wanted was to not think about what a mess her life was. Just for a little while. It wasn't as if she was an ugly stepsister or something. She had assets, and she knew how to use them. And that left her right back at He Isn't Interested. She blew out a breath. Okay, then, she wouldn't be interested.

Merle stood behind the bar, still counting the money from the register.

"What do I owe you?" she asked, feeling foolish. She'd just come on—hard—to Collin Tyler and been turned down flat. The old bartender might pretend he didn't see anything in the bar, but she knew he caught it all. God, this was so embarrassing.

"Your friends cleared the tab." He put most of the money into a bank bag, locked it, and then put a few tens, fives and ones back into the register before closing it up.

"Oh." She looked around, not sure what to do. Leave, she supposed. Go back to the ranch.

"When am I going to get one of your songs for the juke?" Merle asked.

"Oh. Um… I just finished cutting my first record." Not that it would be released anytime soon. Genevieve was the star of their shared label. Savannah was the newcomer who'd literally screwed herself out of a tour slot. Not being in front of the fans coupled with Genevieve's pull at the label probably meant a fast and definite death for her career. The career that Savannah wanted for her parents more than she'd wanted it for herself.

The whole time she'd felt like a fraud. Petrified the world would find out she wasn't who she'd told them she was—the normal girl from the normal family from a normal small town—when the truth about the way she came to Slippery Rock or her family was so not normal. Not knowing her actual birth date wasn't normal. Not knowing her biological medical history wasn't normal. Not knowing her racial makeup wasn't normal.

She'd been told as a kid that she couldn't be white because of her hair type. But, she'd also been told she couldn't be black because her skin tone was light, like Jennifer Beals or Zoe Kravitz. None of the kids in Slippery Rock seemed to realize that both of those actresses were biracial. She'd been raised by an African-American family who hadn't cared that her skin tone was several shades lighter than theirs. For the most part, Savannah didn't, either. She just wished she could feel worthy of them. That was the feeling that drove her to Los Angeles and then to Nashville.

Bennett and Mama Hazel loved country music, and had passed that love on to her. Once she arrived in LA, no one seemed to care about anything but her singing, so she'd pretended to be just another small-town girl, trying to make it. Then she stepped on the stage and realized she wanted to be anywhere but in the middle of that spotlight. The crowd was too loud, and the lights were too hot, and she'd just wanted it all to stop.

She couldn't stop the LA circus, though, no matter how much she wanted out. Singing country music had been Mama Hazel's dream as a young woman, but she'd fallen in love with Bennett and given it up. Savannah doing well on the show, doing well in Nashville, would have given a little bit of Mama's dream back to her.

Then the discomfort of the stage turned into fear that some zealous reporter would start to dig into her past. Would make the connection between Levi and her. There would have been questions she couldn't answer, and maybe even accusations that she'd been trying to "pass." In truth, she hadn't considered her ethnicity at all; she had been too focused on finally doing something that would make her parents proud.

Merle's voice brought her thoughts back to the bar. "Well, when you've got that song, you make sure we get a copy. It'll be the most played song in the Slope, I guarantee." Merle winked.

"I will." Savannah backed out of the bar. The thick oak door closed behind her and Savannah leaned against it for a second. She heard the tumblers click over as Merle locked up for the night.

She had no illusions about the perfection of Slippery Rock. There were racial and economic divisions even in the middle of nowhere. Bennett and Mama Hazel were respected landowners, her brother, a beloved football star, but there were other families who weren't thought of in the same way. Families who lived below the poverty line. Some of them also families of color. Ever since the adoption worker had brought her here, Savannah had been caught in the vicious cycle of wanting to be worthy of the family that had chosen her, but of being too afraid to accept their love.

Afraid that they would come to the same realization that her first family had—that Savannah was too much trouble—and would send her back to those cold police station steps.

Getting out of town, finding herself living a very sheltered and artistic California life in which no one questioned her race, had been freeing for the first few days. Then the old fears had come back. What if people turned on her because she might not be the typical, Caucasian country music star? What if people turned on her because she could have been the one to break the musical stereotype but instead had chosen to pass, even if she hadn't consciously thought not mentioning her past was an attempt at passing?

It had been a relief when she hadn't won. It was as if she'd dodged a bullet. But then the Nashville record company had offered her a deal, and then, when one of the biggest country stars opened a tour slot for her, it had all spun out of control.

From the second those offers came in, she'd started to think she really could earn the love of the family that chose her, but she'd still been so uncomfortable under all of that attention. And when Philip Anderson, Genevieve's tour manager and estranged husband, had come on to her, she'd found herself following him to Genevieve's bus.

Why had she gone onto that bus with Philip? She didn't even like the man.

She doubted, deep-in-her-heart doubted, that she deserved her family's love now.

Savannah pushed away from the door, got into Mama Hazel's sedan and pulled onto the highway.

This was one more blinking neon light indicating that she should focus on her own mental health and not start chasing a man who obviously didn't want her. She needed to get her life in order.

She parked the car in the carport and slowly

climbed the steps to the house. The door creaked as she opened it. Savannah flicked off the porch light and climbed the stairs to her old room.

Pretty yellow curtains fluttered in the light breeze and the familiar blue of the walls soothed her. She didn't bother with pajamas, just unzipped the party dress and climbed between the cool sheets in her undies. She pulled a pillow to her chest and closed her eyes.

She fell asleep dreaming she was still swaying in Collin's arms.

CHAPTER FIVE

A HEAVY KNOCK sounded at the front door. Collin pulled a couch pillow over his head. Big mistake. His hands still had Savannah's flowery scent on them and he could smell it through the feathers.

"Go away, Savannah," he muttered. He'd turned her down once already tonight, he wasn't sure he had two turn-downs in him.

The knock sounded again.

It couldn't be Savannah. First, he'd walked out on her and she had never been the type to go running after rejection. Second, he was sleeping on the couch in the main house tonight, not in the barn that he'd turned into his office-slash-apartment a couple of years before. If Savannah wanted him, she would be at the barn, not the main house. Of course, Savannah wouldn't know about the apartment in the barn, so it made sense she was knocking on the front door.

Collin scratched his scalp as he started for the door, tripping slightly over the light blanket he'd pulled over his hips when he'd sank onto the couch a couple of hours before.

Another knock.

If she didn't stop trying to demolish the front door with her knocks she would wake up the rest of the house. Wait, what rest of the house? Gran took out her hearing aids at night and Amanda slept like the teenage dead. She hadn't moved a muscle when he'd checked in on her after arriving home to work on the books.

Collin reached for the door, prepared to send Savannah on her way. At least he hadn't been dreaming about her. He unlocked the dead bolt, opened the door and his jaw dropped.

It wasn't Savannah.

It was James.

And his baby sister in handcuffs.

Collin glanced at the grandfather clock in the hall. Just after two thirty.

"Sorry, man, found her using these—" James held up two rolls of pink-camo duct tape "—to cut off the streets leading to the town square."

"I wasn't cutting off traffic, I was funneling it in a way that actually makes sense." Amanda blew out a breath, making the wispy blond fringe around her face float up and then back down. Her eyes were green, rather than the blue of his or Mara's, but the stubborn set of her jaw was all Tyler. For Collin, that stubbornness led to a foot-ball scholarship and a degree in Agri-Business.

For Mara, it led to a top technical university and a job as a cyber-security expert.

In Amanda, that stubbornness was likely to lead straight to jail. He couldn't let that happen.

"We have one-way streets that funnel traffic just fine," James said. He elbowed Amanda gently. "And we don't have the money for a middle-of-the-night traffic cop."

"There's no traffic to direct." Amanda, likely realizing she'd just ruined her own excuse for taping over the streets of downtown, began talking quickly. "Except during the day, and then all Slippery Rock has are one-way streets that make it impossible to get from Maple to Franklin without making a detour down Main."

James, one strong hand at Amanda's elbow, directed her through the front door, gentle despite his height and weight advantage over the teen. Collin felt like a largemouth bass left on the bottom of a boat, gasping for air and getting none.

"You taped off downtown?"

Amanda shrugged. Her blond hair hung in a ponytail down her back, and she wore his old hunting jacket, dark yoga pants and shirt. She'd obviously considered the best way to go undetected during her trek. She'd been planning this for a while. And just who had he said good night to a couple of hours before? She slouched on the leather sofa in the family room, putting her booted feet up on the coffee table. Collin knocked her feet off the table and stood over her.

"What the hell, Amanda! What are you thinking?"

His sister straightened on the sofa and shrugged. "It isn't like I took a jackhammer to the pavement," she said sullenly.

"It isn't like we have the budget to take a street crew off their job to take down your five rolls of duct tape, either." James tossed two remaining rolls to Collin and put three emptied rolls on the entry table. "Look, I'm not filing a report. This time," he said sternly. "But this isn't like the fire you helped to put out. This is a straight-up nuisance, and it's the third time I've caught her out with her tape. The last time, she taped a giant maze through the courthouse square, and the time before that she taped the high school principal into his house."

Collin caught a hint of mirth in James's eyes. But this was so not the time to go easy on Amanda. Even though Old Man Tolbert had been running Slippery Rock High with an iron fist since before Collin's high school days.

"I deconstructed the maze and you can't prove I was the one to tape Troll-bert into his house," she said and then mumbled, "On the third snow day he screwed us out of last year."

"Col, I know you've got your hands full with the orchard and all, but I can't keep covering for your kid sister. It could mean my badge."

"No, I'll take care of it. This won't happen again," Collin promised his friend, wondering how long he would be able to keep it. He hadn't even realized Amanda was gone tonight.

Or any of the other times she'd snuck out of the house since he'd grounded her.

He wasn't good at this stand-in-father thing.

"If you think it'll help, I'll take her to the station house. She can spend the night in a holding cell."

Amanda's eyes widened. "You can't send me to jail."

"Au contraire," James said. "I can. And if your brother wasn't one of my best friends, you'd already be there."

"I've got this one," Collin said. He walked James to the front door. "I'll make sure this doesn't happen again, man."

"I'm not always going to be the one getting the call about her antics, Col. I know you guys are going through some stuff right now, but if one of the other deputies catches her, she'll do more than spend a night in our county lockup, you know?"

Collin nodded. "Yeah, I know."

"This isn't us painting the mascot on the water

tower or Mara resetting the stoplight so it taps out an SOS in Morse code."

"I know." God, did he know.

Collin had once thought the rebellious Tyler gene had skipped his baby sister, but Amanda seemed to be making up for lost time. And he didn't know how to help her.

How the hell was he supposed to come down hard on her when he'd done worse than she had on so many other occasions? The difference was he didn't get caught. She not only had the Tyler Rebel gene, but their mother's Bad Timing gene.

"Thanks for bringing her home, J. I'll take care of it. This won't happen again."

James stepped out onto the front porch. "See you for the fish fry Sunday?"

Collin nodded. "Sure. I'm bringing the apples, remember?"

James got into the squad car and backed down the drive. Collin closed the front door and rested his forehead against it for a second.

"What the hell were you thinking, Amanda? What are you trying to do?"

She didn't answer.

"Are you trying to get sent to some halfway house for rejects? Because if Sheriff Calhoun or one of the other deputies catches you out one night, that's where you'll go. It won't matter that I'm your older brother, but it will matter that I don't have custodial rights. That you don't have parental supervision."

Still no answer.

"You could wind up in juvenile hall."

Nothing.

Collin turned around.

Amanda lay on the sofa, a round pillow clutched to her chest, asleep. Her legs were curled up to her chest, the way she'd slept when she was a baby, and the ponytail was fanned out over the sofa cushions.

"What am I going to do with you?" he asked, but her only answer was a soft snore.

Collin gathered his sister in his arms as if she weighed nothing and carried her upstairs and down the long hall to her bedroom. When he pulled back the electric-pink covers, he saw Mara's old doll on the pillow. It was one of those life-size dolls that seemed to walk alongside when a little girl held its hands. Mara had used it to fake out their grandparents every time she'd snuck out as a teen.

"I'm trying, Amanda, but I don't know what you need," he said as he laid her sleeping form on the bed. Collin pulled the covers over her and smoothed her hair off her face. "I wish I could say they're coming back, but I can't. I'm sorry. I wish I could change it. I wish I could make our family like every other family in Slippery Rock, but I can't. I'm what you've got, kid. Me and Gran, and she's not as strong as she used to be. The upside of that is that the two of you are all I've got, and I'm not going to let you down the way our parents let me and Mara down, okay? I'm going to get you through this."

Amanda snuggled into her pillow as another snore escaped her lips. The sullen expression was gone, the rebellious bent to her shoulders nonexistent. She was just a kid. A lonely, screwed-up kid whose parents showed up two weeks after her grandfather's funeral, saying it was a wake-up call, and that they wanted to build a relationship with their youngest daughter. They had actually stayed at the orchard for just over a year, but when Gran needed the hip replacement, things got too real for Samson and Maddie and they'd left in the middle of the night, just before Christmas.

From the second they arrived, Collin wanted to make them leave, but the hope he'd seen in Amanda's eyes, the desperation he'd seen in Gran's, had kept him from kicking them right back to wherever they'd been living. Prior to that visit, the last time they'd been at the orchard had been when Collin and Mara graduated from high school, and that had been a quick trip between what Samson Tyler called "business meetings."

Collin had heard him begging for money from Granddad, though, so he'd known it was a lie.

Collin had caused Amanda's rebellion. If he'd only kicked them out, like Mara had suggested, none of this would be happening. There would have been no time for Amanda to get so attached to them that she forgot they couldn't be relied upon.

He'd been pissed after their mother had called to say they were taking more time in Florida. Even more pissed when the two weeks she'd said they needed turned into two months. He hadn't heard from them since mid-January. Not a phone call or an email. At first, all he'd thought about was what an inconvenience it was to have to look after Amanda while they sunned themselves in Florida. How much time he was taking away from the orchard and his plans.

He'd never thought about the toll this must be taking on her.

Collin closed her bedroom door quietly.

For as long as he could remember, Samson had talked about how things would be different in Florida. How they would find a good life in Florida. Apparently, they had found that better life.

Now he had to figure out how to make a better life for his sister here in Slippery Rock. Before he lost her.

Savannah woke the next morning feeling restless. She showered and dressed and then shoved the sequined number she'd worn the night before to the back of her closet. The last thing she wanted was to be reminded of Collin Tyler's walkout.

Or her own idiocy.

Mama Hazel was in the kitchen when she walked in, squeezing orange juice into a tall carafe. Hazel Walters was sixty-two years and one hundred pounds of feisty. Her hair was steel-gray and she had lines around her eyes, but the backs of her hands were still smooth and rich.

"It's about time you got out of bed. You're back on the ranch now, not in your fancy Nashville apartment."

"So I'm supposed to wake up with the rooster and ride the range?" Savannah teased as she snagged a glass from the cabinet and poured juice from the filled carafe. Hazel began filling a paper plate with biscuits and bacon.

"Wouldn't hurt. Levi and your father have been up since dawn, you know."

"Levi is a paragon of virtue," Savannah said drily. Levi had left the bar early, and alone. Levi hadn't made a play for a woman and been walked out on.

Levi was a football star. Levi made the pros. Levi would have been inducted into the Hall of

Fame if not for a squidgy hit. But even though he'd blown out his knee, he'd kept his opponent from scoring.

Levi. Levi.

Freaking. Levi.

"Pssh. Levi has his bad qualities."

"And I have my good ones. After all, if it weren't for me, the Walters clan wouldn't have a black sheep. And every family needs a black sheep."

"Sweetheart, you're no black sheep. You are my beautiful angel." Hazel reached up and tucked a wayward strand of hair behind Savannah's ear. "When I saw these braids for the first time on television, I wasn't sure I liked them. Your natural hair was always the prettiest of corkscrew curls. I was wrong, though, it's just as beautiful like this." She put the plate of food in Savannah's hands, tucked a thermos between her elbow and rib cage and motioned her to the door. "Take this out to your brother. He didn't bother to come in for breakfast. He'll be in the barn by now."

Savannah walked across the front yard toward the massive barn. It was painted red, as it had been for as long as she could remember, but the black tin roof was new. The last time she'd been home the roof was still shake-shingled. Not that it mattered what the roof of the barn was made from. It just looked funny to her.

The same swing, fashioned from the metal seat of an old tractor, hung from a limb of the ancient oak in the side yard. The same ranch trucks sat before the barn, and the same horses ran in the paddock behind it. At least, they looked like the same horses. Somehow, despite growing up on the ranch, she hadn't learned much about farm animals.

She found Levi in the barn office, clicking through a file on his computer. "Mama said you skipped breakfast," she said, setting the plate on the desk.

"And you're her errand girl sent to make me eat?"

Savannah sat in the hard wooden chair across the desk from her brother. "Something like that. I didn't want to get roped into whatever confection she was starting to make, anyway."

"Fish fry on Sunday. She's probably prepping her apple-caramel pie." Levi eyed the plate as if trying to convince himself not to eat.

"You on a diet or something?"

"No." He stuck a couple of bacon slices into the center of a biscuit. He took a bite. "Have fun at the Slope last night?"

Savannah folded her arms across her chest. "What if I did?"

"Just tell me you didn't go home with Merle, okay?"

"Not that it's any of your business, but I didn't go home with anybody. I came back here."

"I didn't hear you come in."

"Are you my keeper now?"

"No. Dad mentioned—"

"Would you both back off? I'm twenty-seven years old, and I've been living on my own in a major metropolitan area for the past couple of years. I think I can handle Slippery Rock without accidentally falling on some guy's penis and impregnating myself."

Levi blinked. "It isn't that we don't think you can take care of yourself—"

"Sure it is." Savannah stood and began to pace. "You want me to be helpless, but I'm not. I'm like Mama." *At least I want to be.*

Mama Hazel was always calm, always knew what to say and how to fix a hurt. She baked pies and loved her family.

"Mama has a purpose."

"And I don't?" She didn't know why she was picking a fight with her brother. It was stupid and childish, especially when she wasn't sure she wanted the things she kept telling her family she wanted. She liked singing, and she was good at it, but there was a difference between the fun of karaoke night with a few friends and singing in front of an audience in an arena. In having all those people scrutinize her every move. There were good points, too, like meeting little girls who wanted to be singers. A few of them had looked up to her. At least, it seemed as if they had.

Levi just watched her for a long moment. "Mama worked in the Peace Corps, Van. She didn't vagabond all over the world with a hobo sack over her shoulder."

"I'm not a vagabond, and my luggage is Louis Vuitton. I lived in Nashville and I've been on tour with the top artist at the label."

Levi nodded as he finished his biscuit.

"Fine, I have no illusions about world peace and I'm not curing cancer. That doesn't mean my dreams are inconsequential."

She just needed to figure out what her dreams were. Did she want to go back to Nashville and face the music? The one part of the city she liked was the weekend music program the label put together for underprivileged kids. Helping those kids find their music had been the highlight of her months there. Now she wasn't welcome in Nashville and definitely not in the music program.

"They could be so much more, Van. You had

a scholarship to the university. You were talking about med school."

"And then I realized I didn't want ten more years of school. I wanted…something else."

Levi waited, watching her expectantly. "What is the something else?"

"I don't know." She crossed her arms over her chest.

"Is that why you're here 'on a break' now? Because you don't know what you want?"

"Is that so wrong?" She didn't wait for his answer.

Savannah stalked out of the barn and started down one of the trails leading to Slippery Rock Lake, which separated Walters Ranch from the Tyler's orchard. Through the trees she could see sunlight dancing over it.

What was wrong with her? Getting turned down by a guy was no reason to take her frustrations out on her family. And keeping this lie that things in Nashville were perfect was ridiculous. Things were so not right in Nashville it wasn't even funny.

She'd gone to Nashville to try to get people to notice her the way that nobody had in Slippery Rock. To validate her in some way. When she was onstage she was more than Levi's sister. Offstage, though, she was still the kid someone had left on the steps of a police station with her name pinned to her jacket.

The truth was that she didn't know what she wanted. She liked singing, but had found out that she detested being on a big stage in front of thousands of people. She enjoyed working with the kids in the music program, but she didn't play an instrument so mostly she'd just encouraged their interest. Now she was back in Slippery Rock, pretending she had her life together, when in truth it was falling apart and she had no idea how to make things right or if she even wanted to.

She'd been wrong to come back here.

Wrong, wrong, wrong.

Savannah should have kept driving and completely reinvented herself in some town where no one knew who she was.

She could use some distraction.

As she neared the lake, she saw Collin sitting on the hood of his old pickup truck, staring out over the calm water. She hadn't realized she'd walked so far.

"Hi," she said as she neared him. Brilliant May sunlight gave his blond hair streaks of white, which was just unfair. Women in Nashville paid hundreds of dollars to beauticians for streaks like that.

"Savannah."

"You say that like you're unhappy to see me," she said, leaning against the fender of his truck and shooting a flirtatious look his way.

Collin glanced at her. "I'm not."

"Not unhappy to see me? I figured," she said, pretending she couldn't read the disdain in his expression. He might have turned her down last night, but she couldn't seem to stop herself from flirting with him again. "What brings you to my side of the lake?"

"Technically, you're on my side."

Savannah grinned wickedly. "Do you want to know what brought me to you, then?"

Collin sat straighter. "No."

It was the panic in his eyes that did her in. It was fun flirting with a man who was reluctant to flirt back. It wasn't fun to flirt with a man who was not only not interested but potentially afraid of her. Although why Collin would be fearful of her, Savannah couldn't quite figure out.

"You don't have to look at me like that. I'm not going to jump your bones out here." Savannah stood straight, smoothing her hands over the thin tank top she wore. It was royal blue and she knew it contrasted nicely with her skin.

"I can take care of myself, whether or not you want to jump my bones," he said, and she thought she caught a hint of laughter in his voice. It seemed like progress. She didn't want him to hate her, after all. They could be friends. "Well, I didn't come here to see you—"

"And I didn't come here to see you," she put in.

"So how did we both wind up here?"

"I needed a break from Levi the Lecturer." She shook her head when Collin started to say something. "Or maybe he deserved a break from me. I was in a mood."

"And now you're not?" Collin seemed genuinely curious.

"I'm trying to not be in a mood. Being in a mood gets me into trouble. By the way, he has no idea about last night, and he's not going to." And maybe, if she really was going to make a change, it should start now. "I should apologize for all that. I…um…" She wasn't quite sure how to explain last night without laying bare those old insecurities.

"'Was in a mood'?" Collin asked, and this time she definitely caught a hint of laughter in his voice.

"Something like that."

"What caused the mood?"

Nope. Not going there. Collin Tyler might not hate her, but that didn't mean she needed to dump all her baggage on him. He was barely an acquaintance. She shook her head. "Doesn't matter."

Collin nodded. "I was in a weird mood, too," he said.

"So you did want to dance with me?" Savannah leaned her shoulder against the truck and crossed one foot over the other in the dirt.

"No," he said, a little too quickly, a little too harshly. She couldn't ignore the quick hit of pain. Stupid pride.

"Don't go getting all soft on me now," Savannah said. "Tell me how you really feel."

He didn't look at her for a long moment. When he finally spoke, he seemed completely focused on a tree with branches hanging low over the smooth water.

"Savannah, I have… There's a lot." He drew his brows together. "You're Levi's sister. I just don't think about you that way."

Oh. Well, that was way more information than she wanted at—Savannah glanced at her watch—ten o'clock in the morning. The day after she'd made a serious come-on to the man.

"Maybe we could be friends," he said.

The feelings she felt around Collin were definitely not the friendship breed of feelings. Good thing she was decent at covering up her true feelings. That was the one thing in life she'd always been good at.

"Sure, whatever. I just wanted to apologize because I had a little too much to drink last night. But I'm going back to Nashville in a couple of weeks, so we don't have to pretend we're friends or anything. We can just go back to being Levi's sister and Levi's best friend. It's all good," she said, hating the words even as she said them. Hating the intentionally careless tone she'd pushed into her voice.

Savannah was pretty sure she didn't want to be Collin's friend.

He might not think he wanted her as his girl-friend—not even in the short term—but she definitely didn't want to just be his friend.

And if no one ever called her Levi's sister for the rest of her life, it would be too soon.

She backed away from the truck, feeling Collin's gaze on her the way she'd felt his hands the night before.

"See you around, friend," she said and then turned and walked away from him as quickly as she could.

CHAPTER SIX

COLLIN WANTED—BADLY—to adjust the tie trying its best to strangle him. He liked farm work because most days the dress code called for jeans and a T-shirt, like he'd been wearing last Saturday when Savannah had found him at the lake. God, he'd like to be at the lake now instead of this conference room talking to the head of a regional grocery chain about the next step in his plan to expand Tyler Orchard. Even if being there meant lying some more about how Savannah being Levi's younger sister was the reason he'd walked out of the Slope that night.

Walking out of the Slope had had zero to do with Levi and one hundred percent to do with the things he'd been thinking while breathing in Savannah's sweet perfume. He'd been thinking they could take a drive out to the lake, or maybe just a quick run to his truck, so he could strip her down to see if her skin was that glowy, coppery tone everywhere, or if it was just a trick of the lighting. Yeah, there was no way he was telling

Savannah any of that. He didn't need her kind of distraction right now.

Collin focused on the question Jake Westfall asked about growth averages for the past three years. Luckily, he only needed half of his brain to talk growth averages, as the other half was still firmly in the imaginary bed of his truck. He needed to get his mind fully into this office building in Joplin, an hour west of Slippery Rock. With effort, he pushed Savannah all the way out of his brain, imagining he and the other executives were walking one of the ruler-straight rows of apple trees instead of sitting in this conference room, with its wide windows looking over the downtown area, the potted ficus in the corner, and its granite-topped table.

Damn, but he'd like to loosen this damn tie. Suits and ties were for bankers and insurance salesmen, not orchard owners. The last time he'd worn a suit, this very suit, had been his grandfather's funeral a year and a half before. The only other time he'd worn it had been to the party his grandparents had thrown after he'd graduated college with his degree in agri-business.

The other suits in the room didn't appear to be suffering from the same issues as he was, though, so he kept his hands away from his neck as he wrapped up his presentation about how he'd taken the orchard from a small, family-run business to a larger business, still family run but with more ties to the community.

Adding peaches and pears to the apples Tyler Orchards was known for had been a risky move, but it was paying off. The fruit stand his grandfather had run had become a fruit market, and then other local farmers had joined in, creating a full-fledged farmers' market with locally grown vegetables, dairy products and locally sourced honey. Going into business with a regional grocery company was a logical step in his plans to take Tyler Orchards to the next level. It would increase the family's financial stability. Money might not buy happiness, but it definitely made it easier to enjoy life.

If the deal went through with Westfall Foods, maybe it would ease whatever was stressing Amanda out to the point she was using duct tape to reroute traffic downtown and getting caught up with a group of high school firebugs.

"We've gone down this road before with local growers. They promise us the moon, but then they deliver late or give us sub-par goods."

He wouldn't risk his reputation or the reputation of the orchard his grandfather had built from nothing. That's what made the difference, Collin wanted to say. He didn't think Jake Westfall, the lead partner in the chain, would be swayed by an impassioned plea about personal reputation or work ethic, though. Especially if he'd been burned by someone making the same impassioned plea in the past.

"I could send you to our pages on Yelp or Facebook or any of the review sites, and you'd see thousands of satisfied customers' comments. I could make a fifteen-minute speech about personal integrity. But I have a feeling you've read those comments and heard that speech before. I can only stress…" He paused. Because what else did he have except his word? These corporate executives didn't know him, and they didn't know how important this move was for his business. His family.

He handed another paper-clipped bunch of papers across the conference table. Recommendations from a few local restaurants and B and Bs he'd begun supplying three years before.

"I'm going to give that speech to you anyway. My family has been growing organic apples for a local fruit stand for more than forty years. Quality has always been important to us, and that isn't going to stop if we begin contracting with you. If anything, that focus on quality will increase. You have to make the right decision for your stores. I can only tell you that contracting with Tyler Orchards is a good move for both our businesses."

The three executives exchanged a look and

then Westfall said, "If you could give us a few minutes, we'd like to have the room."

Collin nodded, picked up the leather attaché case he'd carried in college and left the conference room with its broad table and leather executive chairs. Alone in a tiled hallway with photographic prints of the Ozark Mountains and Mark Twain National Forest, he considered his options.

The worst they could do was say no. If they did, he would continue his search for a regional grocery chain, and continue supplying local businesses and the farmers' market. If they said yes, he'd do all those and keep expanding the orchard.

He didn't want to spend more time in his office researching potential partners instead of in the orchard, but he would do what he had to.

Collin ran his index finger along the inside of his collar. He didn't want to wear his funeral suit to another meeting. He'd do that, too, though, if it meant more stability for the orchard, for Gran and for Amanda.

He would do anything for them.

Collin rolled his shoulders. Anything.

A few moments later Westfall opened the conference room door and waved Collin back inside.

"We've been looking to increase our organic produce section, as you know, for some time.

We like what we've heard from the local businesses you contract with, and we've followed the orchard's reviews on social media. We also like the proposal you brought in today—with one addition.

"Grove Markets, our main subsidiary, can't risk its reputation on a small outfit like yours, especially one that is already spread thin." He held up his hand when Collin started to interrupt. "As I said before, we've been taken in before by the stake-my-reputation-on-this promises of other growers. The changes you've made to the orchard over the past seven years are tremendous. What we are proposing is a four-month trial period.

"You have four months to prove to us that you are, indeed, staking your reputation on this partnership, and we have that time to see if our customers like your produce as well as your local customers do.

"During the trial, we expect you to withdraw Tyler Orchards produce from the local farmers' market. We would also like you to consider closing the orchard stand for the trial. If both parties are happy with the partnership at the end of the trial, we'll revisit your involvement in both."

Collin swallowed. Not work the stand? Not spend most weekends at the farmers' market? Those were things his grandfather had done for decades. Businesses the elder Tyler had helped to start. Tyler Orchards would be nothing without those things. Of course, it was only for a few months, and if those months led to more business, that wasn't a bad thing. Was it?

"What about the local restaurants and B and Bs?"

"We understand you have contracts, and don't expect you to break them. If things go as well as we're hoping, you may decide being our primary organic source for apples, pears and peaches is more lucrative than those smaller ventures."

"Primary source?" Collin flexed his hands as a quick hit of adrenaline made his heart beat faster.

"That's the deal, Mr. Tyler. We aren't just looking for another bag of organic apples or peaches. We're looking for a business that can become our main resource. Tyler Orchards would, of course, be noted on the packaging, but the branding would become Grove Market or Westfall Foods."

Collin's heart beat a little harder. A primary-source contract was so much more than he'd considered. It meant multiple thousands of dollars. It could mean expanding the orchard sooner than he'd planned. Maybe even expanding the small greenhouses where Gran raised her plots of broccoli and carrots into full-fledged fields, too.

Giving up the local businesses for a windfall contract from a regional grocery chain could change their lives. He wanted to pump his fist in the air. Those first small contracts had been his babies, his idea, his plan to transform the orchard as a small, family-run business into a bigger player in the organic marketplace. Now those initial plans could be paying off much faster than he had anticipated.

The clipped-together recommendations from the local restaurants and B and Bs caught his eye, and he felt his elation leaking like air from a broken balloon.

Those local businesses depended on Tyler fruit for their menus. Collin's stomach knotted. Sourcing organic fruits for a grocery chain was a big deal. It could mean so much more in the financial column. But…

Collin was on a first-name basis with everyone he contracted with. He saw them running into the bank or fishing on the lake during the summer months. The fruits of his labor literally made their businesses stronger. He couldn't take that away from them. Could he?

"Tyler Orchards is a family-run business. I make the final decisions, but I would like the chance to discuss this with my family before signing anything."

"Of course. We can give you thirty days, and then we'll need the decision."

Collin nodded. He collected his things and walked out of the four-story building in downtown Joplin, Missouri. Westfall Foods had lost its three main Grove Market stores in that tornado and the storms that followed. He looked up. This building had been reduced to a pile of rubble, but Jake Westfall had rebuilt his company bigger and better than it had been before. Partnering with him would be a boon for Tyler Orchards.

Two days later Collin stood in the fruit stand at the end of the lane leading to Tyler Orchards, still contemplating what he should do about the offer from Westfall Foods. Go all-in with the grocery chain? Or continue as a small-potatoes fruit operation with ties to a farmers' market, a few B and Bs and some local restaurants? He hadn't talked to Gran or Amanda about the option because he wanted to have a firm idea about what he personally wanted first.

His professors would tell him to go with the chain, but he'd never really liked any of the professors. They'd been too comfortable in their pressed suits and wingtips for his liking.

What was it Granddad had always said? *If a man doesn't leave a little of his work on him, how can you know he's doing the job?* Collin pondered the question.

Partnering with Westfall would mean more office and paperwork time for him. He'd need to hire a manager for the orchards, more labor for harvest times, and that would mean not having the dirt of the orchard in the treads of his shoes or the smell of the blossoms in his nose. Instead he'd have ink on his fingers from contracts and harvest forecasts. Would Granddad think ink was a good substitute for dirt?

He still didn't have an answer, but he knew several people who always seemed to be in pristine condition, without a speck of dust on them. And yet he knew they worked hard.

He picked up a few more jars of Gran's apple preserves, stuffed them on a shelf and winced as the jars cracked together. Inspecting them closely, he saw that there was no actual damage done and breathed a sigh of relief. His garbage can was already overflowing because of his carelessness earlier this morning. A deer had jumped into the road and Collin had wrenched the old truck's steering wheel to the side to avoid it. As the truck swerved, he heard the sickening crunch of a few jars of peach jelly and blackberry preserves. He'd have to hose down the back or bees would start making a new hive where the remnants of those jars stuck to the sides of the truck.

There had to be a way he could serve both the local businesses and the regional chain. Working with the grocer didn't have to mean the end of the Tyler Orchards stand, his partnership in the farmers' market or the other contracts. Even with the grocer contract, if he signed, the orchard would have more than enough to fulfill that and still work locally. He just needed to figure out how to present a solution to the executives. That meant he needed a solution that was workable from both sides.

He picked up an oddly shaped apple and tossed it into the basket he would take to the house once his shift at the stand was finished. People stopping by wanted perfectly shaped produce, not a misshapen apple with a stem area that appeared to be grimacing.

He had twenty-seven more days to figure out the solution. He wouldn't sacrifice his family's financial security.

And he wouldn't go back on his commitments to his community, either.

A BRIGHT RAY of sunlight shafted through the barn window, blinding Savannah for a split second. She sat on a three-legged stool, staring at the udder of one of the dairy cows. She'd found this one, already gated in an area of the barn away from the other cows. She wasn't sure why it was here, and she didn't care. She was going to figure out how to milk the darn thing if it was the last thing she ever learned.

"That one's been a little under the weather lately. She had trouble calving last year, and doesn't like the machines."

Savannah nearly fell off the little three-legged stool at the sound of Bennett's voice. His big hand steadied her shoulder, and slowly, she swiveled to face him.

"I was wondering why she was over here and not with the others."

"She just needs a little extra attention, don't you, girl?" Bennett asked, patting the cow lightly on the rump. The cow didn't respond, just kept chewing on the hay in the trough before it.

"I can teach you how to milk, if you want." She shot him a look. "You think Levi and I haven't noticed you skulking around the barns?" He winked at her. "Fine, *skulking* isn't really the right word, but every time you saw us, you'd hightail it in the other direction. Do you want to learn?"

Savannah nodded. "I want to be useful."

"People are useful in different ways, Van." Bennett, nearly as tall as Levi, but slighter and more wiry, squatted down beside her. He took her hands in his and put them on the smooth udder of the cow. "You start at the base of the teat," he said, putting her hands at the small crease between the cow's teat and the udder. It felt weird. Warm and smooth and weird. "Make a ring with your index finger and thumb and then you bring your other fingers in, kind of like you're making a fist around the teat but in a slow, kind of rolling motion."

Savannah focused on the udder, making a ring with her finger and thumb, and then squeezed her hard as if she were making a fist. Nothing happened. She tried again, and again nothing happened. Bennett put his hands over hers and squeezed. A steady stream of milk squirted into the pail beneath the cow. Savannah shot a glance at her father.

"Okay, I've got this." She placed her hands in the proper position, closed her eyes and squeezed her hands in the same rolling motion Bennett had used. Nothing happened. She tried again, but only a few drops of milk hit the pail.

"You'll get it. It takes time."

Frustrated, Savannah stood, leaving the cow with its head in the gate.

"I don't know why I even tried. I'm not a—a milkmaid," she said. "I'm not…I'm not any-thing."

"Sure you are."

She crossed her arms over her chest. He was wrong. She wasn't anything. Not a singer, she wasn't even sure her label wanted her anymore. Or, maybe worse, if she wanted the label to want her. Did she want to sing? Was that what would finally make her feel as if there was purpose to this life?

She couldn't cook like Mama Hazel; cooking for people served a purpose. She couldn't milk a freaking cow; cows provided milk and dairy products to people. That held purpose. Hell, she couldn't be trusted to take her car to the shop when the check engine light came on and, maybe worst of all, remember to fill the tank with gas when she was on a road trip.

"I'm a mess."

Bennett reached out, tugging on a braid. Savannah turned to face him. "You're my Savannah, and you're stronger than you think." A smiled spread over his dark face, and his eyes, the color of walnuts, seemed to brighten. "What is your dream?"

"What is my dream?" she parroted his words back to him.

"I overheard you talking to Levi the other day. What is it that you want, sweet girl?"

Savannah mulled the question for a long moment. What did she want? She didn't really care about milking cows, although it would be nice to have something to do at the ranch other than stare out the windows. She loved to sing, but the thought of singing before thousands of people left her cold. Colder than the thought of everyone learning about that last night on the tour. She liked flirting with Collin, had loved being in his arms for that brief moment at the Slope. Savannah kicked at a small pile of hay on the floor.

"I don't know," she said, and the words felt like another failure. How could she have reached twenty-seven years old and not know what she wanted out of life? Bennett started to say something, but Savannah held up her hand to stop him. She didn't want a platitude. This was something she had to do herself. "I think I'll go see if Mama needs help getting the pies and jams ready for the market this morning," she said, and hurried out of the barn before her father could tell her she wasn't a screwup, that she would figure things out.

"Savannah." He called after her, but Savannah kept going. Into the house and up to her childhood room. She sat on the side of the bed, putting her hands to her head. She couldn't milk a freaking cow. What kind of person who grew up on a dairy farm couldn't milk cow?

She had to figure this out. She needed to decide what she wanted, and she needed to decide fast. She couldn't hide in Slippery Rock forever. She wouldn't let herself just float. She'd come home to figure out her life.

"Savannah?" her mother called from downstairs. "I'm about ready to leave. You coming?"

Savannah stood, straightened her shoulders. "Coming, Mama."

Savannah wasn't sure what she hoped to accomplish by working the farmers' market this morning. She'd already failed at her second attempt to milk a cow. It wasn't as if spending a day selling Mama Hazel's state-fair-winning apple pie and telling locals about their dairy farm was much in the way of penance for going into that bus with Genevieve's husband.

It was nice to be here, though. The clock tower on the county building that dominated the town square read 11:05, but it had been broken for as long as she could remember. Bright Missouri sunshine was just beginning to clear the trees on the east side of the marina. Before long, that hot sun would make it nearly unbearable in the brick building where locals sold their pies and jams and things. Not to mention the cracked-pavement parking lot where her father and brother were selling fresh milk, other farmers sold berries, and Collin Tyler sold the first pickings from the orchard.

The scent of fresh produce made the air taste almost magical, peppered with the muted conversations of the farmers working the market, talking about topsoil conditions, the importance of the early rains they'd been having and the potential for severe weather later in the summer, which had so far bypassed their part of southern Missouri.

Savannah couldn't remember ever being at the farmers' market before, which was just another mark against her, she knew. She'd been too wrapped up in her own misery before leaving Slippery Rock to think about weather conditions as more than a bad-hair-day nuisance.

God, she'd been so self-centered.

Through the storefront windows she caught sight of Collin's tight butt in worn jeans, and another wave of regret hit her. She'd been crazy to be so forward with him at the lake last week. Of course, his overly sincere "you're my best friend's sister" excuse was equally idiotic. The man was twenty-eight, not sixteen. The time for teenaged bros-before-hos dating rules was long gone.

He was right, though. They should keep their distance. The last thing she needed right now was another fling. What Savannah needed was to figure out why she kept sabotaging every good thing that happened to her. Getting wrapped up in Collin Tyler was not going to help her figure that out. She wondered if Slippery Rock had a therapist with a couch she could borrow for an hour or so.

Mama Hazel bumped her elbow into Savannah's ribs. "He's turned into quite the nicelooking young man, hasn't he?" Her gaze, too, focused on Collin's butt as he bent to pick up another crate of apples. He stood and Savannah swore she could see his quads and hamstrings ripple beneath the worn denim covering his thighs. She shook herself.

"I hadn't noticed," she lied, and quickly began rearranging the pie boxes on the folding table Levi had set up earlier that morning.

"Psshh," Mama Hazel grunted. "You didn't notice that boy about as much as I didn't notice him." Savannah shot her mother a shocked glance. "What? I'm married and over fifty. That doesn't mean I've lost my ability to recognize Grade A Man Meat when I see it."

Savannah blinked. She didn't think her mother had ever said something so…sexual before.

Hazel giggled like a schoolgirl and the crow's feet at her eyes deepened.

"I don't think you've ever said anything like that to me before."

"Then it's high time I did. For example, and this will deepen that blush on your cheeks a bit, did you know your father—"

"No, don't say it," Savannah interrupted, shaking her head as she put her fingers in her ears. "I'd like to keep my illusions about you and daddy and your abstinent lives intact, please."

"And just how did we get Levi if we were abstinent?"

"The same way you got me. Stork." Savannah finished her pie box pyramid and started on a pyramid of blackberry preserves. Hazel laughed.

"You children are hysterical. Over twenty-five and still believing in the stork and that their parents don't have the sex."

"First, it isn't 'the sex,' it's just sex. And, no, parents aren't allowed to have it. It's in the parenting rule book."

Hazel took apart Savannah's pie pyramid, grumbling about the lattice work denting from the stack. "Hate to break it to you, Van, but there is no rule book. It's just a lot of luck and figuring things out on the fly."

Savannah chewed on her lower lip, considering. This wasn't the place to have a conversation about her childhood, but so far she'd been pretty good at avoiding having it at the ranch. Maybe having it here, where they'd be interrupted occasionally by customers, would make it simpler.

"I made you figure a lot out on the fly."

Hazel chuckled and finished arranging the pie boxes in a pretty fan pattern. "You were a challenge, that's true, but I've always liked a challenge. And I loved you from the moment

I laid eyes on you in the back of that social worker's minivan."

"I wasn't much to look at."

Her mother shook her head. "You weren't. Hair all tangled up because the white officers who brought you in didn't know what to do with it, dirty from head to toe, and wearing not much more than a few rags. You looked at me, and I just knew."

"Knew what?" Savannah asked after a long minute.

"Knew you were mine." Hazel wiped a dark brown hand over the pristine tablecloth. "Just like I knew you needed your space when you were in Los Angeles. Just like I knew you'd come back home when you were ready. The only thing I don't know is how long you're staying."

Savannah wasn't sure how to answer her. She'd left Slippery Rock because she didn't feel she belonged here. Had followed her wandering heart to a reality show, and then a recording studio in Nashville. She had an album nearly finished, had been kicked off a tour and was now persona non grata in Nashville for at least a little while. She'd been back in Slippery Rock for nearly two weeks, and she knew she couldn't hide forever, but for now, it felt right to be here.

More right than it had felt in any of the years she'd lived here as a child, and she thought maybe it was because coming back had been her choice. Sure, she'd been running away from something bad, but she could have kept running instead of stopping here.

She didn't want to tell her mother about Nashville yet, though. If she never had to tell her, that might be for the best. Savannah had a feeling Hazel's support might not survive a blow like that. And where would she be if the one person who had been fighting for her all her life suddenly stopped fighting for her? What if Nashville was the thing that made Mama and Daddy and Levi realize they never really loved her at all?

A few customers began trickling in the doors. Savannah put on her best reality-show contestant smile and focused her attention on the locals buying her mother's pies and jams instead of the unasked questions in her mom's dark brown eyes.

By noon they had sold out of Mama Hazel's pies and had only a couple jars of preserves left. The cool of the early morning had long passed, and when a break in customers occurred, Savannah offered to run down to the bait shop for a couple of cold drinks.

She crossed the street, waving to a family in a minivan who allowed her to cross early. Barrels filled with marigolds, petunias and impatiens were placed every few feet along the main street of town. She'd always thought they were too hokey for words, but the familiarity of them was actually nice.

Bud's Bait Shop, which did double duty as a sandwich shop, was blessedly cool when she opened the door. A small bell hanging over the door tinkled. Air-conditioning poured into the hot street, and Savannah breathed deep.

Bud stood behind the counter, and he seemed shorter to Savannah. He still wore his salt-and-pepper hair in a comb-over, and his overalls were a pinstriped blue-and-white, just as she remembered.

Hand-written signs advertising night crawlers and worms were taped to a glass-fronted cooler on the left side of the counter. On the right was a menu for cold cut sub sandwiches, coleslaw and potato salad. The same brands of fishing lures lined the shelves, and along the back wall were fishing poles in every color, shape and size Savannah could imagine. It was like stepping back in time.

"Hey, Bud, two Cokes, please. From the fountain."

"Savannah Walters. I heard you were back in town. What's going on with that fancy Nashville record deal?" he asked as he shoveled ice into two oversize foam cups and set them under the fountain machine.

"It's going," she said, and ordered herself to come up with something better to say to the question nearly everyone in town had asked since she'd returned. "I cut the last song a few weeks ago." She didn't bother to tell the now-familiar lie that she was taking a break from the tour. Lying made her feel almost as squidgy as anticipating how people would treat her when they learned why she'd really left Nashville. "How's the bait business?"

"Better the bait, the shorter the wait," Bud said. "Be better if we could get some rain in here, cool off the water. Hot lake makes the fish lazy."

"I always thought a hot lake made the fish frisky."

Bud put lids on the cups and punched a few numbers on the register. "Depends on the day, I suppose. That'll be two dollars."

She handed him the money, stuck straws in her back pocket and picked up the drinks. "See ya later, Bud."

"See ya, Savannah," he said as she pushed the door open with her hip. "You tell Hazel if she has any preserves left, I'll take 'em."

Hot, sticky air assaulted her, making her wish she'd put the straws in the cups for a quick sip before leaving the air-conditioning of Bud's shop.

She hurried across the street, handed her

mother one of the Cokes and shoved her straw through the plastic lid before taking a long drink. She closed her eyes, letting a few of the bubbles tickle her nose, enjoying the taste. The advisors for the reality show had told the contestants to back off sugary drinks and fried foods during the show, hoping to keep everyone svelte and looking good on the cameras.

Savannah had kicked her Coke habit cold turkey. Until today. And she didn't even care that the cup in her hand represented about three hundred bad calories. It tasted like heaven.

Finally, she looked around. Most of the other vendors were tearing down tables and displays. Their table was completely empty. "Darn, Bud was hoping for a jar of preserves," she said.

Hazel nodded. "I swear, that man has to be about fifty percent preserves by now. I saved him a jar, and I'll have your father drop it off when he stops in there for his usual Saturday cheat meal." Bennett's cheat meal consisted of a sub with every kind of lunch meat Bud had on hand, a slathering of mustard, and Colby Jack cheese. Savannah's stomach growled. Not a good idea. Cheating with a soda was one thing; a sandwich like Bennett's might send her into a deep food binge.

Savannah took the white cloth from the table

and began folding it. Hazel took it from her. "Don't do that, sweetheart. I can get it. Why don't you go see if your father or brother needs anything?"

Savannah felt a little like a teenager, being told where to go, but Hazel had always been particular about how things were folded and put away. She figured letting her mother do the grunt work would actually save time. And give her a moment to apologize to Collin Tyler for…whatever that had been at the lake.

Okay, so she didn't want to apologize to him so much as just talk to him again. The man was like a denim-clad, dusty magnet, and maybe if she talked to him her brain would wrap around the fact that he was just another guy.

Nothing special.

She caught a glimpse of him through the plate-glass window fronting the inside of the market, and her heart thumped in her chest. So maybe he was grumpy and uninterested in her, but there was definitely something attractive about Collin Tyler. Maybe she would just ogle him a little.

She found a stall that had already been emptied out in the parking lot, sat on the table and watched. Levi and her father had things clearly in hand at the dairy table. A couple of farmers loaded their leftovers into the beds of their pickup trucks. Collin sat on the gate of his truck, feet dangling inside dusty boots, and a tight T-shirt covering his torso. He was chewing on what appeared to be a piece of straw, making Savannah laugh.

Only in Missouri would a twenty-eight-year-old orchard owner sit on the gate of his truck chewing on a stick of straw like some actor in one of those black-and-white comedies from the 1940s.

Only in Missouri would the man not look ridiculous doing it.

Okay, maybe cowboys in Texas or Wyoming could look that good being a stereotype, too. But still.

"He looks ridiculous," a sullen voice said to Savannah's left. A young girl with long blond hair in a French braid, wearing a faded T-shirt, ripped jeans and Chuck Taylors rolled her eyes when Savannah turned in her direction. "Like we're living in the eighteen hundreds instead of the twenty-first century."

"I take it you don't like farmers' markets?"

The girl scuffed her shoe against some loose gravel. "Not when I'm here under duress. He says I owe him compensation."

"Amanda Tyler, right?" The girl nodded. Savannah didn't remember her exactly, but her features were too similar to Collin's to deny, and since she was too old to be his secret love child, she had to be his sister. His other sister. Savannah and Mara were the same age, although they'd never been close friends. Amanda was clearly several years younger. "Savannah Walters."

"I know who you are. You almost won that singing show last winter." Amanda breathed a heavy sigh. "Even people who get out of this town don't really get out of it."

Oh, she could so relate to the teenager. The last place she'd wanted to be when she was sixteen was Slippery Rock. People either called her Levi's sister, ignored her completely or made not-quite-whispered insinuations about her adoption and the possibility that either Bennett or Hazel had a love child. Or that she was a drug baby from Springfield who needed to be saved by the wholesome Bennett family. The speculation was endless. She patted the table beside her.

"Pull up a corner of the table and we can plot your exit from the oppressive Slippery Rock."

That got a grin from Amanda. She sat beside Savannah, swinging her legs.

"Why do you owe him compensation?"

She mumbled something Savannah didn't catch, but before she could ask again, Collin interrupted.

"I said five minutes, not fifty." Annoyance laced his words and his expression, which was focused on Savannah rather than his sister.

"There was a line at Bud's and I was barely gone fifteen," Amanda retorted. She shoved the cup in her hands at her brother and stomped off. "I'll be in the truck if my penance is over."

"What did she do?" Savannah couldn't resist asking.

Collin looked from her to his sister's retreating back, and then winced when she slammed the door of his truck. "She shouldn't have been—" he squeezed his eyebrows together as if searching for the right word "—bothering you."

Savannah sat straighter, reading between the lines. He didn't really see this situation as Amanda bugging someone, he saw it as his innocent baby sister being led astray by Savannah Walters, Screwup. "You really think in the two minutes we were talking I could have convinced her to...what? Run away from home?"

"Isn't that what you did?"

"I tried out for a reality show. I was over twenty-one. It isn't the same thing."

"That isn't what I was talking about."

Savannah blinked.

Collin watched her for a long moment, and then said, "I was talking about homecoming night, my senior year, your junior."

Her breath caught in her throat. She didn't think anyone outside the family knew about the time she really had run away. The night the boy who'd asked her to the homecoming dance, the boy who'd made her feel like she might finally fit in here, had called to tell her he couldn't take her to the dance because she was mixed race. She'd been waiting by the front door in the pretty peach gown she and Hazel had found in Joplin, she'd straightened her hair and spent an hour on her makeup.

And she'd wanted to die.

She'd run as far as she could, gotten lost in the woods between the ranch and the lake, and spent most of the cold, rainy night hugging a tree trunk and hoping there were no wolves or bears in Missouri. Bennett had found her at dawn the next day. He'd carried her home, but no matter how gently they'd asked what had happened, Savannah hadn't been able to tell them.

People in town trusted and liked the Walterses, despite racial tensions in the area, but she wasn't really a Walters. She was different, and that boy made sure she knew it.

"How did you know about that?"

"Who do you think drove all the country roads with Levi that night while your dad and my grandfather and Sheriff Calhoun searched the woods?"

She swallowed. He'd helped look for her. God, no wonder the pristine Collin Tyler wanted nothing to do with her. Collin, who had the perfect life with his perfect family whose roots went back further than the Walters clan. Collin, who was a Tyler by birth, unlike her, a Walters by adoption.

"I should thank you for helping Levi that night. And it was no bother talking to Amanda. Mama Hazel sent me out here to get out of her way and into my dad's. I decided to steer clear of both and enjoy a cold drink. Amanda made for a little company."

"Still. She had her orders."

"And I'm not the kind of influence you want around her. Well, from what I recall, teenage girls don't do so well with orders. You didn't answer my question. What did she do? Skip curfew?" Savannah knew she should drop the subject, but she couldn't. Despite Amanda's obvious annoyance at Collin, there was something very connected about the two of them. Family dynamics fascinated her.

Collin rubbed a hand over the back of his neck. "What hasn't she done? Cut class, skipped curfew. She was with the kids who set that fire downtown just after you got back into town. Last weekend she duct taped the one-ways downtown to run the way she thought made more sense. She needs a keeper."

Savannah chuckled. "Sounds like some of the stuff you guys did back in high school." Pranks and raids she'd never been invited into, not that she was bitter. Even if Levi had asked, she would never have gone.

"Totally different."

"Because you were boys and she's a girl?"

Collin's mouth twisted to the side and a little stab of attraction hit her belly. Lord, but a man twisting up his mouth shouldn't be so hot. Especially when said man was once again dusty from head to boots. At least he'd dropped the piece of straw.

"We never taped off downtown. We didn't set any fires—"

"I didn't see her name in the police blotter."

"Technically, she was trying to put it out, but that doesn't—"

"I remember something about the five of you absconding with the sheriff department's boat," she interrupted him.

"We were pretty sure there was a drug deal going on at the sandbar at the time. And no one would listen to us."

"So five high school football players were going to do a citizen's arrest, at night, on potential drug runners in the middle of the lake?" She tilted her head to the side. "You guys wanted to take your girls out on the lake that night, admit it." He beetled his brows again. "In the grand scheme of things, your prank was a lot more dangerous than taping off a couple of streets."

"It's still not the same."

"Of course it isn't. She's your sister. Doing idiotic things is part of growing up. It isn't like she's on the fast track to the supermax prison in Colorado."

Collin exhaled. "I thought you were an aspiring country music star, not a headshrinker."

"Yeah, well, I'm multitalented," she said, not wanting to get into the therapy sessions they'd attended when she was first adopted, and that Mama Hazel had gotten her into again after the homecoming dance. She could talk the talk, but if Nashville was any indication, the Walterses' money hadn't been well spent in regard to her mental health.

She needed to get out of there before she forgot this was Collin. The guy who disliked her so much he made up a lame excuse about a bro code so he didn't have to spend time with her. "I'm sure my family has had enough time to empty out the stalls and prep for the trip back out to the ranch. See you around, Collin," she said, stepping away from the table.

"Sure, I need to pack things up, too." He

looked at her as if unsure what to say. "I'll see you around, Savannah," he said.

Savannah couldn't resist watching him walk away.

She picked up a few foam cups that had been left behind by either vendors or shoppers, and hurried to the trash can near the corner of the building. Mama Hazel was picking up some of her empty boxes. If she hurried, she could take them off her mom's hands.

Voices around the corner of the building stopped her in her tracks.

"Did you see her slinging jams and pies with her mother?" Marcy's voice cut through the afternoon air, stopping Savannah in her tracks. She giggled a little. "She never would have bothered with that in high school."

"Because she was too busy pretending to be just like the rest of us," Dana, Marcy's best friend and co–head cheerleader, said. At the Slope a few nights ago, Savannah had been surprised at how much Dana had changed. The tall, thin woman, who had had frizzy red hair and an addiction to Little Debbies in high school, now straightened her hair and looked as if no sugar had passed her lips in the past decade. "When she's nothing like us," she added.

Savannah pressed her back against the brick wall. She told herself to walk away, but couldn't make her feet move. It was as if she was right back at Slippery Rock high, hiding in a bathroom stall while the other girls talked about her crazy hair or her unusual coloring or, in the very worst of moments, speculated about her life before she landed in Slippery Rock.

"As true as that is, I meant she wouldn't have bothered because she was so over-the-moon for Vince Honeycutt. She was too busy skulking after him to do anything productive."

"Selling jams and pies is productive? Come on, Marcy, it's a step down from being a clerk at Mallard's Grocery."

"How is it a step down?"

"Because the Mallard family has a choice in who they hire. Her family is stuck with her because they saw her as some kind of waif in need of saving. But not even Bennett and Hazel Walters could make her into anything good. I mean, she couldn't even win a silly talent contest."

Walk away, Van, walk away.

"Come on, you bought her single."

"Because she's from Slippery Rock. What is someone going to think if they click into my music app and the one person from here who has a song on country radio isn't in my playlist?" Savannah could envision Dana rolling her eyes and shaking her head as she spoke. "I am the daughter of the town mayor. People expect us to be civic-minded."

One of them giggled, but she couldn't tell which one. Maybe both of them because the sound seemed to morph and grow into something much uglier than a simple giggle as Savannah listened. God, and she'd been the one to call them about girls' night out. How they must have laughed about that. The abandoned and adopted Walters girl calling two of the most popular, former cheerleaders at Slippery Rock high to go out for drinks.

Savannah fisted her hands and pushed off the wall. She'd pretended to be oblivious to the Marcys and Danas of Slippery Rock high school all those years ago. The truth was, she'd let them feed her fears about the past, and look where that had gotten her. Possibly blackballed from Nashville, sleeping in her childhood bedroom without a clue what she might want to do with her life. She was twenty-seven years old.

She was too old to sit back and take this kind of…of meanness.

Savannah pulled a bill from her pocket and stepped around the corner of the building. Marcy saw her first, and her eyes practically bugged out of her head. Dana turned slowly, but where Marcy was now blushing and looking anywhere except at Savannah, Dana simply stared at her, as if daring her to confront them.

In school, Savannah hadn't been strong enough for these kinds of girls. Hell, she wasn't sure she was strong enough now. She knew one thing, though—she was tired of running away from the things that hurt.

"I think coming in third from a pack of more than three thousand people who tried out and the twenty-five contestants isn't such a bad placement. It isn't quite as sad as, say, having daddy call the school when a certain girl wasn't chosen for head cheerleader."

Dana blanched, her body recoiling as if Savannah had slapped her. She kind of wished she had.

"How do you know that?"

"I was in the principal's office, talking about college placements, when your father stormed in. He didn't notice me sitting across from Mr. Tolbert. That's okay. Most people ignored or didn't notice me back then. I kind of liked that because being ignored is so much better than being bullied."

"I never bullied you—"

"You never hit me, and you never said anything mean to my face, but can you honestly say this is the first time you've talked about me behind my back?" Marcy's face flamed a bright pink. Dana narrowed her eyes.

"If we were such bullies to you back then, why did you call us the other night?" she sneered.

Savannah offered the five-dollar bill to Dana. The other woman folded her arms across her chest. "Calling you when I got back to town was a mistake. Kind of like you wasting a buck fifty buying my song when it came out." Dana didn't take the money, so Savannah let it fall to the ground between them. "You can keep the change." She turned on her heel and walked away.

Savannah pasted a smile on her face when she entered the farmers' market, kept her back straight and her shoulders squared. She wanted to slink away and hide, but where could she go?

What was that saying about people like Dana? Whoever is trying to bring you down is already beneath you. There was another one, too. That the person trying to bring you down is insecure about themselves. That one had been on a poster in the office of one of the family therapists Mama Hazel and Bennett contacted when she was a teen. She'd never believed that saying, but when she'd been standing around the corner from Dana and Marcy, something clicked. Marcy had never been outwardly mean to her, at least not in high school, and she'd seemed embarrassed when she first saw Savannah come around the corner.

Dana, on the other hand, had been. Too many times to count, she had been leading the gossip while Savannah hid in the bathroom stall or simply pretended she couldn't hear what was being said two rows behind her in Biology class.

Calling Marcy had been a gamble.

Not walking out of the Slope as soon as she saw Dana come in with her was a mistake.

If she'd left, though, she wouldn't have that dance with Collin.

Inside the farmers' market, Savannah picked up the last of Mama Hazel's boxes and pressed a quick kiss to her cheek.

"Now what was that for?"

"For being you," Savannah said. And for the first time in a very long time, she thought she might be on the way to finding herself.

CHAPTER SEVEN

SAVANNAH ROLLED TO her side and blearily picked up her ringing cell phone. She checked the screen. Guy Lambert. Her manager. She blinked. At not even eight in the morning. A shot of adrenaline made her sit up and slide her finger across the screen to answer the call.

"Savannah, listen, I know I said get out of town a few days and this will all blow over. I may have been too optimistic," he said. "There are rumblings along Music Row that several new artists are being cut from the label, and your name is at the top of the list."

Never a man to waste time on formalities. At least he hadn't dragged it out.

"Oh, God," she said and slumped back against the headboard of her bed. "Is it all over town?"

"All the rumblings are about money. You know, the label is huge in New York, but this is their first dip into Nashville. So far, their gambles on new talent have only paid off with one star—Genevieve."

"And we know how she feels about me." She

had every right to hate Savannah. Every right. Still, it hurt. Not the loss of the contract so much as the knowledge that she'd hurt someone besides herself this time.

"Well, that part of the story is still underground."

"When will you know for sure?"

"I've got lunch scheduled for next week. I'll talk you up, you know the drill. If we can just get them to release your album, there's a chance. If not, we have to hope when they release your contract, they also release the tracks."

Savannah blew out a breath. "Thanks for calling."

"Sorry it isn't better news," he said. "How's Mayberry?"

"It's Slippery Rock, and it's okay."

Okay was maybe too strong a word, but she doubted Guy would care. He was her manager, not her friend. "Hey, do you know what they're planning to do with the music program?"

"You are not coming back here to volunteer with the rug rats, Savannah," he said. "We need you out of town until Genevieve remembers she isn't the grieving spouse, she's just the embarrassed spouse."

"No, I know. I just thought if there are money problems it might impact the program. It's a good program."

"I never thought of that."

Of course he hadn't. Guy thought about making and collecting money, not using it for charity.

"Do you think, if they don't release me, that I could start something like that on my own?" Savannah wasn't sure where the idea had come from, but once she spoke it aloud, it was as if the idea had always been in her subconscious. She wasn't a teacher, but she'd liked volunteering with the music program.

Fostered and adopted kids like her could use an outlet like music.

Guy laughed, the sound harsh in her ear. Savannah winced. "Why would you want to waste your money on kids who won't appreciate what you're giving up? Listen, Savannah, I'll call you after the lunch. Stay out of trouble, okay?" he said and ended the call.

Savannah sat on the bed for a long moment, then swung her legs over the side and pulled her robe across her shoulders.

The program idea was a good one, despite Guy's dismissal. She had a little money saved from that first song release and the winnings from the reality show. Maybe she could use it to do something good.

Stay out of trouble. Guy's voice echoed in her mind.

Savannah Walters wasn't the kind of role model troubled kids needed in their lives.

She smelled bacon frying and her stomach revolted. She couldn't eat. Couldn't face her family over the breakfast table. Savannah closed her bedroom door, threw her pajamas and robe on the unmade bed, and pulled on a pair of faded jeans and a yellow T-shirt.

She needed to get out of there.

COLLIN DROVE THE orchard four-wheeler through the grove of peach trees, happy with the new growth and the shape of the fruit beginning to come in on the branches.

If only raising a teenager was as easy as raising fruit trees.

That wasn't quite fair. All a tree wanted was rain and sunshine. Teenagers needed a lot more than that, and he'd been so wrapped up in the rain and sunshine part of his life that he had ignored just how much Amanda was being left behind. Not just by their parents, but by the whole family.

Mara hadn't been back to Slippery Rock, other than a few one-day trips at Christmas, in several years. She blamed the absence on her job with the cyber-security firm in Tulsa where she worked, but Collin knew there was more to it.

He would have to dig deeper with her the next time she called home.

Just as he was learning to dig deeper with Amanda.

He had assumed since their parents were always unreliable that it wouldn't bother Amanda when they came and went, but obviously their most recent disappearance had done some major damage. No surprise since it had followed on the heels of their grandfather's death a couple of years before, and their grandmother's decline in health.

Even though they shared an orchard, a dinner table and a grandmother, Amanda had been virtually abandoned since Granddad died. He'd made a promise, on the day Granddad had brought them to the orchard, that neither Mara nor Amanda would ever feel that kind of abandonment. He'd dropped the ball on that, but he could pick it up. He could keep doing the work that would ensure they had financial stability. Financial stability would lead to emotional stability, too. Collin had made promises to the girls all those years ago that went deeper than money in the bank, and it was time he started to make good on those promises, too.

With school out for the summer, he'd put Amanda to work with one of his hired hands in the greenhouses this morning. She'd only grumbled a little and he considered that a fill-in-parenting win.

He came to the edge of the grove, which backed onto Slippery Rock Lake, parked the four-wheeler under a tree and looked out over the blue water.

Promises he hadn't kept.

Oh, he'd made sure the orchard was profitable, he'd worked with Granddad to learn the basics and then learned more in college, but the important things, the never-leave-anyone-behind things, he'd set aside.

Then he'd gotten all bitchy with Savannah at the farmers' market last weekend. He'd nearly told her he didn't want her befriending his sister when, God knew, his sister needed a friend.

Sunlight glinted off another vehicle closer to the shore. Collin leaned forward, wondering if Levi had come to the lake to cool off, but those curves didn't belong to his buddy.

A quick hit of lust fired in his veins as he watched Savannah strip out of her jeans and tee, revealing a tiny bikini that made the smoldering fire combust into a roaring blaze.

She tossed her clothes over the handlebars of the four-wheeler she drove, ran to the small dock Bennett had built when they were teenagers and dived into the water. She surfaced a moment later, flipped onto her back and stretched her arms and legs out to float over the surface.

Collin gripped his handlebars tightly, telling himself to start the engine and go back to the orchard. His hands remained tight over the rubberized grips as he watched her float. She disappeared behind a tall oak only to reappear near a poplar. In a few minutes she would completely disappear behind the tall fir trees that dominated the forested area on the south side of the lake.

He pulled at his collar. Suddenly the light breeze seemed stifling. Maybe the pear and apple trees could wait while he cooled off in the water, too. He glanced down at the cargo shorts he'd pulled on this morning after the local radio host said the temperature would top ninety. They weren't board shorts, but they were better than the boxer briefs he wore under them. Or the Speedo that Mara sent him as a gag gift on Valentine's Day. She'd attached a note—"Go show off your stuff and find a woman already"—and a goofy card with speed-dating jokes on it.

He should continue with his day.

Collin started back down the path, but at the fork where he told himself to turn right for the return to the trees, the four-wheeler turned left.

This was a bad idea, he told himself, but he couldn't get his hands and body to obey the instructions to turn the four-wheeler around and get back to work. It took only a couple of minutes to get to the dock area.

It had grown over a bit. When they were kids, he and Levi had kept the area free of weeds. One especially enterprising summer, they'd bought sand to make a beach, but a storm blew through and the sand wound up at the bottom of the manmade lake. After that, they'd stuck with weeding and mowing.

And since Savannah hadn't realized he was there yet, he would turn right around.

"Hey, stranger," she called, and he wondered how he'd missed her swimming back to the dock. She pulled herself out of the water, muscles beneath her light brown skin bunching and releasing as she did. Water dripped around her, and she lifted a towel to her face.

His mouth went dry. The bikini bottoms were emerald green, held together on the sides by four thin strings that met in the middle in a tiny triangle several inches below her flat stomach. A matching green jewel winked at him from her belly button, making his toes curl.

No woman had ever made his toes curl.

One more reason to turn the four-wheeler around and get away from the lake.

He didn't need this right now. He had enough on his plate with the offer from Westfall Foods and his sister. He didn't need raging hormones pushing him to make a wrong decision.

She squeezed water from her hair and then bent at the waist to gather the mass of loose curls on top of her head in a ponytail. Savannah started toward him, bare feet leaving a trail of footprints behind her. She slipped her narrow feet into flip-flops at the edge of the dock and neatly tied an oversize beach towel around her waist like a sarong.

That only served to focus his attention on the green-and-white-striped triangles covering her pert breasts and her nipples making little points beneath the wet fabric.

"I figured straight-arrow Collin Tyler would be hard at work in the orchard, it being a Monday and all," she said when she reached the four-wheelers. "What are you doing slumming it on a lakeside beach?"

"Saw you from the ridge," he said, pointing dumbly as if she didn't know there was a ridge behind them where the orchard began. "Wanted to make sure it wasn't some kid from town trespassing."

Savannah nodded, shaking her head. "Figures you'd come down here like the police to throw out someone who doesn't belong. You know, sometimes people just want to have a little fun."

Collin blinked. What did that mean? If she

had been a townie, not that he'd been in any doubt, she would have been trespassing—an illegal activity. "People shouldn't swim alone," he said. Then he considered her words. "And if that was a straight-up slam against me, I know how to have fun."

"Playing lifeguard is your definition of fun?" Her soft voice sounded musical to him, which was odd since her rigid stance and folded arms screamed that this time she wasn't flirting. She was annoyed.

When she put it like that, no. But practicing his CPR skills on her suddenly seemed like a good way to pass some time. Not that he would do that. This was just about talking, being friendly so that whatever this was between them moved firmly—and only—into the friend zone.

"Actually, I thought a swim seemed like a good idea. Why are you in such a foul mood?" Not that he could blame her. He hadn't exactly rolled out the welcome mat since Savannah had come back to town.

Something flashed in her chocolate eyes and, for a split second, Collin thought she must be hurting over something. Possibly over someone. Then the emotion was gone and she shook her head.

"I don't know how to milk a cow."

Collin blinked and then tugged on his earlobe

as if he could tune his ear the way he tuned his car. There was no way Savannah Walters was upset about not knowing how to milk a cow. She'd never seemed at all interested in the Walterses' family business.

"Did you say till a plow?"

She folded her arms over her chest.

"Lick a towel?" He couldn't resist teasing her.

"Milk a cow," she said, enunciating each word carefully.

"Why would you want to milk a cow?" He was curious now, wondering what had gotten into this woman who used to be the girl he thought he knew everything about, even though he'd never really spoken to her.

She shrugged and wouldn't look him in the eye. "It's what my family does. Figured it was time I learned."

"You're twenty-seven and you want to learn how to be a dairy farmer? You could have started with something easier."

"Like what?"

Collin opened and closed his mouth, trying to think of something simpler than milking a cow. Nothing came to mind.

"See? I'm inept." Savannah sank onto the seat of her four-wheeler, shoulders slumped. "I don't give a fig about milking cows, but after being raised mostly at the ranch—and why do they call it that, anyway? It's a dairy farm. No one calls it a dairy ranch—"

Collin interrupted. "Your grandfather raised beef cattle. Bennett is the one who made the switch to dairy. The name stuck, though."

She blinked at him. "Oh. How did I not know that?" She shook her head. "Don't answer that, I already know. I was a scared kid who turned into a stubborn, angry, self-absorbed teenager who never bothered to ask questions. Still, I should have picked some of it up, right? I couldn't even get one of the cows to follow me into the milk barn this morning."

There was a lot to key into in those few sentences, but Collin stuck with the actual farming bit. He had no business giving anyone personal advice, but he was good at the business side of things.

"No one learns dairy farming by osmosis, Van," he said, her nickname slipping from his lips as if he'd always called her by her family's pet name. "If you really want to learn, I'm sure Levi or your father would be happy to show you the parlor."

She rolled her eyes and the expression was so similar to the Savannah he remembered that he grinned at her. "No one calls it a 'parlor' anymore. It's just a living room."

"The 'parlor' is what they call the milking room."

She blushed, a pretty pink color that made the light sprinkling of freckles over her nose stand out. Collin swallowed.

"See?" she said. "Inept."

"Is there a sudden need in Nashville for milkmaids?"

Savannah shook her head, as if his question didn't matter, but there was an emotion he couldn't quite read in the depths of her big brown eyes. He had a feeling the question did matter. A lot.

"I'm just feeling disjointed, I suppose. Being back here when I've been touring for a while." She fanned her face with her hand. "I'm going back in for another dip before I face round two in the milking parlor."

"Here's one tip. If the cows have already been milked this morning, there's no way in hell you'll get anything else out of them until at least midafternoon."

"Then there's plenty of time for another swim," she said, and pulled the elastic from her head, making all that thick hair frame her face. She looked about twelve with her hair pulled back, but with it all in her face, she was pure siren. Collin ordered his libido to back off.

It didn't listen.

"Well, are you coming in or not?" Savannah stood, took the towel from around her waist and laid it over the seat of the four-wheeler.

He should go back to the ridge and refocus on his business and his family.

He always did the right thing. He was the one to hide his sisters when children's services came to the tiny apartment in Kansas City when they were little. The one to call their grandparents when he realized CPS would keep coming back, and that their parents wouldn't. He worked hard at the orchard so his grandfather didn't have to hire additional help, worked hard on the football field to get a scholarship, worked hard in college because he knew keeping the orchard growing would fall to him. He was glad he'd done those things. He'd carved out a nice life from the mess his parents began all those years ago.

As much as he had messed things up with Amanda, the two of them would find a rhythm and she would find her purpose.

Taking the morning off to swim with Savannah wasn't the same as blowing off work for an afternoon at a strip club, but a voice in his head still warned him to turn the four-wheeler back toward the orchard.

The hot summer sun beat down from the sky, and the beautiful woman slipped off her flip-flops and walked to the dock. It was just a quick swim, and then right back to the orchard and he would finish his weekly survey of the trees. Maybe it wouldn't be so bad to do the wrong thing just this once.

Collin pulled his old T-shirt over his head and threw it across the handlebars. Ten minutes, and right back to work.

His body cut through the water in a smooth dive, and the cool water instantly made him glad he was off the four-wheeler and out of the sun. He blew air out through his nose and then surfaced, cutting his arms through the water as he stroked toward the middle of the narrow lake.

This wasn't showing off. It was swimming. Enjoying the late Monday-morning sunshine and heat. If Savannah was impressed with his stroke, there was nothing wrong with that.

Not a damn thing wrong with that.

He came up for a breath and realized Savannah was right beside him, cutting through the water with a strong freestyle. Of course she could swim. Bennett had probably taught her just as he had taught Collin and Levi when they were kids. They swam side by side for a while. Collin's arm brushed hers a few times, and a little zing of heat seemed to sizzle the water around them.

Finally, Collin flipped onto his back so he could see the clouds lazily floating in the crystal-blue sky.

God, he loved this place. He looked beside him. The company wasn't bad, either.

Savannah flipped, too, breathing heavily. "It's been a while since I swam like that."

He watched her for a long moment, staring at the sky as he had been. Her breasts rose unevenly as she slowed her breathing. Her long brown hair floated around her in long, skinny braids. She looked so inviting. It would be easy to close the space between them and taste those full lips. Feel her body under his hands.

No. Kissing Savannah was a step past bad, straight into terrible.

To occupy his hands he waved them gently in the water, putting a little more space between them. "Me, too. Usually when I come down here it's to jump in the water and get right back out."

"Seems like a poor way to spend an afternoon at the lake," she said. Savannah gently kicked as she floated, sending a few ripples his direction.

Suddenly, jumping into the water with the intention of getting right back out did seem like a poor excuse for relaxation. Well, he was making up for that now, he thought as he spread his legs and arms wide.

He turned his head to look at her again. "Yeah, well, you're a bad influence," he said, joking. But he caught that fleeting expression again, a darkness that almost turned the brown of her iris black, and that made him want to draw her to him. He regretted the words. "That was a joke. You're not actually a bad influence. On me or... anyone else." He didn't want to have this conversation looking at the sky, so Collin turned his body around to tread water, but she remained on her back, not looking at him.

"No. I am a bad influence, or at least, I've done some things I'm not proud of."

"We all have. I shouldn't have said that, and I shouldn't have implied it at the market, either. You were just talking to Amanda, and she obviously needs someone to talk to."

"Yeah, well, I didn't exactly make a great impression on you that night at the Slope. Coming on to Adam, then making a ham-fisted play for you." Savannah changed position to face him, too. "I was doing what I've always done. Being the good-time girl. I'm tired of being that girl."

Savannah blew out a breath. She shouldn't be talking about this with Collin. She knew that, but she couldn't seem to stop the flow of words. She did want to change, and she didn't care all that much about dairy farming or milking parlors, but after that call with her manager she needed to figure out some way to make herself useful. Not just to her family, but to herself.

There was very little chance she would be useful to anyone in Nashville now that her record launch was on hold and the scuttlebutt around town was that the label was considering dropping several new artists. Her name was at the top of their hit list.

Earlier that morning she'd stood in the driveway for a long moment, trying to figure out where she could go. Bennett took her Honda to a repair shop in town, so she didn't even have a working car. The sound of cows in the barns was her inspiration. Maybe she could finally figure out a way to fit in here.

And she'd wound up at the lake, trying to swim off her aggravation at her own stupidity. Now, as she faced Collin in the cool water, she wondered if she'd been right from that first moment in the bar.

She didn't belong here in the long run, but would it be so bad if she had a little fun while she was here? Kissing Collin, feeling his hands on her body, would be more than a little fun. They were both consenting adults. Sure, sex was part of what had gotten her into this mess, but Collin wasn't married or even dating anyone as far as she could tell. No-strings sex with him couldn't make things any worse.

She allowed the current in the water to carry her closer to him. "Well, maybe I'm not completely ready to put Good Time Savannah into the closet."

Collin's pupils dilated, making his light blue eyes darken.

Definitely both consenting adults, she decided when he didn't kick away from her. Her foot touched his leg under the water, and that zing of heat she'd been trying to resist since she'd seen him beside the dock intensified. She swam a little closer, letting her legs tangle with his.

"I've never been interested in being a good-time guy," he said, and although his voice was rough, the look in his eyes told her to come a little closer.

"It has its benefits," she said, closing the distance between them. Legs kicking in the water, arms skulling forward and back, they hung there for a long moment. Savannah couldn't sever the connection between their gazes. She didn't want to. She wanted him. Wanted, just for a little while, to not be Savannah the Screwup.

Collin was a good man. No woman could be called a screwup if she was with him.

That magnet thing happened again. Savannah felt herself being pulled the remaining inches until she was chest to chest with Collin. She stilled her legs, letting him kick for both of them and locking her arms around his waist. She tilted her head to the side and put her lips on his.

His mouth was softer than she had imagined. He didn't smile very much, and somehow she'd thought his mouth would be hard because of it, but his lips were smooth. She slid her hands over his back, his skin slick beneath hers, and couldn't resist sliding her hands over his ribs and chest so she could bury her hands in his hair. Collin's arms came around her waist, holding her in place as he ran his tongue over the seam of her lips.

She opened for him, and he dipped his tongue into her mouth.

God, she should have kissed him a long time ago. Should have made a bigger fool of herself at the Slope. Should have set her teenaged sights on him instead of that troll Vince Honeycutt.

They slid beneath the surface, but she didn't care. Even under the water she felt like she could kiss Collin for a year and not get enough of him. He kicked hard for the surface, and when they broke free of the water, leaned away from her.

Savannah leaned forward, but Collin released her. Maybe it wasn't the same for him. Maybe it was just a kiss, not an earth-shattering, life-changing event.

How stupid could she be?

"If we're going to do this, it isn't going to be in ten feet of lake water," he said, his tongue tripping over a couple of the words and his breath coming in ragged gasps just like hers. He watched her for a minute, but Savannah couldn't make her voice work. She could only nod.

Collin's big hand captured hers under the surface and he began a slow kick back toward the dock. Savannah kicked alongside him, feeling as if she were in a daze.

When they reached the dock, Collin pulled himself out of the water before reaching for her hand to help her up. When her feet were on the dock, he pulled her into his arms and this time his lips weren't soft. They were devouring.

His big hands played the sensitive skin along her rib cage while his mouth nipped at her lips. Savannah put her thumbs through the belt loops of his cargo shorts, holding him close to her. She could feel the thickness of his erection through the layers of his clothes, and the hardness sent a wave of heat between her legs.

"Not here," he said against her lips.

"We're not in the water," she said, pressing her mouth to his once more. "No worries about drowning or man-eating bass attempting to feed on our flesh."

"God, Van, this isn't a horror flick," he said, and a chuckle escaped his throat.

Savannah thought Collin's chuckle was one of the sweetest sounds she'd ever heard.

"I mean we aren't getting naked here on the dock. This is private property, but between your ranch and my orchard there are about thirty different people who might decide to go for a swim this afternoon."

"Where do you suggest we go on a Monday afternoon when we both still live at home? I'm assuming you live at the orchard?" He nodded. "How pathetic are two twentysomethings who can't have sex because their mommy—in your case sister—might catch them?" Savannah giggled.

"There's a hunting cabin on the east side of the pear grove that no one uses anymore."

"Too far." She couldn't do this, not if she had to walk or drive to do it. It would give her too much time to think, and thinking would make her second-guess, and second-guessing would leave her with a set of raging hormones. She could get off by herself, but it was never as fun as getting off with someone else.

And that, right there, was the number-one reason to say goodbye and run like hell away from Collin's fabulous chest and very talented mouth. The last time she'd had sex for the hell of it she'd blown her life up. There was a chance having sex with Collin would blow up in her face, too, but there was a bigger chance, based on that night at the Slope, that it wouldn't. He wasn't tied to anyone; he didn't want ties to her. No one had to know.

She slid her fingers through the belt loops on Collin's cargos and pressed her lips to his mouth, demanding a response. Collin wrapped one hand around her neck as he devoured her lips. She could feel the coarse hairs on his chest through her wet bikini top, and it pushed the fire in her veins to another level. She wanted to feel his skin against her, wanted to wrap her legs around his waist and lose herself for a little while.

"We're not going to make it to the cabin," he said against her lips.

"And we're not doing this at noon on the dock, either." Her breathing was heavy, and she tried to push aside the lust fogging her brain to figure out a solution. Her gaze caught on the tree line near the shore, and she remembered a small grassy area where she'd liked to sunbathe.

Savannah grabbed his hand, leaving her flip-flops and clothes on the ground near the dock, but grabbing her oversize towel as they passed the four-wheelers.

She was going to have sex with Collin Tyler, and there were a million reasons to say no, but she was determined to ignore every single one.

It only took a moment to pass through the

trees near the dock. She laid the towel beneath the spreading branches.

"I think this is out of the way enough, don't you think?"

"I'd forgotten about this little area."

"I guess it wasn't my secret hideaway, hmm?"

He shook his head. "We're not going to talk about that."

She nodded. "No, we're not." She didn't want to talk about past sexual partners or teenaged—or adult—trysts either of them had here before.

His fingers walked up her spine, and she shivered. She was thinking too much again, and it annoyed the hell out of her. Yes, she wanted to change her bad habits, but couldn't her newly found conscience shut the heck up for the next fifteen minutes?

There was one way to shut it up.

Savannah stepped up on her toes to press her open mouth to Collin's neck. She could feel the pulse there accelerate. He pulled on the top string of her bikini top and then the bottom string before tossing it to the side. He walked her backward until her back pressed gently into a tree, and she didn't even care that the bark was rough against her skin. It was merely another stimulating part of this moment with Collin. His rock-hard chest at her front, the tree at her back, and as much time as they wanted to take. The waves of heat rolling across her senses intensified.

God, but she didn't want to take this slow. She wanted fast and hard and breathlessness.

Savannah buried her hands in the hair at his nape and kissed her way up his neck until her lips met his. His hands found her breasts, and when he nipped at her lower lip, she arched her neck so he could do the same to the sensitive skin there. His thumbs flicked against her tight nipples, and Savannah couldn't hold back the low moan that escaped her throat.

She had to touch him, had to do more than leave her hands buried in his hair. She loosened his belt and unbuttoned his shorts, letting them fall from his hips. His erection was hard against her hip and she couldn't resist reaching past the waistband of his boxer briefs to feel his length.

He was warm in her hand, despite the cool lake water. Warm and hard and, God, she couldn't see him, but based on the feel there was more enjoyment to be had in a few minutes.

She worked her hand up and down his shaft, squeezing lightly as she did.

A *lot* more enjoyment.

"Do that much longer and this is going to be over before either of us wants it to be," he said against her collarbone.

Savannah released him, but only to push the

boxer briefs past his hips. Collin shimmied them down his legs but before she could reach for him again, he went to his knees on the grass beneath the tree.

Hands at her hips, he pressed kisses to her abdomen, focusing on the little gem that dangled above her belly button. He was close, so close to her core. Her knees nearly buckled when he dipped his tongue into her belly button as if he might drink from her. She fisted one hand in his hair and kept the other firmly against the trunk of the tree, trying to keep herself upright.

With a flick of his wrist, Collin disposed of her bikini bottoms, and she was naked before him. He pressed a kiss below her belly button and then another farther down her belly, and then his mouth was at the junction of her thighs and he pressed a kiss to the curls there.

"So sweet," he said as he pressed a finger inside her.

Savannah caught her breath and when his thumb found the tight bundle of nerves near his mouth, she forgot to breathe completely. She could only feel. With his fingers and his thumb, he set a rhythm that was as close to torture as Savannah ever wanted to be. She was perched precariously on the fine wire between awareness and blessed oblivion, and she didn't want it to stop.

Collin's mouth replaced his thumb, his tongue teasing her, and it sent her crashing over the edge. The orgasm shook her, made her feel weak and boneless, and if Collin didn't still have his body against hers, she would have collapsed onto the ground.

He kissed his way back up her body, his hands hard against her abdomen, and when he kissed her mouth she could taste herself on his lips.

"More." She didn't know where the word came from. She only knew this couldn't be the end. She wanted more of him, wanted more kissing and touching and, heaven help her, she wanted to feel again that blast of electricity that hit just before he'd sent her crashing into that orgasm.

She pulled him down onto the towel with her. It was barely wide enough for the two of them, but she didn't care that she was partially on the soft grass. She only cared that the intricate patterns he drew with his fingers on her belly were making that fire in her veins burn hotter again.

Collin grabbed his shorts, pulled out his wallet and the plastic-wrapped packet inside.

"You went swimming with your wallet still in your pocket?"

"Grabbed it when we passed the four-wheelers," he said as he opened the packet.

"Boy Scout."

He grinned wickedly at her. "Always Be Prepared has always seemed like a good motto to me." He rolled the condom over his considerable length, but she didn't want him taking the lead this time. Savannah pressed her hands against his shoulders and, when his back was on the towel, straddled his hips.

Savannah put her mouth over his nipple, biting lightly, and Collin hissed in a breath. "I'm no Girl Scout," she said, "just in case you wondered."

"Technically, I was never a Boy Scout, either," he said and rolled his hips so that his penis teased at her opening.

Savannah sank down, letting his length fill her. Warmth spread through her. His hands returned to her breasts, kneading and caressing. Savannah began to move, her hips in rhythm with his, sliding up and down his length.

One of his hands moved to her core, and his thumb found her clit again. The stimulation both inside her body and out was too much, and once more she went crashing over the edge. Collin's hips pumped into her once, twice more, and then he grunted his own release.

Savannah sank down on his chest, and listened to his rapid heartbeat.

It thumped in time with her own. That warmth spread through her chest again, and she slid to the side. Collin's arms came around her, holding her to him, their legs intertwined. He slid the condom from his length and laid it carefully on top of his briefs.

When she could speak she said, "Wow." The word felt inadequate.

"Yeah," he said, his breath whispering through her hair as his fingers traced along her shoulder.

Savannah drew her index finger over his chest, liking the feel of his short, wiry chest hair against her hands. She thought she could lie like this, with this man, forever.

Collin shifted beneath her. "But this should probably not happen again," he said. And she went cold.

She hadn't expected a declaration of love, not for a one-morning stand. She wasn't sure what she had expected, but it wasn't this…this…blow-off.

"Another lame excuse about me being Levi's sister?"

He was quiet for a long moment, and Savannah sat up. "You realize this isn't high school, right?" she asked.

"Yeah. This wouldn't have happened in high school."

"Because you never gave me the time of day back then. But then, I guess you're really not giving me the time of day now, either, are you? You're just here to get down and dirty so you can keep presenting the perfect facade you've got going to the town." Savannah stepped into her bikini bottoms and then tied her top with shaking fingers. She couldn't look at him. "God, I'm an idiot."

Collin grabbed his shorts, pulling them over his hips. He stuck the wadded-up boxer briefs in his pocket along with his wallet. "That isn't what I meant." He shook his head. "You're here on a break from your life in Nashville, and as you saw at the farmers' market, I've got my hands full playing the part of father for my teenage sister." He grabbed her wrist when she turned away. "I didn't mean I'm sorry this happened, I just meant I need to keep my focus on what's real and permanent around here."

"And I'm not permanent." The words hurt more than Savannah wanted to admit. She wasn't here permanently, that was true. Whether her career was over or not, she couldn't see living in this place where people looked at her as if she were different.

As if she didn't belong.

"Van," he said, but she shook her head.

"No, you're right. I'm leaving, and you have your own things to deal with. You shouldn't have to add me to that mix." She picked the towel up off the ground and folded it carefully.

"Savannah, don't be angry."

"I'm not mad. I'm not anything." *Anything but sad*, she added silently. Because, just once, it might be nice if someone like Collin thought she was worth the trouble of getting to the real Savannah. Whoever the real Savannah was. She stepped away from him. "Have a good afternoon."

"Savannah—" he said, but she turned to walk back to the four-wheelers.

At the dock she pulled her T-shirt over her head but threw her jeans and the towel into the little basket on the back of the vehicle, started it up and sped back along the path to the ranch.

Savannah brushed her hand along her cheek, angry that she was crying over Collin Tyler. Angry she'd had sex with him. Angry she thought coming back here would help her come to terms with the past. She should leave. Find the place where she did belong.

She stopped the four-wheeler when the path along the lake met the lane that led to the ranch house. Savannah used a corner of the towel to wipe the remnants of her tears from her face. She pulled her shorts over her hips, and did her best to finger-comb her hands through her mass of braids. She wished she had a mirror, just to make sure when she reached the house that she didn't look like she'd just had sex.

For the first time since she'd first come to

Slippery Rock, though, the prospect of leaving held no shine. She wanted to stay. Not because of Collin. Because of her. People here knew her, and some, like Dana, hated her for reasons she couldn't fathom. More people, she was beginning to realize, just knew who she was, and didn't judge her for what might have brought her to the Walters family or Slippery Rock. Being famous in a small town was different from the paparazzi attention that came with being famous in a big city.

Maybe she didn't belong in Slippery Rock right this second, but that didn't mean she couldn't belong here in the future.

Maybe, if she worked hard enough, the future could come sooner.

CHAPTER EIGHT

HE COULDN'T GET Savannah or that morning at the lake out of his head.

It was just sex. Amazing sex. With an awkward conversation at the end because, while he knew he shouldn't stay with her, he'd been tempted to do just that. To stay right with her in their little clearing for the rest of the day. To turn that day into a week or maybe a month or… however long he could make it last.

But he couldn't blow off work just for sex with Savannah Walters. He had responsibilities. Collin Tyler did the right thing. Responsibilities were the right thing.

Having sex at the side of the lake on a beach towel with Savannah Walters might have felt right, but it was all kinds of wrong.

And thinking about it like this was all kinds of obsessive. It had been three days. Three long days and three interminable nights in which he fell asleep imagining the feel of her body under his hands, and woke up sweaty, tangled in sheets he'd dreamed were made of terry cloth. With a raging hard-on.

He hadn't taken as many cold showers since he was a sixteen-year-old.

Collin checked the soil in a few of the greenhouse saplings, but the feel of the soft dirt reminded him of those moments on his knees in front of Savannah. He withdrew his hand as if he'd been burned. Maybe he'd check on things outside the greenhouse. Or he could go to his office to figure out a way for Tyler Orchards to become the supplier for Westfall Foods without losing either their farm stand or the market in town. Both were integral pieces of the orchard that had saved Collin and his sisters all those years ago. He couldn't turn his back on them now.

He started for the barn, but saw a blond head in the garden.

They'd planted Gran's berry garden a few weeks before and he found Amanda kneeling in the dirt, harvesting a few ripe strawberries.

"Hey, kid, grabbing an afternoon snack?"

The strawberry plants were looking good, and the raspberry and blueberry vines, too, he noticed. In another couple of weeks, Gran would have a good harvest, and they would have berries to add to the offerings at the farmers' market.

Amanda looked up, bitten strawberry in her

hand. "Gran was going to teach me how to make a strawberry pie." She frowned and then sighed. "But she got tired and went up to take a nap. I thought maybe I'd figure it out on my own." There was a hopeful glint to her clear blue gaze.

Collin shook his head. "I know how to grow and pick the food around here. Baking it is beyond me." Her gaze fell.

"Can't be too hard," she mumbled, and snapped a few more strawberries off the plant, dropping them into the bowl at her knees.

Maybe he could struggle through an afternoon in the kitchen. It would take all his concentration, which would mean less time for thoughts about Savannah. And he still had three weeks to come to a decision about the Westfall offer.

Collin bent and snapped off a few strawberries.

"Maybe I could figure it out."

"You don't have to."

"I know."

"I don't need a babysitter. Seventeen-year-olds know how to cook without burning down a house." She picked up the bowl of berries, holding it to her chest.

"Did I ever tell you about me, Levi and Adam, Home Ec class and a cherry cheesecake that looked like something someone had vomited up?" He put his arm around Amanda's shoulder and began walking to the house with her.

"We'd mixed all the main ingredients, but Adam thought the cherries should be combined into the mix. It was already beginning to mold so Levi grabs a mixer from another station, Adam dumps the can of cherries into the bowl, and Levi starts mixing them. And the cheesecake is starting to look pink, like Pepto-Bismol, and I'm thinking there is no way this can be right. But there was no turning back."

Amanda giggled. "The cherries go over the cheesecake. You guys were idiots."

"Yeah, that goes without saying. So we pour the three or four cherries that were left in the can over the cheesecake and stick it in the fridge."

"Did you fail?"

"No, our teacher gave us a C for creativity. It didn't taste half-bad, if you could get past the look of it. Gran banned me from the kitchen after that."

"And so you never learned how to cook?"

"I can do toast. Eggs. Some pasta, as long as the sauce is from a can. Stuff that doesn't call for a recipe." They reached the kitchen, and Amanda began washing the strawberries. "Speaking of, do you have the recipe?"

She pointed to the wooden recipe clip shaped like a small iron that Collin had made their grandmother for Mother's Day one year. He read the recipe. Didn't seem too daunting. He arranged pots, a pie plate and the other ingredients.

"You don't have to waste your day spending time with me. I'm used to entertaining myself," his sister said.

"I don't mind," he said absently as he read the recipe.

When Amanda plopped the bowl of berries on the counter, droplets of water sprayed the paper and Collin's arms.

"You want to cut the berries, and I'll start mixing dough for the crust?" She shrugged, which Collin decided was as close to a yes as he was going to get. He handed her the cutting board and began mixing the crust ingredients.

"I haven't asked what your plans are for the summer." School released the day he'd met Savannah at the lake. Three days ago. Damn it, he needed to stop using sex with Savannah as a time measurement device. Collin punched the dough in the mixing bowl.

"I assume I'm still on work duty for the farmers' market and the roadside stand."

"Of course, but you don't have to be at either 24/7."

Amanda scraped the tops of the cut strawberries into the trash, checked the recipe and

began making the sauce while Collin rolled the
dough into the shape of a piecrust. It was cool
and smooth, like Savannah's skin when they'd
first left the water.

Cooking sucked.

"You don't even listen to me when we're working on something together." Amanda dumped
the strawberries into saucepan on the stove and
stormed out of the kitchen.

What had he done now? Collin sighed. He
wiped his hands on a red-checked towel, clicked
off the stove burner and removed the pan from
the hot element. He turned off the oven and hung
the towel over the handle on the oven door.

He found her sitting in the gazebo swing in the
side yard. Their grandfather had built it to look
like a miniature version of the big barn, with
swings on two sides. Collin slipped through one
of the open ends and sat across from her.

"I'm sorry I wasn't listening. I had…" He considered his words. "Something else on my mind.
It's a terrible excuse. I'm sorry."

She wouldn't look at him.

"Amanda."

She curled one leg under her, leaning against
the arm of the swing as she pushed her other foot
against the floor. "It doesn't matter."

Except that it did. He sucked at parenting.
He'd been using his sister as a distraction from

Savannah when the two of them had already decided not to go any further with whatever was pushing the attraction between them. He'd never been one to get preoccupied with sex, but since that morning with Savannah it was all he could think about.

"You matter, kid, and I'm sorry I screwed up the kitchen thing. I'm not sure how to be your parent, but I'm trying."

"You could start by not being my parent. I've already got two lousy ones." She chewed on her lower lip.

Collin lightly kicked her foot with his. "You need someone, and while Gran's still sick, I'm what you've got."

"Great."

He sighed. With any other teen, he might think the attitude was overly dramatic, but he'd never known Amanda to go for that kind of thing. And he had been a jerk in the kitchen. For longer than that, actually.

"Maybe I'll go back to being your brother, then?"

She shrugged.

"I know I missed it in the kitchen, but how *do* you want to spend your last summer as a high school student?"

Finally, she looked at him. "Work with you?"

"I meant other than working at the market and the farm stand."

"Yeah. I thought, maybe, you could teach me about the trees."

"You want to know how the orchard works?"

She nodded, her nearly white-blond hair flying around her face as she did. "I want to know when to transplant the saplings and how you know a tree has finishing providing fruit and how you can tell a fruit is ready to be picked. I want to learn about the sustainability things you do, and what our carbon footprint is—"

Collin held up his hands. "That's a lot to take in in a single summer." Her interest was surprising. Any time he'd asked her about the orchard before, Amanda had seemed completely bored by how an organic orchard worked.

"I can learn it, and I can keep working with you in the fall. I checked with the guidance counselor, and I could do a work-study thing where I go to school in the mornings and work here in the afternoons—"

"You checked with the guidance counselor?"

Amanda nodded. "I have all the credits I need already to graduate, so if I'm working here half the day, I only have to figure out two morning classes instead of a full class load."

"So you want to work here by default? So you don't have to take a bunch of classes you aren't interested in?" That made more sense than her sudden interest in farming.

But Amanda surprised him again. "Yes to the uninteresting classes part, but no to the default part. There was an assembly earlier this year about environmental protection and green initiatives. It was really inspiring. That's when I started to get interested in how things run here, but you've been pretty busy."

Collin was stunned. "It means being in the orchard by six every morning."

"I can do that."

"And it's a lot of hard work, running an organic orchard. No pesticides, so we have to do other things to keep the pests away."

"I know, I've been reading about it."

"You're not going to have a lot of extra time to hang out with your friends."

"I don't care. This is more important."

God, she sounded like him. Although he'd always made time for the guys and fit "orcharding" around them. He had one more question. "If you're so interested in the environment, what's with wasting who knows how many rolls of duct tape downtown?"

"The one-ways are wasteful. There are only about ten thousand people in town. Making them all take extra laps around the courthouse square to find a parking space just because all those streets only go one direction wastes gas and puts more exhaust into the air."

Collin blinked. "You tried to re-route town traffic to be less wasteful?"

Amanda nodded. "But you and Officer Calhoun wouldn't listen to me."

"I'm not sure you actually tried to explain your actions."

She shrugged. "If I'd tried to explain, would you have listened?"

"Probably not." Definitely not. Until this conversation, he'd thought Amanda was oblivious to global warming, eco-friendly farming and carbon footprints. "But I'm glad I listened today. You want to go finish that pie?"

"Yeah. We can surprise Gran at supper."

They walked back to the house, and Collin thought maybe the two of them had turned a corner. Now to turn that corner with his sudden obsession with Savannah.

Maybe after a little more dough-pounding he would find a solution to the Savannah issue, and the Westfall offer, too.

Savannah pulled Mama Hazel's car to a stop at the farm stand near the turnoff for the orchard. Hazel had sent her over for irregular apples so she could bake caramel apple pies for the farmers' market coming up on Saturday. Why she needed irregular apples, Savannah didn't know.

She wasn't even sure what irregular apples *were*, but after secluding herself at the ranch for the past three days she had run out of things to do. She'd cleaned out her old closet, tossing most of the things she'd left behind when she'd left home—like the yearbook her cheerleader "friends" had signed, a pair of tennis shoes that had seen better days and an especially embarrassing rhinestone-embellished, fringed blouse she'd worn to sing the national anthem at the county fair rodeo the summer she graduated from Slippery Rock High. She'd helped Hazel with spring cleaning in the house, pretending she was too focused on the work to talk, and attempted one more time to figure out the milking apparatus in the parlor.

She'd failed. Maybe she should just ask her dad or her brother how it all worked. YouTube videos and online tutorials were certainly not working.

She'd also spent way too much time thinking and dreaming about Collin.

Getting out of the house was a good thing. She could reassure herself that Collin was merely a man and not a Thor-like sex god. Added bonus, she could let him know that she wasn't hung up on him.

Much.

Well, for all he'll know, she decided as she checked her reflection in the mirror, *I'm not thinking about him at all.*

She put a few dollars in the pocket of her shorts, picked up the reusable grocery bags from the passenger seat and left the car.

Amanda sat inside the booth.

Damn. Now Collin would have no idea how not-hung-up on him she was.

"Amanda, right?" The younger girl nodded. "I'm here for about ten pounds of irregular apples. Think you can help me out?"

She shook her head. "We keep all the irregulars in the barn. Customers get the best of the stock. You could go up there to get some, though, we have plenty."

Savannah leaned against the counter. "Could I ask you a favor?"

"Sure." She seemed happier today than she had Saturday at the farmers' market.

"What's the difference?"

"That's not a favor."

"The favor is don't tell your brother I asked."

Amanda grinned. "Irregulars look different. They're not bad apples, mostly they're just misshapen or their color is off. Most people think bad color means bad taste, so we don't bring them to the stand or the market."

That made sense. Savannah didn't cook, but when she picked up an apple or a tomato or any other fruit or vegetable she always picked the prettiest ones. "How much for ten pounds?"

"Oh, we don't sell the irregulars, you can just take them."

"Since Mama Hazel is using them for pies, we'll buy them."

Amanda shrugged, but she took the money Savannah handed over the counter.

"So, up at the barn?"

The girl nodded. "Follow the lane around and go in through the big doors, they'll be open." She tilted her head to the side. "Can I ask you something?"

"Sure."

"Why did you come back here?"

Savannah blinked and then realized Amanda was talking in generalities, not about the incident at the lake. She really had to get her mind off Collin.

"I had a break from the tour—" she began, but Amanda cut her off.

"You could have gone anywhere, but you came back here."

For a teenager, she saw way too much. "Well, I hadn't been back for a while. I missed my family." She was surprised to realize the words were true. She had missed Bennett, Hazel and

Levi. More than she'd ever imagined she could miss anyone.

Amanda nodded. "Yeah," she said, and it was as if the weight of the world were in that single syllable.

Savannah started to turn away but then asked, "Did that answer your question?" She knew it was a lame question, but she didn't really know Amanda. She didn't want the girl to feel as if Savannah were prying into something that was none of her business.

The girl shot a look over her shoulder and then nodded. Savannah would have pushed, but Amanda had picked up the magazine on the counter and focused her attention there. Savannah had been dismissed.

It only took a minute to drive Hazel's sedan up the orchard drive. She parked in front of the massive red barn and took a couple of reusable grocery bags from the seat. She didn't bother to check her appearance. Obviously she'd been obsessing about nothing. Collin was probably out checking his trees or something.

The interior of the barn was dark as she walked in through doors big enough that a tractor could pass through them, and she blinked to adjust her gaze. Tractors and other farm equipment was arranged on one side of the structure, and tables filled with wooden bushel baskets and other paraphernalia filled the other. Savannah crossed to the side with the tables. Several of the baskets were filled with apples that looked odd.

Some had strange color markings, and a few were so misshapen around the core they looked like they were squinting. She filled both bags and returned to the car to put the apples in the trunk.

She was in the clear, she should go.

Savannah looked back at the barn. She didn't want to leave.

She wanted to talk to Collin. Not have sex. Just talk. And let him know he wouldn't be getting any more sex from her.

That seemed a bit childish. She shook her head, slammed the trunk.

Things were going to be weird if they didn't talk. With Collin being buddies with her brother, they were bound to run into one another often while she was back in town. She didn't want those interactions to be uncomfortable or weird.

He was probably in the orchard, anyway, but she could at least check the door near the back of the barn with the sign reading Office.

Before she could talk herself out of it, Savannah marched back into the barn and knocked on the door. No answer. Just like a man to not be around when a woman wanted him to see how not-hung-up-on-him she was.

Probably for the best, anyway. Chances were she'd say something she would regret later. Or find it impossible to not kiss him again.

"No one uses that office anymore," Collin said from behind her.

Savannah whirled, putting her hand to her chest. "What are you doing here?"

"I work here, and I own the place. What are you doing here?" He looked scrumptious in another pair of cargo shorts, this time olive-colored, and a black T-shirt. The man had to have stock in some cargo shorts company, as often as he wore them. He had old Nikes on his feet, and a Slippery Rock High ball cap on his head. His sunglasses were perched on the bill. "Finished with your inspection?"

"I was buying apples."

"Nice try. The apple stand is at the end of the drive."

"I needed irregulars." He raised one eyebrow in disbelief. "For Mama Hazel. She's making pies. For the farmers' market. Caramel apple."

"And the apples are?"

"In the trunk." She pointed to the blue sedan.

"And you're knocking on the office door because…?"

"Because I don't want to have sex with you." Savannah immediately wished the words back. "That came out wrong." She fisted her hands at her sides. Well, she'd started this. She could finish it. "I, uh, wanted to let you know I'm okay about how things ended the other day. I'm not interested in starting anything up with you, either. So, we don't have to avoid one another or feel weird around one another or...tell anyone else about what happened."

There, that *almost* sounded like something a self-confident adult would say. Collin looked bewildered. Or something. She couldn't quite read the expression in his clear blue gaze. He tilted his head to the side and the movement reminded her of his sister. The Tyler family definitely had that resemblance thing down. Longing squeezed Savannah's heart. She'd spent so long pretending to find resemblances between herself and her adoptive family, and then so long pretending it didn't matter that she was so different from them. Her skin lighter, her hair different.

She wasn't like them, though. Her parents and her brother always did the right thing. Savannah made all the wrong moves, although it was hard to remember that having sex with Collin was a wrong move when he was standing three feet away from her, the embodiment of a bunch of her teenage fantasies.

"I'm glad you cleared that up."

"Yeah, well, I'm trying to...be more responsible about things, and since we'll be seeing one another at the market, I didn't want things to be awkward."

"Okay." He waited a long moment, watching her. Savannah switched her weight from one leg to the other. "What happened to the Honda?" he asked finally.

Savannah glanced outside toward Mama Hazel's big blue sedan. "Turns out that check-engine light was an actual thing. It's out of commission for a while."

Collin nodded. "I'm glad you had it checked." He moved past her to the office door.

"Where are you going?"

"To the office to go over some paperwork."

"Oh." This was awkward. She should go. *Walk to the car, Savannah, and drive away. Far, far away.* "Why are you going into the office if no one uses it?" she asked, following him inside.

The room was dusty, the window looking out over the orchard streaked with dirt. There was a big wooden desk along one wall, old filing cabinets along another. The chairs were old but didn't look rickety. No phone, no computer. Collin reached into the filing cabinet and pulled out an old ledger.

"Needed to go over some old numbers," he said. "I don't use the office, but it's a good place to store the old files."

"You should transfer them to the computer."

He tilted his head to one side. "When I figure out how to get twenty-seven hours out of a day instead of twenty-four, I'll consider it."

"You sound like Levi. I tried milking again. That osmosis thing still isn't working."

Just leave, Savannah. Just go, she told herself, but she couldn't get her feet to obey her brain's orders.

"Watch a YouTube video. You'd be surprised what you can pick up."

"Have you learned anything by watching YouTube videos?" All she'd learned from the videos so far was how to make a fool of herself in front of some cows.

He shook his head. "No. But I've heard." Collin leaned a hip against the dusty desk. "For someone who isn't here to have sex, you're finding a lot of reasons to stick around."

"I'm testing the awkwardness level. If we can have a conversation alone, we can have a conversation when people are around us." And maybe if they kept talking, her feet would get the unspoken message to move. "So what are you working on that you need a ledger from 1950?"

That brought a smile to Collin's lips, and Savannah relaxed. Maybe they could get past the post-sex awkwardness. He might already be past it, but this was good practice for her. She didn't want to let another I-don't-want-sex comment to pass her lips when people were around.

"It's actually from '99. The year my grandfather expanded the orchard. He bought forty acres from a neighboring farm and put in another ten acres of apple trees. I need to look at yield totals and do some estimating." He stood.

"Why?"

"Because it's what farmers do."

"I've never seen Bennett or Levi go back more than five years." At least, she didn't think they had.

"Look, seeing you is going to be awkward, and not just because we had sex. Talking to me about orchard totals isn't going to ease that awkwardness." Collin shook his head. "I'm sorry I was abrupt the other day. I'm not…in a place to start anything romantic or personal, and having sex with you was…" He trailed off.

"Personal?" she asked hopefully.

He took off his baseball cap and twisted it in his hands. "Yeah, it was personal. I should have handled it better, and I didn't."

"I'm a big girl, Collin, and I'm not sorry it happened. We can just be friends, though. Or just hey-how-are-you merchants at the market."

"Good," he said.

Savannah moved to the door and, before she could talk herself out of it, turned back to him.

"It was personal for me, too. If you get past whatever it is you're doing with the old ledger, I'll be around." And then she walked as quickly as she could to Hazel's car, telling herself she was a million kinds of fool for telling him she would be around. He didn't need to know that. It was bad enough she'd said it was personal for her, too.

She wasn't going to be around, at least not for him, whether or not her manager called with good news. Slippery Rock was just a place to get her feet back under her, nothing more.

She put the key in the ignition but instead of backing away, sat looking at the big barn for a long minute. Savannah couldn't afford to let herself get too comfortable here. She wanted to, but she'd let herself get comfortable once before with Vince Honeycutt. He'd been as suave as any high school boy could be, and she'd fallen for every line that came out of his mouth. And that got her pressed against a tree in her formal dress in the rain. All she'd wanted from Vince with a little bit of teenage normalcy—she hadn't been foolish enough to think a homecoming dance would lead anywhere important.

Getting comfortable with Collin would be so much more dangerous. He didn't say the right things, and he was grumpy. She still wanted normal, and he was ridiculously, sexily normal.

He could shatter the pieces of her heart she was finally trying to glue back together.

CHAPTER NINE

SATURDAY MORNING DAWNED bright and clear at the orchard. Collin woke to the sound of cardinals in the trees outside the window, and for the first time in more days than he cared to count, he wasn't waking up thinking about Savannah.

Much.

He showered, lukewarm instead of ice cold, and pulled a pair of jeans over his hips. He grabbed a Tyler Orchards T-shirt and his favorite ball cap, but skipped the boots. It would be too hot for boots today. He slipped his feet into his old Nikes and headed for the kitchen.

His grandmother, Gladys, had made pancakes and she pointed him to the table. "Short stack or tall?" she asked, her slight Missouri drawl more pronounced than usual. She wore orthopedic shoes on her feet, jeans, a Tyler Orchards T-shirt, and her hair was held back with a colorful scarf. She looked like a shorter, older, female version of him. He studied her closely. The paleness of the last few weeks was gone. Her eyes were alert. The post-surgery limp remained, but he thought it didn't seem as pronounced.

A wave of love and relief rushed through him.

"Short. How are you feeling this morning? And where's Amanda?"

"She rushed through breakfast a few minutes ago and said she was going to make sure the truck was ready to go. What's gotten into that girl?"

"She says she wants to learn the business."

Gran shook her head. "I hope she stays with it." She brought his plate, only limping a little, and sat across from him. "I'm going to the market with you today."

"Gran—"

"I had hip surgery, not heart surgery. I miss my friends. I need to be around people," she said. "A woman can only take so many naps, and I've already taken far too many."

"That old parking lot is filled with potholes, and you know the building isn't air-conditioned." Not limping was one thing, taking Gran in her condition to the market was another. He took a bite of pancake and then another.

"And you know we didn't have air-conditioning in this house for a lot of years. I can deal with the heat, and I'm going." She set her mouth in a stubborn line that Collin recognized. It was the same expression he and his sisters wore when Gladys or Granddad laid down a law they didn't agree with.

"I'm just thinking of your comfort."

"And I'm just thinking of my sanity. It's been more than two months since the surgery, and the only people I've seen outside of the family are in my doctor's office. Besides, I've got Red Rider."

"Who's Red Rider? And what does he or she or it have to do with the market?"

Gran went into the mudroom and a second later motored into the kitchen on a red mobility scooter with orange flames painted on the sides and a long orange flag swinging from behind the seat. "This is Red Rider, guaranteed to make it through potholes, crowded restaurants and even a sandy beach without an issue," she said, gesturing with her hands like one of those models from *The Price is Right*.

Collin choked on a bite of pancake. "When did you get a mobility scooter?"

Gran turned off the machine, stood and returned to the stove where she flipped another pancake. "A couple of weeks ago. I couldn't sleep so I was watching one of those middle-of-the-night health shows—"

"You mean infomercials?"

She waved a hand. "Whatever. There are people older than me running all over the world on these things, and you know I'm not as fast as I used to be. I figured one might be the answer to my problems. Plus, you won't have to wait on me so much. It arrived yesterday and I tipped the delivery driver an extra fifty to help me put it together."

"Gran, I don't mind waiting." He didn't. He might get frustrated when she asked him to run back and forth all over the grocery, but at least he had her in the store with him.

"I mind." She looked at the scooter as if inspecting it. "I'm not sure I'd have painted it to look as if there were flames shooting down the sides, but then again, the flames are kind of cool, don't you think?"

He sighed and got up to inspect the scooter. The tires seemed fine. It was electric, so no worries about gas or oil. Collin decided to make a deal.

"If I put your scooter in the truck so you can get around easier, you have to promise that you'll use it. No leaving it in the market while you traipse off with your friends," he said, feeling as if he were talking to a teenager rather than his grandmother. He had to, though. Gran might seem excited about the scooter here, but once she was around her friends there was no telling how she would feel. Gran started to say something, but Collin held up his hand. "Do we have a deal?"

Gran drew her brows together. "Fine."

A half hour later the three of them were at the market, Amanda watching the table inside with jams and jellies, and him outside with the apples, berries from the garden and a few early peaches and pears. Gran cruised the aisles on her scooter, the orange flag flying behind her as she motored around, talking to her friends. Collin shook his head.

Maybe he'd been wrong about Gran's mental health. This morning she'd seemed like her old self, not the sad, tired woman he'd been worrying about the past few weeks.

He spotted Savannah inside with Hazel at their table. She wore a white tank top, olive shorts, and had her hair pulled back in a ponytail. Long chains hung from her ears, and he wondered if she still wore the green belly button ring or if she'd changed it. Could belly button rings even be changed?

She laughed at something Mama Hazel said, and the pure joy on her face sent a shiver of awareness through him. Collin couldn't remember her ever laughing or smiling that freely in the past. Whatever had brought Savannah home, it seemed to have changed her from the sullen person she had been all those years ago into someone a little less angry and a little more happy.

Happy looked good on her.

He knew he wasn't being completely reasonable. He hadn't interacted with her enough to know if she were truly sullen or if there was something more to the quiet girl she had been.

"I'll take a dozen apples, please." A young woman with two toddlers at her knees jolted him back to the parking lot. Collin filled the basket the woman carried and then focused on the rest of his customers.

The morning flew. With summer in full swing, even if the calendar hadn't made the official changeover, people were out looking for fresh produce and other locally made goods. By noon he'd sold out of berries and had only a couple of baskets of apples left.

"Hey, stranger." Savannah came around the side of his truck with two large foam cups in her hands. She gave one to him.

"Lemonade. You looked like you could use it," she said, and sat on the edge of his tailgate. Collin joined her.

"Busy today."

"Isn't it every Saturday? I've been here twice now, and both days have been crazy."

"Sometimes I think we could run this market every day of the week and we'd have a crowd. Thanks for the lemonade," he said as he sipped from the cup.

Bud's famous lemonade, always on the tart

side, made his eyes squinch together. It was the best taste in the world. He shot a glance at Savannah. Maybe the second best, but he wasn't going there.

"Any news on the tour?"

"Not a peep," she said, and maybe he was imagining it, but her voice sounded happy about that.

"Got tired of singing about nothing, did you?" he teased.

Savannah shot him an annoyed look. "I don't sing about nothing. People loved that first single."

"Of course they did. It was a song about getting drunk and getting revenge on an ex. Who wouldn't love that?"

"Apparently you." She shot him another look. "Are you trying to pick a fight with me? Because I'll take the lemonade back."

Collin switched his cup to his other hand protectively. He backpedaled. "I'm just saying you don't see King George singing about drunken revenge."

"No, he sings about breaking the law and running off to Mexico. But that's okay because—what?—he has a penis and I have a vagina."

"That's not what I meant." He was losing control of the conversation too fast. It was just a joke.

"Because there's nothing wrong with party songs, as evidenced by where that particular one landed on the charts."

He'd offended her. Collin didn't mean to offend Savannah. Damn it, he should have just drunk the damn lemonade and kept his big mouth shut.

"I just meant...never mind. I like songs that have meaning, that's all."

Savannah shook her head. "What are you, fifty? Not all music has to be about some deep, dark issue. Music can be about having fun and being free."

He was quiet for a long moment. "What's your next single about?"

Savannah took her full bottom lip between her teeth and shot him a sidelong look. "A girl who gets dumped at her baby shower, and takes revenge in a series of diabolical ways." That was, assuming the song or any others ever got released. Savannah laughed. "So that's not the greatest example, but there *are* a couple of ballads on the album, and even one or two George-worthy songs."

"Good for you. When does it come out?"

An emotion he couldn't read clouded her big brown eyes for a moment. "I'm not sure," she said and then shook her head. When her gaze connected with his again, that strange emotion was gone. "What about you? Figure out those twenty-year-old numbers?"

Collin finished the lemonade. "I did, actually. Now I just need to figure out how to present it to a potential business partner."

"Someone's buying into the orchard?" She sounded surprised.

Was he that transparent? Contracting with the grocer was as far as he wanted to go on the partnership route.

"No, it's staying in the family. I had a meeting with a regional grocer who wants Tyler Orchards to become their main organic provider."

"That's amazing. Congratulations."

He wanted to reach out and take her hand in his, but he couldn't. They weren't dating. That one sexual experience didn't even make them friends, which made it even stranger that he was telling her this when he hadn't mentioned it to Gran or Mara or Amanda yet. Collin wobbled his head from side to side, not agreeing with her but not disagreeing, either. "It could be. The thing is, the contract would call for us to only provide to the chain. No more market or farm stand and, after this summer, possibly no contract with the local restaurants and B and Bs. I want to convince them our trees can provide ample fruit for them while still keeping the market and stand going."

It felt good to be telling someone else about his plans, even if the someone he was telling wasn't technically a friend. Maybe because the someone wasn't technically a friend. Savannah was an outsider, not someone like Gran or his sisters who might agree with his decision even if she didn't like the choice. Talking it over with Savannah could be his best chance to get an honest opinion about the choices before him.

"Why not just give them what they want? It sounds like an amazing deal."

He wanted to reach out and take her hand in his, but he couldn't. They weren't dating. That one sexual experience didn't even make them friends. "It would be. More money, more potential for growth. More stability for the family." He paused. "The stand and the market were important to my grandfather, though. It feels almost disloyal to turn away from them."

"But if it's more money for less work," she said as if she were playing devil's advocate with him. "Why not go for it? It isn't as if people won't still get Tyler Orchards' produce. They'll just get it from a bigger store."

He didn't want her to play devil's advocate. He didn't want to think of the ways it would be simpler to give Westfall Foods exactly what they wanted. And this was not the conversation to have with Savannah, the woman he'd screwed on the side of a lake earlier this week. The woman he still couldn't get out of his head. The woman whose hand he wanted to hold, whose neck he wanted to kiss, whose body he wanted to get lost in.

None of those things would help him make this decision; they might muddy it, though.

Savannah had run away from this town twice already. What could she know about the kind of root system that was so important to Collin when, instead of facing whatever bothered her, she ran from it?

Then again, she wasn't running now, was she? She'd come back, and although she said it was only for a couple of weeks, she'd already been here three and showed no interest in leaving. Maybe he hadn't given her enough credit. Running away from pain as a teen was a normal thing, wasn't it? And going on that reality show wasn't running away, exactly, it was running toward, wasn't it? His hand tightened around the lemonade cup. She was still here.

That was dangerous ground. Savannah still being in Slippery Rock right now didn't mean she would always be here any more than the offer from Westfall Foods would always be on the table.

He couldn't deny he wanted the grocer's contract, but he wasn't willing to give up on the market or the roadside stand to do it. Maybe it was selfish, but he wanted all the options. He needed to hold on to more control until he knew Amanda was back on track. Until he knew Gran was truly on the mend and not just having a good day.

If things ended badly with the grocer and he shut down the local sourcing, it would take a long time to build that trust back up.

"We're a local farm. Going into business with a chain is a great opportunity, but it's also a risk. I need to hedge the bets. This isn't anything you would understand."

Savannah blinked at him and anger lit her brown eyes. Collin leaned back. "Nothing I'd understand?" she asked, and her voice had a strange edge to it.

"You aren't a farmer. The people in this county depend on my orchard. I have business relationships with other local owners."

"That's an asshole thing to say. You think because I can't milk cows that I don't know what it means to be a local farmer? I've seen my brother and father get up before dawn for most of my life. Even when he was playing football, Levi would call home to talk about the herd or new techniques."

She twisted her wrist, sending the ice in her cup rattling against the sides. "Leaving Slippery

Rock doesn't mean I don't understand the people who choose to stay here. The fact is you'll still be providing fruits and berries and other produce to the community, it'll just come from a store with air-conditioning instead of the back of your truck."

She didn't get it. Collin blew out a breath. "And what about the people who can't afford grocery-store prices? I sell a bushel of apples for fifteen dollars here at the market. In a grocery store, that price is going to jump to at least thirty."

"What family of four needs a bushel of apples every week? You're acting like all people eat around here are apples for breakfast, lunch and dinner."

"You know, money isn't everything, Savannah."

"You're the one making this about the almighty dollar. Or did you not just say the money from this contract would mean a more stable cash flow?"

Collin wanted to disagree, but he had said that. It had been his main motivator for renegotiating the contract before he signed it. Money didn't buy happiness, but the stability of it made life easier to enjoy.

Savannah shook her head. "It's your business, none of mine, but if you want the security of the big contract you're going to have to let go of whatever it is that is making you put this market above your family's financial security," she said and hopped off the tailgate.

She walked back into the market and began to help her mother tear down the remainder of their display. Like most of the other booths, Mama Hazel's pies had nearly sold out.

Savannah had a point. A family of four didn't need a bushel of apples every week. He could go along with what Westfall wanted and then renegotiate next year when they saw that he could provide for them and the local buyers.

Damn it, this Saturday had started out so well. Gran was having a good day. Amanda seemed to be regaining her balance.

Savannah looked freaking hot in those shorts.

He'd known exactly how to present his counter-presentation to the executives at Westfall, and now he was torn between the immediate security of the deal and the tentative security of keeping things the same.

There was nothing wrong with his grandfather's way of doing business, but Collin wanted more. For the orchard and for the family. He wanted to build something bigger and stronger. Something that couldn't be torn down by anything.

Collin shoved the tailgate closed and stomped to a trash can to throw away the empty cup.

He should have kept the options to himself

to mull over a bit more. Sitting with Savannah on the tailgate of his pickup didn't make her his confidante any more than having sex with her had made her his girlfriend.

He'd wanted an unbiased and possibly uninformed opinion on his plan, and what he'd gotten was a bit of devil's advocacy and sniping about her lack of farming knowledge. She deserved better than that.

Now he'd not only insulted Savannah when he should have kept things light and fluffy between then, but he was back to square one: put all his apples in Westfall's basket or keep doing things the way Granddad had always done them.

HAVING SEX WITH Collin didn't make her an expert, but he didn't seem like the kind of guy who would want a business partner, especially one who told him where to sell his produce and for how much. Savannah tried to wrap her head around Collin's dilemma. It seemed straightforward to her: choose the road with more dollar signs attached.

She knew it was shallow, but it was also true. Money made things easier. She didn't remember much about her life before coming to Slippery Rock, but the things she did weren't pretty. Hunger and anger were what stood out the most. Hunger on her part. Loud words and angry voices from the shadowy people that stomped around the dirty little apartment. She remembered always feeling cold and the smoothness of the note attached to her thin jacket when she'd been left at the police station.

When she got to Slippery Rock it was warm. She was clean. Nobody yelled, or at least not often. There was plenty of food. Money for toys and clothes.

Taking the contract with the big chain didn't mean Collin was turning his back on the community. It meant he was choosing financial security for his family.

Without saying a word to her mother, Savannah began folding the white tablecloth Hazel used every Saturday. She carefully matched the corners, just as she'd seen Hazel do a thousand times, placed the remaining pies carefully in a box, and wiped down the tiered pie display Hazel had brought from the farm that morning. Her mother watched her for a long moment.

"Everything okay?"

"Everything's fine," she said, anger lacing her words. She couldn't breathe. Felt like all the fresh air had been sucked from the room. She had to get out of there. Savannah put the tablecloth in the box and picked it up. "I'll put these in the car."

Outside, she put the box on the trunk and then put her hands on her knees. She took a long, slow breath in and held it for a few seconds. Breathed out.

She wasn't mad at Collin, not even for that swipe he'd taken at her short-lived singing career. He didn't understand that taking that record deal in Nashville was about choosing financial security for herself.

Savannah had no illusions about why she'd accepted the contract with the Nashville label. That decision had been based solely on security, as had the decision to go on tour with Genevieve. Savannah had wanted money and she'd wanted it fast. Money that wasn't given to her in an allowance or because Bennett or Mama Hazel knew she was going out with her friends. She scuffed the toe of her sandal on the asphalt. Money that wasn't scraped together from the two-dollar tips left on the tables at the Slope.

Every single thing she'd done the last few years was for the benefit of Savannah.

She'd wanted to be able to show her family she had something to offer; that she was good enough.

For too long she'd scraped by on part-time waitressing hours at the Slope and using her mother's credit cards when she went shopping. Farm work had seemed dirty all those years ago. Savannah didn't like to be dirty, so she ignored the cattle and other chores. She liked singing because it was clean. Getting dressed up, putting on makeup, entertaining people with the fake fabulousness of her life. Her voice was a means to an end. She didn't go to college like Levi. She didn't know how to be a farm girl. Singing was what she had to offer them.

Then, when all those things she'd wanted were within reach, she'd destroyed the perfect picture she'd been painting. Just like she destroyed everything good in her life. Savannah twisted her ponytail around her hand and pulled.

Now she didn't even have singing. She had a record label on the verge of cutting her, a ticked-off Nashville star against her, and she wasn't even sure she still wanted to sing. Sure, a few of those moments on stage were fun, but most of them were awkward and scary, and afterward it was a blur of people she didn't know telling her how amazing she was, and long days and longer nights on a lonely tour bus. People using social media to talk about her like they knew her. Running the risk of reporters digging into the past she didn't like to think about, much less make into the next headline.

"Hey, Savannah." Amanda walked out of the building, arms loaded with her own box of leftovers.

Savannah released the tiny, braided locks she'd fisted in her hand, popped the trunk and put the pie box inside. "Hey." Savannah looked toward the building, hoping Hazel would be out soon. She wanted to leave. Things were getting a little too close for comfort.

Hazel didn't magically appear in the doorway.

"Do you like my brother or something?"

The question startled her. Amanda stood near her, arms folded over her chest, watching Savannah intently.

"I, uh, barely know him," she said. Having sex with Collin didn't mean she knew him.

"Because you guys looked chummy out in the parking lot for a little while, and then you stomped off. Did he say something stupid? Because he says stupid things a lot."

Savannah grinned. He did say stupid things. But then, so did she. And throwing Collin under the bus with his kid sister was just wrong. She was tired of doing the wrong thing. "He was just voicing his opinion."

Amanda nodded and then sighed. "Yeah. He has opinions."

"Opinions like?"

"He thinks I'm a felon waiting to happen."

"And you're not?" They leaned against the trunk of Hazel's car. Savannah watched Amanda closely. Her white-blond hair was so different from Savannah's nearly black hair. Savannah's skin the lightest of browns and Amanda's nearly peach. But the look in the younger girl's green gaze was as familiar as the look she sometimes caught in her own brown eyes. The look that came whenever she was feeling particularly inadequate. Misunderstood.

She hated that look.

"I just… No one listens to me," she said, and Savannah could understand that, too. Not that she'd ever tried hard to make people listen to her. Still, she'd often hoped people would understand what she couldn't say.

"I felt the same way when I was your age. The thing is, people can only hear what we put out there and sometimes we think we're being clear about things—" like money, security, but those were her battles, not Amanda's "—but we aren't."

"I'm not sure how much more clear I can be."

"About what?"

Amanda didn't say anything for a long moment. She glanced at Savannah from the corner of her eye and bit her lower lip. "Don't laugh."

Savannah used her index finger to cross her heart. "Promise."

Amanda seemed to choose her words carefully. "Saving the world."

Savannah opened her mouth and then closed it. Those three words were nowhere near the words she'd thought the young girl would say.

She'd thought they were talking about boys or maybe taking a year off between high school and college.

"Never mind. Stupid idea." She started to walk away, but Savannah grabbed her elbow, stopping her.

"What do you mean 'save the world'?"

"I mean leave it greener than it is now. Reverse global warming or at least slow it down. Granddad and now Collin run an organic orchard, but one orchard isn't enough. I want to do my part, but no one will listen to me."

"Then you have to find a way to make them listen. You have your purpose. You need to find a way to make that purpose heard."

"Do you think I can?"

She nodded. "I never underestimate the power of a young woman with ambition and goals."

"Like you?"

Pain stabbed at Savannah's heart but she held her smile steady. She'd had all the wrong ambitions, all the wrong reasons for leaving this place. Look where it had gotten her. Back here, yes. Reconnecting with her family, yes. Having a quickie by the lake with a man she barely knew. Not such a smart move. Practically obsessing over said man? An even dumber move.

"I've made a few missteps, but I'm working on finding my purpose."

Amanda grinned. "You make a good listener," she said, and the simple words eased the pain in Savannah's chest.

"Thanks."

Amanda started toward the market. "I'd better go find Gran. Thanks, Savannah."

"You're welcome," she said, but Amanda had already gone.

Savannah had the feeling it was she who should be thanking the younger girl.

She didn't yet know what her purpose was, but she was more determined than ever to find it.

CHAPTER TEN

HE'D BEEN A DICK.

Collin threw a red-tipped dart at the board, but it hit the wall to the side and he watched as it clattered to the floor.

A dick who couldn't throw darts.

"That leaves me and Levi," Adam said, gathering the darts littering the corner at the Slope. It was their usual Wednesday night, and it should be as familiar as going to the barn every morning before heading out to the orchard, but Collin couldn't relax.

He didn't want to follow Adam's inane conversation or to try to figure out why Levi was barely talking at all. James had picked up an extra shift at the sheriff's office, so it was only the three of them.

"I'll get the next round," Collin offered and headed to the bar. Merle wiped down the wide strip of mahogany. "Three longnecks," Collin said.

The bar was mostly empty tonight, but he couldn't stop picturing Savannah sitting at the bar in her tight sequined party dress from the other night. He wondered where she was tonight. Not that it mattered.

He kept making an idiot of himself when she was around, and he couldn't figure it out. She wasn't wrong. She'd basically echoed what he'd been telling himself—the deal would benefit the orchard and his wallet significantly.

So why did he keep coming up with reasons not to take it? As adamant as Granddad had been about how to run the orchard, he'd always supported Collin's plans to make it bigger and better. Hell, he'd put the idea of contracting with a bigger grocer in Collin's head after reading about the farmers along the gulf coast who'd contracted with the big cruise lines for fruit and produce.

Merle put the three cold bottles on the counter. "You boys are my best customers tonight. Summer tourists haven't picked up yet."

"After Memorial Day you'll wish we were your best customers," Collin joked.

Merle pretended to hate the increased traffic through town during the summer months. He pooh-poohed the boaters who came in, complained about the increased wait times at the restaurants and grumbled about mixing the fancy drinks a lot of tourists wanted. Merle was a beer, whiskey and tequila kind of man. But, like the rest of the town, he knew the tourism industry was what kept a lot of the local businesses going.

Slippery Rock Lake was one of many man-made lakes in Missouri, created by damming the Slippery Rock River, in part to ease flooding and in part to provide water for the growing city of Joplin. Merle and many of the older business owners had agreed to the creation of the lake, but insisted on a nondevelopment clause, similar to Stockton Lake in another part of the state, so that the area wouldn't be too overrun with tourists during the summer months.

"You catch that bit in the paper about the fishing tournament?"

"What tournament?"

"Bass Nationals. They're looking for a spot for one of their big tournaments next summer. Apparently our lake made the short list, something about the mayor meeting up with one of the sponsors at that city planning expo in Little Rock in the fall." Merle slapped the white towel he'd been using to wipe down the bar over his shoulder. "We've got some of the best bass fishing in the state." His annoyance at the tourists was apparently at war with his love of fishing.

Collin picked up the beers. "Just think of all those fish cocktails you'll have to learn how to make if the fishermen come to town," he said and started toward the table in the corner.

"Real fishermen drink beer," Merle called after him, making Collin chuckle.

"What was that about?" Levi focused his attention on the dartboard as he asked the question.

"Merle's annoyed the tourist traffic hasn't picked up yet, but he seems to have forgotten how anti-tourist he is once Memorial Day rolls around."

"He'll remember real quick about the fifth time someone asks for a sex on the beach or a fuzzy navel," Adam joked. Levi threw his dart and hit the bull's-eye. "Damn fine shot, Walters."

"That's game for me." Levi took one of the beers from the table and drank. The three of them sat at the table, finishing their beers in silence.

"Speaking of Memorial Day, Jenny wants to you all to come to a barbecue that day," Adam said after a while. "Burgers and brats. The usual. She wants to show off the new house." Adam and his wife, Jenny, had one of the few lakefront lots within the city limits; he'd inherited it from his grandfather.

When Slippery Rock Lake had been created, the town founders had laid out the plans so that it wouldn't become overly commercialized with marinas like many of the other lakes in the state. Locals knew of a few private access points, but the Slippery Rock Marina near the Slope was the only public access point.

"Mama has been working on some new ice-cream flavors, so we'll bring dessert." Levi finished his beer, but made no move to leave the booth.

Before Collin could answer, James walked in the door wearing his department uniform. He slid into the empty seat and tilted it back against the wall.

"Sometimes being a cop sucks," he said.

"Who'd you have to ticket tonight? Maggie Hall out running the stop signs again?" Adam quipped. Maggie was the wife of the mayor and since his election three years before had decided stop signs, stop lights, yield signs and most other traffic signs didn't apply to her.

"I wish." He sighed. "For the last three hours I've been scrubbing paint off the sidewalks. Someone painted murals all around the courthouse square."

Collin shot James a look, but he shook his head. "It doesn't have the cachet of duct taping the streets, so I think Amanda's in the clear."

"That's a first."

The door opened, and Savannah walked in. She wore blue jeans and a gauzy tank top that flirted with her narrow hips. She'd left her hair down and a couple of silver bangles glinted in the low light from the bar. No cheerleader friends with her tonight.

She crossed to the bar and settled across from Merle. She crossed her legs, and one low-heeled sandal dangled from her foot. Her foot didn't jiggle, it swayed, and Collin found himself mesmerized by the movement. She didn't give the corner table a single glance, and when she laughed at something Merle said, Collin frowned.

The man was too old for her by about thirty years.

"There he goes again, folks, distracted by the pretty lady at the bar." Adam's voice brought him back to his section of the bar.

"I'm not distracted," he objected.

Levi snickered. "Son, that's my sister you just lost yourself in for about ten minutes. We've already decided the full menu for the barbecue. You've got ice duty and James is going to go hunt down some firebugs to see if they also have artistic abilities. And you're watching my sister as if she's the oasis to your desert."

"She's flirting with Merle," Collin said, disgust ringing in his words.

"That's not flirting, it's called talking," Levi said.

"She's your sister. You don't see it."

"Because she's my sister I know all her moves. That laugh, that posture—those aren't Savannah's come-ons." He looked more closely at Collin, and Collin couldn't hold his gaze. "Since when do you care who Van flirts with anyway?"

Apparently since now, not that he was going to say that. He didn't want to feel it, much less say it. Collin threw a few bills on the table. "Mark down three for the barbecue," he said to Adam and walked out of the bar.

He didn't get far. Collin leaned against the brick out front, trying to wrap his head around the annoyance—no, the jealousy—he'd felt when he saw Savannah chatting up Merle at the bar. God, he was an idiot. He wasn't going to get involved. Not with Savannah, not with anyone, until his financial future was set. Now here he was, telling her his business plans and getting jealous when she talked to her old boss and feeling—what? Hurt?—when she didn't spare a single glance in his direction.

He ran his hands over his face, wishing he had a bucket of ice-cold water he could stick his head in. Maybe that would wake him up.

He started to walk in the dim twilight. Streetlights were just beginning to come on, and he glanced at the broken clock on the courthouse out of habit. As if a broken clock could give him answers...

Collin ignored his truck and instead cut across the street to the pier leading into the marina. The lights were off at Bud's Bait Shop, but there were several boats in the permanent slips on either side of the pier. Collin walked to the end, sat and dangled his feet over the edge while he watched the last rays of sunlight disappear into the night.

"Hey," Savannah said, sitting beside him.

"You must have ESP to find me out here in the dark."

Savannah knocked her bare shoulder against his and he could swear he felt her heat through the cotton of his T-shirt. "I saw you leave and decided to come out here to tell you I'm sorry."

She was sorry? For what? He was the one acting the fool where she was concerned. Picking fights with her, making light of her talents and generally being a jerk every time she showed up.

Unless he was kissing her silly and having sex with her beside the lake.

"I was a jerk at the market the other day. You following your dreams and making them come true is commendable, not something to be held against you. This grocer deal is making me a little crazy."

Almost as crazy as sitting next to her but not touching her was making him. Maybe that was what this was all about. The last time he'd been relaxed around her he'd been inside her, and that had been probably the best mistake he'd ever made. But that didn't mean he should make it again.

"No, I was projecting my needs onto you. I don't remember a lot about my life before Slippery Rock, but I do remember a little bit about what it is to have no money." He felt her shoulder shrug in the darkness, and the contact made that buzz of attraction start up again. "You should do what you think is right, regardless of how much money you may or may not make."

"How about we forget that conversation ever happened?"

"Can we forget the part about you comparing my one-hit-wonder to George Strait's fifty-odd number ones?"

"I still think he sings amazing songs."

"I don't disagree."

"My sister had your single on repeat for about a month back in the winter. You did a good job with it."

"That almost sounds like a compliment, Collin."

"Well, you're no King George," he said and bumped his shoulder against hers.

"Of course not. George has a penis. I have a vagina," she joked back. "And boobs, don't forget the boobs."

"I haven't been able to forget about the boobs in about a week."

Something sizzled in the air between them. A bit of awareness, Collin thought, or maybe it was just the heat of the Missouri summer night.

"So what brought you into town tonight? Desperate for Merle's scintillating conversation?"

"No." She laughed. "He said something about wanting my single for the juke. I had my manager send a copy of it for him."

"You've just made it onto Merle's permanent nice list."

"Doesn't that mean I get free beers at Christmas?"

"Doubtful. But he might let you snack on the cherries and lemon and lime wedges he puts out between Thanksgiving and New Year's."

"The only time of the year he likes to make girly drinks," Savannah said, and Collin thought he detected a hint of nostalgia in her voice. "I used to love Christmas in Slippery Rock."

"The faux snow or the tinny elf music they pipe into the streets?"

"Don't forget the hot cider, the light displays and the polar bear plunge."

"Maybe you should come back this year."

He thought she nodded, but the moon had hidden behind a few clouds and he couldn't tell.

"Maybe I'll stay through the holidays."

They sat together looking out over the water for a long time. Cicadas buzzed in the low grass near the shore, and a few cars passed slowly on the street behind them.

"Why didn't you leave?"

"Tired of me already?" She tilted her head to look at him, and he thought he saw a bit of uncertainty flash across her gaze in the moonlight.

"College. Levi, Aiden and Adam took the scholarships at the big schools. James did, too, and then went straight into the police academy. You chose the small school and commuted instead of living on campus."

There were so many reasons. His parents had been in one of their let's-be-a-happy-family modes and were staying at the orchard that fall, and he'd been convinced they would drop everything, leaving his grandparents in the lurch again—which they did. He and Granddad were planting the first of the pear and peach trees. Mara wanted the big school with the great tech department, but the scholarship she'd gotten hadn't covered all the expenses. Him living at the orchard had meant more money going to her.

Those were the reasons he'd used to convince Granddad and Gran to let him commute.

He'd never told them the real reason: he belonged at the orchard. It was the place that made him feel strong, the place that made him feel as if he belonged.

It was the place that had saved him and the

girls when they were children. The thought of leaving it, even if it was just during the school semester, had left him cold.

"From the time the three of us came to the orchard, it's the only place I wanted to be," he said, not wanting to tell the same half-truths to Savannah.

"You didn't always live there?"

He shook his head. "We lived with our parents in a small apartment in Kansas City until I was ten. Samson, my father, was a traveling salesman." That was one lie he'd gotten good at telling and it slipped from his mouth before he could stop it. Collin blew out a breath. "Actually, my parents weren't big on the family thing. They were always looking at how much easier it would be without kids. So we came here and they kept going."

She reached for his hand, and her skin was cool against his. "I didn't know that."

"That my biological parents were deadbeats? It's one of those secrets most of the people in town know but no one talks about. Mostly, I think they've forgotten that Granddad and Gran are technically our grandparents and not our parents."

Collin laced his fingers with hers, content to watch the moon slide from behind the clouds to shine down on the dark lake. Savannah laid her head against his shoulder. She was the first person to whom he'd told that much about the past. He didn't want to dig any deeper into it. Didn't want to open the wounds of a terrified ten-year-old, so desperate for help that he'd called a stranger's number from a ragged address book.

"Parents suck."

"Some of them," he said. Then there were the people like his grandparents, who'd gone above and beyond to be parents when no one else had wanted the job.

He didn't care that Savannah wasn't the right person for him, or that she would possibly leave at some point in the near future. He liked the feeling that he could be honest with her, and not because she didn't have anyone to tell his secrets to, but because he trusted her to keep them. He didn't understand a lot about Savannah, but he understood she wasn't the type to kiss and tell. For a while longer, he just wanted to enjoy his time with her and maybe tack on a few more memories for the days after she left.

"Do you have plans tomorrow?"

She shook her head against his shoulder. "No. Why?"

"Since you're no good at the milkmaid thing, but you're interested in rural life, I thought I could show you around the orchard. Apples, peaches and pears just have to be picked. No milking machines involved."

"It's a date," she said.

Collin placed a soft kiss against her forehead. "It's a date," he echoed.

"So what you're looking for is an apple that is firm but not hard, with good red color."

Savannah reached above her head. She was standing on a ladder at the tree next to his and drew a branch down before snapping off a piece of fruit. "What about the gold flecks?" she asked as she dropped the apple in the bag hanging from her shoulder.

"We grow Honey Crisps here, so yellow and gold flecks are good."

"I thought you ran an organic orchard. Aren't these GMO?"

"You know about genetically modified crops?"

"I picked up a few things during high school, yes. So?"

"Honey Crisps are a hybrid, not a GMO, so they fit here. These are the apples the chain will want, but we have other fields of heritage apples. A few acres of Arkansas Blacks, Cortlands and Orange Pippins. Those were Granddad's favorites."

"What is your favorite?" she asked, putting a few more apples into her bag.

"For pure sweetness, the Orange Pippins are my favorites. You?"

"I don't really know the difference. At the store, I usually pick up Honey Crisps, though."

They continued picking, a job Collin usually farmed out to local high schoolers. They had already worked most of the weekend, though, and only a few trees were left for this week's picking, so he'd sent them to the garden to pick berries.

It was nearly eleven and Savannah had been picking apples with him for more than an hour while the hot May sunshine pushed the temperature gauge up several degrees. Collin wiped his face with the hem of his T-shirt before pulling his ball cap from his back pocket.

He'd grabbed one of Amanda's old caps from the porch when Savannah had pulled up, but she'd stepped from Mama Hazel's sedan with a floppy gardener's hat, making him laugh. The straw thing had looked unwieldy as hell when she was carrying it around the farmyard, and she'd had to hold it in place when they'd driven up here in the four-wheeler, but she hadn't complained once about it since they'd started picking.

Collin reached for the last apple ready for the farmers' market and then climbed down from his ladder. He reset it next to Savannah's.

"I think this is it," she said, putting one more apple in her shoulder bag.

On the ground, she dumped the bag into the bushel barrel. Collin inspected the tree from the ground.

"You do good work," he said. "If you'll work for eleven dollars an hour, you're hired."

Savannah stretched her arms over her head and swayed her body left to right. She flexed her hands. "I can't feel my fingers and my back may never unstiffen, and I only earned twenty-two dollars? You need to rethink your pay scale."

Collin shrugged. "On the plus side, you get to be outside in the sunshine instead of cooped up in a dark recording studio."

"True. I've gotten more vitamin D in the last three weeks than I probably got in the past two years." She brushed her hands down her pants, lifted the floppy hat from her head and hung it by its string over her shoulder. "Plus, I get to wear Mama Hazel's gardening hat. It's like a giant umbrella right over my head."

"And the jeans, don't forget the jeans."

"Well, capris." She glanced down at the denim pants that reached just past her knees. "I noticed the other day that you wear shorts a lot."

"Ninety-plus temperatures and long jeans don't mix well. Speaking of…you want to take a break under a shade tree? I think we've done all the picking we can over here."

"What about the peaches and pears?"

"They need a couple more weeks yet, but I'll take you over there later, if you'd like."

She nodded. "I would like. Now, what about that break?"

"Gran made sandwiches and I have cold sodas in the cooler. Can I interest you in a picnic at the lake?"

"Sounds perfect."

They climbed in the Gator and drove down the dirt track that led from the orchard grove to the beach. Being here didn't mean another midday swim or sex. It was just lunch.

But the water looked awfully inviting.

Collin parked beneath an oak. Together they sat on the little tailgate of the recreational vehicle. Collin passed Savannah a wrapped ham sandwich and a cold bottle of soda.

"So what is the official title for an orchard owner? Orcharder? Orchardist?" she asked after a while.

Collin finished his sandwich and took a long drink. "Orchardist. Pomologist. Usually, I just go with farmer. It covers the basics, even if my fields are groves."

"I'd go with one of the 'ists.' Sounds more professional. You could charge more for apples from a pomologist," she said, and there was laughter in her voice.

"Unless someone called for a pulmonologist

and I came running. Somehow I don't think choosing an apple has the same educational background as diagnosing lung diseases."

"What's that saying? An apple a day keeps the doctor away?" Savannah finished her lunch and kicked her feet under the tailgate. She shot him a sideways glance. "And I'll bet some doctors wear shorts under their white lab coats."

"Shorts would be a prerequisite for me."

She watched the sunlight play over the blue water for a long moment.

There was a light breeze near the shore that rippled through the oak trees and pushed the water against the shoreline. These were the kinds of summer days Collin liked best. The heat was nearly unbearable, but the breeze and the inviting water meant a respite was never far behind.

"Can I ask you a question?" she asked after a while.

"Shoot." He figured she had more questions about the orchard, but her question floored him.

"Was it hard to figure out where you belonged, once you were here, I mean?" Her hands rested against the tailgate and her knuckles were pale, as if she was gripping the underside of the metal tightly.

"I never gave it a lot of thought, actually," he said. He'd been too relieved to have a place where social workers didn't knock on the door at all hours and where the adults didn't disappear for days on end.

The last thing he'd wanted was to go back to that dark apartment as the main caretaker for his younger sisters, so he'd set out to make himself indispensable to his grandparents. He'd followed Granddad around the groves asking questions, watched as he'd noted the yields, paid close attention when he'd pruned the branches that no longer bore fruit. And every night he'd thanked the God he very nearly didn't believe in for bringing them there.

"We came at the end of a school year, so there was a lot to do. I liked being outside, and every boy loves climbing trees. We had our own lake, or that's how it seemed to me."

She nodded, and the movement was sharp. "Sounds like perfection."

He considered that. Not always. Not when Mara stubbornly refused to help with their baby sister. Not when Amanda cut her two-year molars. Not when Samson and Maddie would randomly show up at the orchard, stay for a few months and then disappear again without as much as a goodbye hug. He told her as much, leaving out the part about his parents. No need to go down that road. He was over it.

"Your grandparents sound like saints."

In his opinion they were more like saviors.

"They loved us, and we loved them. That made the difference. What about you? I'll bet Mama Hazel was just as hands-on when you came to the ranch."

"Definitely. I wanted to stay with her forever before she said a word to me. There was such gentleness in those big brown eyes, and her hands were soft, and she smelled like sugar cookies." Savannah closed her eyes as if experiencing the memory. "Bennett scared me at first, I'm not sure why. Probably his deep baritone. And Levi seemed like he'd been made for me to climb all over, which I'm sure he hated."

She'd stopped talking, and Collin had a feeling there was more. He wondered if her transition to Slippery Rock had taken a more twisted turn than his own.

She'd been younger than him, but he didn't know anything about her life prior to the ranch.

"You were seven when you came here, right?"

She nodded. "I was nine the first time Levi brought you home, and I knew from the second you walked in the door there would be no more wrestling around with him. Girls weren't allowed into the boys' club."

That would have been the fall after the three of them had come to live at the orchard. He, Levi, James and the twins, Aiden and Adam, had bonded on the monkey bars during that first recess.

"So that's why you never spoke to me before that night at the bar." It made sense. He'd stolen her best friend, her brother, in a way.

Savannah shook her head. "You were the one who never spoke to me. Those blue eyes of yours never seemed to recognize when I was in the room."

That wasn't exactly true. He'd noticed the quiet girl with the light-colored skin and the big brown eyes and the riot of messy black curls. She'd grown into the hair and eyes, and her skin had darkened a little, but he still saw the little girl hanging behind the doorjamb from time to time.

"Well, I've noticed you now," he said, and the words sounded huskier than he intended. He twisted a lock of her hair around his finger. It was soft, silky, and felt a little bit like a tiny piece of rope. "This is different."

She twirled another strand around her finger. "I had it micro-braided once I got to LA. It's a little edgy. I like edgy. Plus, I could never get the natural curls to do what I wanted when I wanted."

"I like it," he said.

Savannah's gaze met his, and her eyes darkened. She swallowed. "We should maybe get out of this heat before we do something we'll regret."

He leaned a little closer to her, but she slid off the tailgate and ran toward the lake, stripping off her shirt and dropping her capris at the edge of the dock. She wore another bikini, this one navy, and she slipped into the water in a smooth dive.

Collin tossed his T-shirt in the bed of the Gator, threw his wallet on top of it and toed off his Nikes at the dock before slicing through the water.

It felt blessedly cool in the blue depths, and he stayed under until his lungs burned before kicking for the surface. He'd swum quite a distance from the dock, but saw Savannah farther out along the shaded shoreline.

He flipped over on his back, watching puffy white clouds skim across the bright blue sky. Jumping in the lake was the better idea, and he'd have to thank Savannah for that. They barely knew each other, had had all of two significant conversations. They couldn't just jump into bed again.

Speaking of, the next time they did…he wanted a bed. A big bed with soft pillows and all the time in the world to explore her curvy body. He felt himself harden despite the cool water. Collin kicked his legs and started for shore, trying to push the image of Savannah naked on a big four-poster from his mind.

Collin forced his brain onto farm work rather than Savannah work, hoping to deflate the raging hard-on the cold water of the lake couldn't.

He reached the dock and pulled himself up, watching her swim along the tree line. She'd turned back while he was floating and was nearly to the dock herself.

His mental calculations of organic pest control methods didn't work. He still wanted her.

Savannah pulled herself up onto the dock and sat, dripping, beside him. She'd changed the belly button ring to a blue stone, and he wondered if she always matched her body jewelry to her clothing. She seemed like the kind of woman who would.

He'd never imagined he would be the kind of man who would like the kind of woman who did something like that. And yet here he was, sitting on a dock, wanting her.

"Savannah…" he started to say. But before he could say more, she pressed her mouth to his. Her small hands wound through the hair at his nape, holding his head in place while she nipped at his mouth with her teeth, sending a jolt of heat through him.

Collin put his arms around her waist, pulling her over his lap. One knee on either side of his hips, Savannah settled over him, her tongue jousting with his while he ran his hands over her slick body.

"I still say this dock isn't the place to do this," he said, pulling his mouth from hers and breathing unevenly. "But if you kiss me like that again, it's going to happen right here, right now."

"That clearing is just through the trees," she said, and the want in her honey-brown gaze nearly undid him. Who cared about a big, soft bed when he had a woman with wicked curves in his lap?

"There's another option."

"I'm living in my childhood bedroom, and it doesn't matter that I'm twenty-seven, Mama Hazel is not going to react well to us defiling that childhood bed."

"I was thinking of the hunting cabin at the back edge of the orchard." She raised an eyebrow. "It has the bonus of being private."

"Private could be good."

"Private will be amazing," he said.

She stood, and Collin took her hand, leading her to the Gator.

They were going to get that bed, rustic though it was, after all.

CHAPTER ELEVEN

IT ONLY TOOK a couple of minutes to reach the small hunting cabin, set in a clearing near the corner where the grove of pear trees met the apple. Behind it, tall fir trees soared toward the sky and the branches of two massive trees laced together.

When he'd built the cabin, Collin's grandfather had taken great care to make sure it would be comfortable for both summer and winter dwelling. There were the massive trees along the ridge to break the winter winds, and the trees on the back side of the house provided summer shade. They parked under one of the trees, and Savannah picked up something that looked similar to a cucumber. There were more hanging from the branches of the trees above.

"It's a cucumber magnolia," Collin said when he saw her looking at the thing in her hand. "Granddad planted them for Gran when they were first married. This was their first house."

"They're beautiful," she said and walked to the small porch, turned the doorknob and went inside.

Collin followed.

The interior of the cabin was sparsely but comfortably furnished. There was a small kitchenette with outdated but clean appliances along the back wall, a couple of comfortable-looking rocking chairs and a plaid sofa near a fireplace along one side. On the other side of the room behind a small screen was a small bed with an old iron frame. A patchwork quilt covered the mattress. His grandmother had made it before arthritis had made quilting difficult for her.

There were no pictures on the walls, just large windows offering views of the orchard in front and the forest in back.

He'd never actually used this place as a hunting cabin, instead preferring it when late frosts threatened the orchard. There was little he could do about late frosts, but it made him feel better to be with his trees. He made a point to check on the place every few weeks, wiping down the surfaces for dust and checking that no rodents had gotten inside.

Collin swallowed. This wasn't just some random shack where they could expend a little excess attraction and energy. This place had been a home to his grandparents, and he still used it or at least visited it often.

Savannah ran her hands over the smooth wood of the small kitchen table.

And now she was going to be part of it.

Maybe he should have thought this through a little more.

"It's beautiful," she said, her voice soft. "Levi and our dad hunt, but they just go out in the morning and are home by noon."

"It was my grandparents' home first, and later Granddad used it as a hunting cabin. Mostly I use it when I'm watching the weather."

"You take good care of it."

Collin shrugged. "I don't like to see things go to waste. It's a useful place when quick summer storms blow up or frosts threaten the trees. Keeping it clean and in good shape means it'll hold up under bad conditions."

He didn't want to talk about it anymore. He wanted to stop talking and thinking, and just be with her. So Collin took her in his arms and pressed his mouth to hers. Then he pushed her back against the wall, ravishing her neck.

"I guess the small talk is over," she said with a chuckle.

"I've never been enamored of it," he returned as his hands found her breasts. Her suit had mostly dried, but her nipples were hard beneath the fabric. He pinched and rolled them, liking it when a little moan escaped her lips.

Savannah pushed her hands past the waistband of his cargos, squeezing his buttocks, and Collin's brain short-circuited for a second. He insinuated one leg between hers, feeling the heat between her legs against his upper thigh.

He unbuckled his belt and pushed his cargos past his hips. No boxer briefs today—not that he'd been expecting sex, he'd simply been preparing for the heat.

And the possibility of sex.

Savannah reached her hand behind her, pulling the strings and loosening her bikini top. It fell to the floor, and he couldn't resist a taste of her breasts. Savannah's hands fisted in his hair, and he was content to focus his attention there.

She banged her head against the wall, muttered an, "Ow," but didn't release her grip on him. He kissed his way back up her chest to her neck and then to the sensitive place behind her ear.

"More," she said, wrapping one leg around his, pulling his hips more firmly against her own.

He reached one hand down, pressed her bikini bottoms past her hips and then cupped her center, feeling her slick heat against his skin.

The thought rolled around his brain that if this moment never ended it would be okay.

THIS PLACE WAS part of Collin. And he'd brought her here.

Savannah's heart melted, not in anticipation

of the sex that was already happening, but because they could have just had sex in the shade of the trees or taken their chances on the dock. But instead he'd brought her here, to this sweet little cabin with its rocking chairs and patchwork quilt.

She didn't care that this was stupid. She just knew that having sex with Collin was like no other sex she'd had, but getting involved with him...that was dangerous. She'd come to terms with the very real possibility that Nashville likely wasn't part of her future, but she remained unsure if Slippery Rock was part of it. Having sex with him again would make it so much harder to leave.

Right now, making things harder for Future Savannah wasn't nearly as important as being with Collin in the present. Not when his mouth was doing amazing things to that spot beneath her ear, and not when his hands were hot against her skin.

She liked the way she felt with Collin.

And she wanted to feel more of it. He sucked at that spot behind her ear again and her head lolled back, banging against the wall, the pain warring with the pleasure his hands were giving her.

But she didn't want a concussion.

Savannah wrapped her arms around Collin's

neck, reached up on her tiptoes and took his lips with hers. She twisted them away from the wall and then began walking backward.

When the backs of her legs hit the soft cotton of the quilt, Savannah sank onto the comfortable mattress. Collin rested one knee between her legs as he followed her down, down until her head rested on a small pillow.

"Savannah." He said her name quietly as his hands played with the sensitized skin of her lower abdomen. His gaze caught hers and, for a moment, it seemed as if time would stop. She could only look into his clear blue eyes and wonder what he was thinking. Then his mouth descended on hers and time seemed to speed back up.

First his hands were on her belly then one hand was over her breast. He'd left his shirt outside, so her hands were free to explore his ridged abdomen. Unlike the men she'd known in California and Tennessee, a light mat of hair covered his chest, tapering down to a vee that disappeared beneath his cargo shorts—when he wore cargos, anyway. She took his length in her hand, liking the feel of him. Soft at the surface but hard beneath. She wrapped one leg around him, bringing his hips up hard against her own.

"Better?" he asked, grinning at her.

"Immensely," she replied and pushed her

hands against his shoulders until he rested on his back. She lay atop him for a while, their legs tangled, chest to chest, pressing little kisses along his collarbone, the way he'd done that day at the lake. Collin's hands explored her, and she let her fingers walk down through his chest hair. She felt his abs clench when her hand passed his belly button, and when she wrapped her hand around his length again, he growled.

Savannah grinned. "You like that." It was nice to know she affected him physically, especially when he affected her in so many different ways.

"What's not to like?" he asked as she ran her hand gently along his length and then squeezed.

"I definitely like," she said, but her voice just missed the playful note she'd been going for. He was too much. Too good with his hands. Her eyes closed when he closed his mouth over her breast. Too good with his mouth. "Oh, God."

Too good to be with a girl like her, but she wasn't about to tell him that. Telling him that would mean those hands and that mouth would be gone from her life. It would mean no more moonlit conversations at the marina in which she was just a woman. Not a woman with baggage. Not the teenager who'd run away.

Not the singer who should have never allowed herself to become so uncomfortable with the life she led that she was easily taken in by the enticing words of her tour-mate's husband.

Savannah shoved that thought out of her mind.

She wasn't that person from those few weeks ago. She wasn't. Even on the tour bus, she'd known she didn't want to be there. Before the tour bus, she'd known she didn't want to be in the spotlight, on a stage, or in any more interviews. She'd wanted to be…here. In Slippery Rock.

Most of all, right now she wanted to be with Collin, and she wasn't going to mess that up by bringing the past into this pretty little cabin at the edge of the orchard.

Savannah buried her hands in his thick blond hair and pressed her mouth to his. He tasted sweet, like the sodas they'd had with lunch. Smelled like the lake and sweat and sunshine and everything good in her life right now.

"I like this," she said against his mouth.

"So do I," he said and flipped her onto her back.

His hands were big and rough, and the sensation of his skin against her sensitized breasts was magnificent. He pressed his flat palms against them, making her nipples tingle at the contact. She tangled her legs with his and felt him settle more comfortably between her legs.

"I like this a lot," she said.

Collin tweaked her nipples with his fingers and the cabin seemed to sizzle with the heat. "And you'll like this, too," he said, and she could only nod because Collin then put his mouth on her, soothing the sensual burning from his hands.

"A lot, a lot," she said, and the words brought another grin to his face.

"Let's see what else you like," he said, his blue gaze locked on hers. But he didn't move. His hands were warm against her waist, his mouth set in that silly grin for a long moment, and although their legs were tangled atop the quilt they were both completely still.

"I like you," she said, trying for light and breezy but knew the catch in her voice gave her away.

She hadn't been a virgin in a long time, but it was as if Collin's hands were different. The reactions he elicited were new and a little uncomfortable because Savannah already knew she couldn't hold back when she was in his arms. When the world came crashing down around them, she was like one of those rowboats wrecked on the lakeshore.

No man had ever wrecked her before.

"I like you, too," he said, and she was glad his voice sounded just a little unsteady. It made them even.

She pressed her lips against his, trying to lock

in every scent and taste and feel because this couldn't last. Collin Tyler, good guy and football star and orchard owner, couldn't want Savannah Walters, bad girl and screwed-up ex-singer, not for long. He kissed her back, his hands caressing her ribs and moving over her hips. Savannah thought it had to be the most delicious kiss she'd ever shared.

His thumb found her entrance, and he teased the opening. Savannah sucked an unsteady breath between her teeth, arching her back and burying her hands in his hair as if she might hold him in place. Then he slipped two fingers inside her, and she thought her body might explode from the exquisite touch.

Collin bit her nipple gently, and the pain was the most pleasurable thing she had ever experienced. It sent a wave of wetness between her legs and, sweet God, his mouth might be her favorite part of his body. Savannah began to feel wobbly on the razor wire of desire.

God, he felt good.

She tried to hold on, tried to think of anything that would slow her body's reaction to Collin, but he surrounded her. His skin against hers, the smell of him—all sunshine and fruit trees and lake water—was everywhere.

He flicked his thumb against her clitoris, and

she went over, her internal muscles in spasms as his hand continued to work her core.

Savannah's hands tightened against his head and then everything went soft, from the sunlight coming through the windows to the way her body seemed to melt against his. It was all she could do to drag rough breaths into her lungs.

Collin rolled onto his side, resting on one elbow as he kissed his way down her belly, stopping for a long moment to play with the blue stone dangling at her belly button.

"I liked the green one, but the blue was a nice surprise."

She'd changed it because the color of the stone reminded her of his eyes. And how lame was it to wear a piece of jewelry because it reminded her of the man she was in bed with?

"You like?" She levered her eyes open to look at him. He had a satisfied look on his face, and maybe it was because she'd just had the best oral orgasm of her life, but the expression was almost sweet. He took pleasure in giving her pleasure, and she couldn't wait to give it right back to him.

He shot her a glance. Nodded. "Holy hell."

Savannah laughed. "If you like that, you might just die when you take a closer look at my hip."

"A man can dream." But his hand stilled on her hip. "What do you mean a closer look?"

She shook her head.

Slowly, his gaze traveled down her body and it was as if he could touch her with the molten heat she saw there. She trembled despite her tensed muscles.

His hand caressed her hip, his callused fingers gentle against her. He paused above her right hip bone to trace the lace hummingbird she'd had tattooed there in white ink when she'd graduated from Slippery Rock High. A flower rose up before the bird and it held an infinity loop in its feet. It was several shades lighter than her own caramel skin tone, but most people still didn't notice it, not even when she wore a bathing suit.

"It's beautiful," he said, placing a light kiss on the bird.

Her stomach muscles quivered. Savannah reached for him, pulling him to her until their lips met again.

"Why no ink on this amazing body?" she asked. "It's practically a rite of passage for our generation."

"George Strait, remember? Old school is my favorite school. I'm am pathetically, boringly un-inked," he said, not really answering her question as he nipped her lip. "And I'm perfectly okay with that."

Somehow, not having a tattoo seemed absolutely Collin.

Savannah let her hands drift down his torso to

the almost pointed edge of the vee of hair covering his chest and abs, liking the feel of his flat, trembling muscles beneath her hands.

She had brought this man to his knees—well, his side—and the sight of him hard and full and long made Savannah bite her lip.

God, he was beautiful. His skin tanned golden by the summer sun, that light smattering of wiry blond hairs covering his body. Hands that were work roughened, but the most gentle she had ever felt on her body. And he was hers.

For now.

Collin left her, grabbed his shorts from near the wall and pulled his wallet from the back pocket. He sheathed himself and then returned to her.

"You prepared again."

"I've never found my penchant for preparation more useful than this moment. Or the one by the lake."

He sank down on the mattress, taking her breast in his mouth as he thrust inside her, making her catch her breath. Despite the toe-curling orgasm of a moment ago, she was ready to plunge over that ledge with him again.

Collin withdrew and when he thrust back inside her, Savannah raised her hips to meet his. She locked her legs around his hips as he plunged deep inside her once more.

"Collin," she said, his name a whisper against his shoulder. He reached his hand between them, finding that bundle of nerves easily. "Holy. Hell," she said, echoing his words from a moment before. The two words were part plea and part exaltation. She raked her hands down his back, wanting more of him. Collin gave it. He caught her mouth with his and the wave of her orgasm crested once more, taking her over the edge and toward oblivion.

"Savannah," he said, her name a fierce growl from his lips as he thrust in and out, in and out. He grunted his own release a moment later, his body tensed and he collapsed on top of her.

Savannah was lost, somewhere between dreaming and wake, listening to Collin's harsh breaths soften and calm. He moved to the side, burying his head in the pillow but leaving an arm across her torso. Their legs remained tangled atop the soft quilt, and Savannah ran her fingers lightly over his arm.

They should maybe take the rest of the day inside this perfect little cabin, away from the world and phones and bad news. She could stay in this little piece of heaven for the rest of her life, maybe. The thought made her nervous, but the feelings he brought out in her were calming.

"Someone's going to have to do some laundry."

"I'll take care of it. Pretend Boy Scout, re-member?" Collin raised his head from the bed. "I would have aced both the preparation and laundry merit badges. If I had been a Scout."

"You have all the trademarks without any of the merit badges," she teased. "Poor Collin."

"Hey, you have to admit me being prepared was a good thing in this particular instance. And the last one." He rose from the bed, disposed of the condom in a small trash can beside the bed, and reached for his shorts.

So much for spending the rest of the day with Collin, his amazing hands and a few more orgasms.

Savannah found her bikini bottoms and pulled them over her hips. She stuck the top in the pocket of her shorts and pulled her T-shirt over her head before stepping into them.

Unsure of what to say—she had a feeling an offhand thanks would be rude—Savannah made her way to the door and slipped her flip-flops back on her feet. She hadn't realized she'd worn the sandals into the cabin.

"Why a hummingbird?" he asked, stopping her. "I was thinking some kind of tribal symbol or a butterfly. Most girls like butterfly tattoos, or so I've heard."

"There you go with the old-school thing again. This isn't the '90's. Even if it was, I'm not most girls," she said, smiling at him as he straightened the quilt on the bed and glanced around the room as if he expected something to be out of place. Nothing was.

"No, you're definitely not. So why the hummingbird?"

She didn't want to talk about the hummingbird, not yet. Maybe not ever. She tried to change the subject. "Why no tattoos?"

"Granddad was of the opinion that only soldiers should have tats, and those tats should be their unit numbers or mascots." He shrugged. "I never found anything important enough to me to make it a permanent part of my body."

They walked outside into the bright sunlight and it was as if time had stood still. The sun was still high in the sky, a light breeze filtered through the trees and the scent of pears, apples and peaches filled the air. Somehow, Savannah had expected it to be twilight.

"Not even your precious fruit trees?"

He shook his head. "I love the orchard, but it's part of me here." He put his hand over his chest. "I never figured I needed it anywhere else." He waited.

Finally, Savannah said, "It's to remind myself to be courageous and strong." That wasn't everything about the hummingbird, but Savannah wasn't sure she could put all of her reasons for the tattoo into words. For the first time, though, she wanted to try. Having sex with the man was one thing. Telling him all her secrets was quite another, but maybe she could tell him just this one.

"There's an old legend that Mama Hazel told me once, about hummingbirds being time travelers, because they are the only birds that can fly both forward and backward. The first time she told me the story I was little, maybe only eight. I can't really remember, but I'd had a nightmare that the people from the state had come to take me away. She said no one was going to take me away. She sang me that old Seals and Crofts song from the '70's, 'Hummingbird' and after that she started calling me her hummingbird."

Savannah sat on the little porch step. "Along with the time-traveler thing, a lot of people believe hummingbirds help us to open our hearts to the impossible. To love. I wanted to remind myself of that."

Collin sat beside her and reached for her hand. He didn't say anything for a long moment and Savannah wasn't sure what to say. Why had she told him so much? Having sex—twice—didn't mean he was her confidant. It didn't even mean he was her friend. He was just… He rubbed his thumb over the back of her hand.

She wanted him to be her friend. If she were

completely honest with herself, she wanted him to be more than her friend. She wanted to be the kind of woman who might be worthy of a man like Collin Tyler. God, she wanted that.

"Why white ink?"

Maybe he could have one more secret. She'd already told him the rest.

"Because it's pretty and because I wanted it to be mine. White ink is definitely visible against my skin, but not as much as black. So unless someone is looking for it, it's mostly invisible."

He held her hand as they sat on the porch. "Most people get tattoos to show them off."

"And I'm not most people. I don't mind people seeing it or knowing about it, but it's for me. My reminder. My inspiration." Her hope, too. Because for most of her life she'd closed herself off to love. She'd been afraid to let people in— she was still afraid, to some extent. The hummingbird was a reminder to herself to be strong. Sometimes she was better at remembering that than others. Nashville, really the last two years, were the neon-blinking examples of that.

He nodded. "We should probably head over to the pears, if you want to see the difference between nearly ripe and ripe."

Collin released her hand when she climbed into the four-wheeler, but once she was settled in the passenger seat, he took it again, bringing a smile to her face. He started down the little dirt track, the Gator driving in and out of the dappled sunshine.

"Savannah?" he asked after a while. She tilted her head toward him and he said, "If I called you sometime—"

"Yes." She cut him off before she could think too much about it. "Yes, I'll answer."

Her intention in having sex with Collin was to forget, just for a little bit, the mess that her life was in. Somewhere between that first kiss in the lake, the argument at the farmers' market and this afternoon in the cabin, and that sweet bed with the old quilt, it had become more. The thought of more Collin made her giddy.

She ran her fingers lightly over the tail of her T-shirt covering the tattoo. Maybe this time she could fully embrace the hummingbird legend.

Maybe this time, the hummingbird would truly lead her home.

CHAPTER TWELVE

AT THE RANCH, Savannah sat on the slanted roof outside her window, watching the sun sink into the forest surrounding Slippery Rock Lake. She knew it was silly to come out here to think, but climbing out the window was habit. She'd been doing it for more than half of her life.

In the distance she could see the navy metal roof of what would become Levi's house once construction on the inside was finished. A last brilliant ray of sunlight glanced off it, and she squinted at the glare.

She'd left Collin's little cabin in the woods a few hours before. Had driven with him through the pear orchard, and still wasn't positive she could see the difference between ripe and not ripe. What she was positive about was the man she'd been with.

Collin was different from men she'd known in the past. He listened when she talked, for one thing. He was careful in every aspect of his life, from the orchard to the high school friendships that were still part of him. He was confident in who he was and what he wanted, and he made her want to be confident about what she wanted.

So what was it that she wanted? Other than him, of course.

She pulled her knees to her chest, circling her arms around them.

She wanted to do something that mattered. Her father and brother ran an organic dairy. That mattered. Collin ran an orchard. Providing food to people mattered. Her mother baked sweet things that people enjoyed. Even Amanda had a passion and a purpose. If a seventeen-year-old could figure those things out, surely a twenty-seven-year-old could.

What could Savannah do that mattered?

She heard the windowsill behind her scrape against the casing as it raised.

"You haven't been out here in—what?—ten years," Levi said, his voice quiet in the growing dusk. He climbed out the window and settled beside her on the steeply pitched roof, but instead of setting his feet the way she had so that she wouldn't slide right off, he sat with his legs crossed, as if he were on solid, level ground. It was like the laws of gravity didn't affect him or something.

"More like five, but you were off playing the football hero for a few of those years."

"Deep thoughts?" he asked, nudging her shoulder with his.

"How's the new house coming along?"

"Putting up the last of the drywall next weekend, then it's just cabinets and the last of the painting."

"Excited about not living in your childhood bedroom?" Savannah nudged his shoulder back.

"It hasn't been so bad."

Savannah raised an eyebrow and speared him with a look. "You've been back for a couple of years now. Living with Mama Hazel and Dad has to have cramped your style a little."

Levi shrugged. "As much as it's cramping your style."

He had a point there. Not that he knew he had a point. She didn't think Collin had told Levi about their rendezvous at the lake, and she definitely wasn't going to.

"It's nice being back here," she said after a while. "I didn't realize how much I had missed this place until I decided to turn left."

"Decided to turn left?"

Whoops. Probably not the best choice of words. Savannah took a breath. "I, uh, was considering…not coming back here," she said and swallowed. She should probably keep the whole left-turn, right-turn debate she'd been having with herself that night on the highway to herself.

But then, her typical response to everything was to pack it deep, deep inside and pretend whatever the "it" was wasn't actually there. She wanted to be better than that.

And she could be better than that. "I messed things up in Nashville. Really messed them up."

"I thought you were taking a break." He tilted his head to look at her, and Savannah was thankful for the growing dusk.

"It isn't so much a self-imposed break as being asked to leave the tour." He cocked an eyebrow at her. "I did something I'm not proud of, and I did it because part of me wanted off the tour and out of the circus I'd made of my life when I first went on the talent show," she said, rushing the words out before she could second-guess her decision to tell her brother. It was crazy to think it had all happened just three short weeks ago.

"Do you want to go back?" he asked after a long moment. Savannah shook her head. She didn't want to go back. Not because of the scandal that was certain to come if she tried, and not just because of her past.

"I don't want to be a singer."

"You love singing."

She raised one shoulder. "Loving to sing and wanting to be on a stage are two very different things. I just didn't know that when I started this whole thing." She threaded her hands together around her knees. "Do you think Mama and Daddy will be disappointed?"

"I think they'll be confused. I know they'll want to know what you plan to do next."

"How did they take it when you didn't go back to football?"

"That was different. I was injured."

"A partial tear in your hamstring isn't a career-ending injury."

"It was the meniscus, and it was a full tear, requiring surgery." He waited a beat. "But I could have gone back. Done the rehab thing, made it back on the team roster."

"Why didn't you?" If she knew why Levi had left the limelight of professional football, maybe she wouldn't feel like such a failure for not wanting the music career that had been at her fingertips. For being so afraid that she'd nuked it instead of calmly walking away.

"I love football. High school and college and the pros, I loved all of it. But I always knew there was more to life than football. I like being here. I like the work and I like the familiarity. I like that what we do here matters."

Savannah nodded and watched as the sky made the final change from purple-gray to nearly black. A few stars twinkled to life over the treetops.

"I want to do something that matters." She

whispered the words, testing each as she let them slide off her tongue. They felt right. "There was a music program I got involved with in Nashville. I liked that program."

"You want to run a music program in Nashville?"

"No." Definitely not in Nashville. "Maybe it isn't a music program at all. Maybe it's…something else."

"What else?" Levi pressed.

Savannah lay her head on her knees and looked at her brother in the darkness. "I don't know. I just know that I don't want to do whatever it is on a stage with thousands of people watching me."

"Not even if those people adore you?"

"Especially not then. I'm not adorable." She was broken and messy and all the other things that weren't adorable.

Levi tweaked her nose. "Sure you are."

"Levi."

"You're my sister and I think you're adorable."

Savannah rolled her eyes.

Levi pulled his knees up, to sit like her on the roof. "Is the thing that matters and that doesn't think you're adorable a person? A Collin-type person?"

Savannah's eyes widened.

"What? I've got eyes. You walk into the bar

and he loses his shit. Quietly, because he's Collin, but he loses it. You keep disappearing with the four-wheeler, and every time I see you leaving, it's in the direction of the lake and the orchard. Then, there's last weekend at the farmers' market."

"You saw that?"

"I think the whole town saw the two of you. So?"

"I like him."

"Of course you like him. He's Collin. He's likeable."

"Is it so bad that I like him?"

"Van," he said, and then he sighed. "You're an adult. You can like whoever you want. But Collin's complicated. From what you've told me, you're already in a complicated situation. Maybe you try to figure that out before you add him to it?"

"Too late for that," she said.

"I figured. Okay, you want my advice? I think, no matter how much fun you're having with him, you need to figure out what you want in your life before you get too deeply involved."

Yeah. Except she was already involved, and not just physically. Savannah twisted her mouth. No, she wasn't going to lie about this, not even to herself. For all she knew, it was physical for Collin, but it was more than that for her. The physical was good, but just being with him, talking to him…that was the best part.

Collin Tyler was a good, strong, sexy man. The kind of man she never thought she would have because she had never considered that she had anything to offer a man like him. Still, he was the kind of man she wanted in her life. She hoped he was the kind of man she might deserve.

HE DIDN'T CALL the ranch line. Collin felt weird calling the ranch and asking to speak to Savannah; it was just too high school. He texted her instead, which he acknowledged wasn't all that different.

At least he didn't have to first make small talk with Mama Hazel or, God forbid, Levi. Although he'd have to talk to his buddy sooner or later, Collin knew. Not for permission, just to let him know, man-to-man, that Collin was taking this thing with Savannah seriously. At least as seriously as it could be taken when she wouldn't talk about her future plans.

He lay in bed on Wednesday morning, hands behind his head, looking at the barn ceiling. With Amanda back on track, he'd moved back to his loft apartment on the second floor of the big red barn.

Hell, his moving to the barn had had little to do with his sister. It was because of Savannah.

He didn't know what the rules were about older brothers bringing girls home when his impressionable, teenage sister lived right down the hall. Having his personal life enclosed in this small space, assuming he ever brought Savannah here, seemed like the mature thing to do.

His phone bleeped with a text from Savannah.

Busy?

He smiled as his thumbs flew over the phone's key pad.

At six o'clock in the morning? What are you doing up? I thought Nashville starlets slept until noon.

This starlet decided to conquer the milking parlor. Turns out, Levi has the cows on a regimented schedule that includes a predawn milking and a second just before dinnertime.

Collin grinned.

Should we alert the presses?

How about we celebrate with a breakfast picnic at the lake?

Sounds perfect, but I promised Amanda we'd

check on the pears and peaches this morning, then we're transplanting some of berries from the greenhouses into a new outdoor garden.

There was a long pause.

You want to tag along?

Amanda won't mind sharing her brother time?

Of course she won't.

By nine the three of them had driven the Gator through both the peach and pear groves, with Collin pointing out the budding trees. Because of the warmer than usual spring, he expected harvesting to begin earlier than normal this year, and he made a note to bring that up in his renegotiation with Westfall Foods at the end of June.

"What's over there?" Savannah asked, pointing toward a low area off to the side of the main peach grove.

Crisp white flowers dotted the limbs of five squat trees that looked similar to the peach grove where the three of them were driving.

The little wooden fence his grandfather had put around the trees needed a fresh coat of paint, he noted. Collin shook his head. Those five trees were funny now, but he'd been mortified by them just a few years before.

"Those are Collin's peaches," Amanda said, laughing.

Savannah looked at Amanda and then at Collin. "I don't get it."

Collin sighed. "And this is where I lose my orchardist title."

Amanda held her belly and her laughs began to sound like wheezes. "He… Granddad…" Amanda couldn't get the words past her mouth, so Collin took over.

"We had a project in 4-H about diversification. It gave me the idea to add peach trees to the orchard. Granddad didn't like the idea and shut me down."

Amanda interrupted, having regained a little control. "So Collin orders the trees online, but they arrive dead. He sends them back before Grandad notices, and uses the refund money to buy trees at the nursery in town," she said, and then lost it again. Tears streamed down her face.

"I don't get it. Obviously the trees grew," Savannah pointed to the little grove off to the side of the main peach orchard. "And now you have a whole grove of them."

"No, he doesn't," Amanda said, still holding her sides. She slid down the seat, and Collin reached into the backseat to grab her before she could fall out of the side of the stopped Gator.

Savannah looked bewildered.

"I was in a hurry. I'd taken Granddad's truck and I needed to get back and get them planted before he realized I was gone," Collin said with a sigh. "So I grabbed four healthy-looking trees with what I thought were the right blossoms and headed back here."

"And?" Savannah asked, drawing out the word.

"They're plum trees," Amanda hooted with laughter. "Mr. I Know How to Build A Peach Orchard tried to start it up with plum trees." And then she really did fall through the open side of the four-seater Gator, which only served to make her laugh harder.

Savannah chuckled, whether at him or his sister, Collin wasn't sure. "Plums?" She glanced at him, and her brown eyes were warm with laughter.

"Plums. In my defense, plum and peach trees have very similar blossoms. Also, I was only sixteen."

"So those are Collin's Peaches," Amanda said.

"Granddad bought the first real peach trees for my eighteenth birthday. I think the sweetness of the plums are what made him change his mind about adding the peaches," he said with a shrug.

Savannah chuckled. "Why not start a whole plum field?"

"This isn't the best area for plum trees, although those have fared really well. Maybe someday," he said.

Amanda finally got her laughter under control and got back into the Gator. They arrived at the greenhouses a little while later, and the three of them loaded the back of the Gator with strawberry, blueberry and raspberry plants, along with a small tiller he could use to get the soil ready. He motioned to one of the teenagers he'd hired for the summer, Troy, and the young boy got into the backseat.

Gran's garden was on the back side of the house, and his plan was to add on to it.

He and Troy unloaded the tiller, and he set the boy to work preparing the soil while he went over how to set up the different berry areas with Amanda and Savannah. Savannah looked at her manicured nails and frowned.

"So much for a week's worth of Passion Berry Pink," she said and picked up a flat of strawberries.

"I can run the Gator back to get you a pair a gloves," he said, but Savannah shook her head.

"I managed to milk cows with this manicure, I can handle a little dirt."

Collin was beginning to think Savannah could

handle almost anything. She'd worn a pair of running shorts and a tank top today, and her hair fell in a mass of twirled locks around her face and past her shoulders. She'd conquered the milking machines; now she was about to plant strawberries. She was about to ruin a manicure.

This Savannah was so different from the girl he had imagined her to be all those years ago when he'd been intent on ignoring her.

This Savannah was a Savannah he'd like to spend a lot of time with. Collin shook himself.

Not going there. She wasn't staying, so whatever this was between them, it was only temporary. No need to start thinking about a nonexistent future.

He sent Troy back to the barns to continue sorting produce for the market, handed Amanda a trowel and took one for himself. She was already digging in the area he'd marked for blueberries.

He could hear music from Amanda's headphones while they planted. After showing her how to prep the soil for the strawberries, Collin left Savannah in that section and began working on the raspberries. Content in the warm sunshine and fragrant earth, it surprised him when he reached into the box for another raspberry plant and his hand found only cardboard.

Amanda had grabbed a bottle of water and

was sitting with her back against a tall maple, her feet tapping along with the music in her earbuds.

Savannah put the last strawberry plant in the dirt and settled it with the back of her trowel. She sat back on her heels. Dirt caked her knees and she'd smeared some over one cheek, too. She clapped her hands together, removing some of the dirt, and then examined her hands.

"Didn't even lose a nail," she said. "Although I think the Passion Berry Pink is done for." Savannah turned her hands so he could see the chipped paint. "Are manicures covered in your benefits plan?" she asked with a grin on her face.

Collin shook his head and joined her at the edge of the garden. He could feel her warmth through the sleeve of his T-shirt, and it started a slow burn in his belly. "We have other benefits," he said, and took her mouth with his.

Savannah wrapped an arm around his neck, settling into the kiss. She twined her legs with his.

"God, you guys, get a room." Amanda's voice broke through his consciousness, and Collin pulled back. Savannah rested her forehead against his, her breathing rough.

"Saved by the teenager," she said.

He grinned. "For now."

"Promises, promises," she said.

Amanda left the shaded area, tossed her empty

water bottle into the bed of the Gator and began picking up the berry flats and cardboard.

"So you guys are together, huh?" she asked as she worked.

Collin looked at Savannah, unsure how to answer. She shrugged, which didn't make it any easier. "We're, ah, dating," he said finally, and made a mental note to actually take Savannah somewhere not orchard-related in the near future.

Savannah cocked an eyebrow at him. Clearly, she thought the term *dating* was a loose definition of what was happening between them, too.

"Cool," was Amanda's response. She tossed the refuse into the back of the Gator and then Collin loaded the tiller.

The three of them got into the vehicle, and Collin began the drive back to the barn area. Too soon, the utility vehicle was unloaded and the cardboard flats disposed of. Collin glanced at the sky. A few fat drops of rain fell, and Amanda started for the house.

"I can't drive home in this," she said, motioning to the four-wheeler she'd arrived in this morning.

"For once, the weatherman was right on the money." He grabbed Savannah's hand and started for the house as heavier rain began to fall.

Inside, Collin handed Savannah a towel, and

she dried off her arms and legs. "It'll pass quickly, just a light shower. Good for Amanda's berries."

"I thought they were for the orchard, not just Amanda?"

He shook his head as he led her into the kitchen. "Expanding Gran's little garden was her idea, so they're Amanda's Berries."

"Like the plums are Collin's Peaches?"

He grimaced. "Something like that."

"Somebody has to bring in new ideas," Amanda said from the kitchen, where she grabbed another bottle of water. She took two more from the shelf and handed them to Savannah and Collin. "You guys want to play cards while the storm passes?"

It wasn't Collin's first option for spending a rainy afternoon with Savannah, but it was probably the mature thing to do.

But sometimes doing the mature thing sucked.

The three of them sat on the screened porch, looking over the garden they'd just planted. The rain brought a cool breeze into the porch, along with the smell of freshly turned soil. A satisfied feeling filled him as he looked out at the new garden. His thigh brushed Savannah's and a different feeling took over.

Before she took the four-wheeler back to the ranch, he was going to finish that kiss.

She elbowed him. "Your draw," she said, motioning to the cards, but her leg remained beside his and her eyes darkened.

Definitely, definitely going to finish that kiss, he thought.

"So cucumber magnolias, apples, plums and peaches. Your grandfather was definitely into trees," Savannah said as she threw a queen into the discard pile.

Bad move, Collin thought, picking up the card.

"Don't forget the pears," he said, pulling a second card from the draw pile. He added a jack of diamonds to jacks of clubs and hearts already in his hand. *Nice*, he thought.

"And the twisted willows at the pond," Amanda put in. She looked at Savannah. "He planted those for Mara when she turned eighteen. Granddad said they were complicated, just like her."

Savannah sent him a questioning look.

"Mara was always busy learning computer programming codes, scribbling new code ideas into her notebooks. Granddad didn't understand how she could find computers more fascinating that nature."

"So he gave her trees that were complicated. Makes sense."

"Not really," Collin said as he drew another card. The fourth jack. Just what he needed.

Collin laid down his cards. Savannah threw her cards onto the middle of the table, as did Amanda, and Collin began shuffling. "Twisted willows are simple, like most trees. Give them sunlight and water, and they're happy. Mara took to coding under them, which made him happy."

"What about Amanda's trees? What did he plant for you?" she asked.

Amanda's face clouded. "He died when I was fourteen. Gran and Collin and Mara got their trees when they were eighteen. So, no trees for me," she said, and pressed her lips together.

Shock hit Collin low in his belly. He hadn't thought about it before, but Amanda was right—she wouldn't get her trees. Granddad had left list after list of how Collin should do things when he was gone, but nowhere was there a note about Amanda's trees. Then their parents had come back. And then they left again.

Amanda would be eighteen in September.

Not having trees hadn't sent Amanda over the edge, but it could have played a part in her behavior changes over the past few months. Damn it, one more thing he hadn't noticed.

Savannah looked from his sister to him and back again, seeming to sense the tension that had come into the room. "What kind of tree would you like, if you could pick?" she asked.

"Virginia live oaks, and I wouldn't just want

one, I would want at least fifteen," Amanda said without hesitation.

"That's specific." Obviously she'd been thinking about the tree thing for a while now. He shuffled the cards, then began dealing. "Why live oaks and why fifteen?"

Amanda drew a card and nodded. Collin wondered if she'd drawn a good card or if her happiness was because of the tree conversation.

"Carbon footprint. Virginia live oaks are one of the best trees to absorb CO_2." Collin blinked and she continued. "That assembly I was telling you about? Some of the fir family are good, too, and maples, but I like the look of the live oaks best. Plus, they stay green nearly year-round."

"You've thought about this a lot." He was impressed. And shocked. How had he missed this serious environmental streak in his baby sister all these years?

"I think about a lot of things a lot," Amanda said.

Savannah drew her card, rearranged the cards in her hands and laid down a set of queens as well as a flush.

"Dang it, I was looking for that one," Amanda said, pointing at Savanna's ten of clubs.

Savannah grinned. "Better luck next time. And I, for one, love live oaks. They're very ethereal, I think."

Collin shot a look at her. "You like live oaks?"

"They're the ones with the branches that can reach down to the ground, right? Like in *Forrest Gump*?"

He nodded. Savannah continued. "All those big, spreading branches, the thick leaf canopy. It's kind of like a real-life fairy-tale tree."

"And it's good for the environment," Amanda put in, as if he could have forgotten her reasons for wanting fifteen of the massive trees so quickly.

"I got it. An environmentally and romantically-sound tree species."

Now to figure out where to put Amanda's trees, because he couldn't just not give her the trees. Granddad would have wanted her to have them. More than that, Collin wanted her to have them, too. The young girl could use a strong root system.

They played two more rounds of rummy—Savannah won both—before the rain began to fade into the distance. Collin was still thinking about the trees and that look on Amanda's face when she said she didn't have a tree. That look that said she wasn't important. The two of them needed to talk, that was certain.

Thunder rumbled in the distance, breaking Collin away from his thoughts. He should load up her four-wheeler and take Savannah home before the storm hit. The air around them had become very still, the humidity spiking after the gentle rain.

"I'll take you home," he said, putting the cards back into the little box Gran had cross-stitched one year for the farmers' market. The little boxes had flown off their table.

"I can take the lake track."

"That storm brewing looks like it could turn bad quickly. I'll load your four-wheeler onto the trailer and take you. Just to be safe."

"I'll go help the guys get the stand settled for the night," Amanda said and left the porch.

"Really, you don't have to drive me home. I'm a big girl."

"And you can handle a milking parlor and plant a berry garden without breaking a nail. But I wouldn't want to be out in that—" he pointed to the low-hanging gray clouds "—on a four-wheeler."

It only took a couple of minutes to hitch the trailer to the truck and secure the four-wheeler, and then he was driving down the orchard lane with Savannah sitting beside him on the truck's bench seat.

"Thanks for letting me hang with you guys today. I had fun," she said after a while.

"Me, too." It had been fun. More fun than he'd expected, but he was surprised it had been fun for Savannah, who was used to Nashville and celebrity parties and performing before thousands of fans. "Are you bored with the country life yet?" He put a teasing note in his voice, but the question was more serious than he wanted to admit.

He was getting too close to her, and they'd only just started spending any quality time together. He had no idea what plans she had for her life. What she wanted to do, outside the whole singing thing. Hell, he knew her tattoo better than he knew Savannah. Those lacey white lines on her skin still fascinated him.

Savannah was quiet for a long moment. Finally, she asked, "Can I ask you a serious question without you immediately thinking I'm some kind of stalker girl trying to hitch her proverbial wagon to yours?"

"Sure." Questions were good. Questions were personal. But that "hitching her wagon" thing? That sounded…a little uncomfortable.

"I'm not sure I'm made up for Nashville or singing. This break…" She paused, took a deep breath. "I'm considering making it permanent."

Collin looked at her, trying to read her expression in the gloomy afternoon light. He couldn't tell if she meant it or not, and it annoyed the hell out of him. Almost as much as it annoyed the hell out of him that his heart did that pitter-pat thing women talked about in those silly romantic comedies he watched with Gran and Amanda.

His heart shouldn't be missing beats because of Savannah Walters. He wasn't even sure if there was anything between them except two of the hottest sessions of sex he'd had in his twenty-eight years.

"Come on, you sparkled on stage." It was Savannah's turn to shoot him what he imagined was an incredulous look. "We watched at the Slope. Merle had that reality show blasting every time it came on. He offered free drinks to everyone who dialed in your contestant number, and he checked to make sure they called the right one."

A slow smile spread over Savannah's face. "I didn't know that."

"Every night you were on, the bar was packed. Levi figures if we'd moved a few thousand more people to town, we could've gotten you through to the final round."

They just made it into town as a few fat drops of rain splattered the ground. The wind picked up, and Collin flicked on the windshield wipers.

"Thank you."

"You did the hard work. Your voice was…angelic," he said, and she laid her head against his shoulder for a brief moment.

"Thank you for that, too. I do like singing,

just not the stuff that comes along with singing in a thousand-watt spotlight. Legitimate reporters and gossip blogs and people willing to sell anything about you to the press."

"What do you have to hide? No one gets up to anything truly bad in Slippery Rock." Not even his sister, he was beginning to realize. Taping off streets was a bit extreme, but if that was the worst she got up to, it really wasn't that bad. Not compared to the kids who'd started the fire with their prank or whoever had taken to painting graffiti on the downtown sidewalks.

Savannah hadn't answered, and he glanced at her in the dim light. She was chewing on her bottom lip and had her hands clasped in her lap.

"There is the fact that I don't know who I am."

He harrumphed. "You're Savannah Walters." His best friend's sister. Daughter of one of the most respected couples in the county. Talented singer. Aspiring milkmaid and berry farmer.

"Yeah, but who was I before they gave me the last name of Walters? I don't even have a real birthday. I don't know my astrological sign. I'm not sure I believe in astrology, but maybe I would if I knew for sure."

"Sure you do, January 1. New Year's baby." She shot him a look. "It's why Levi always skipped out on Aiden and Adam's bowl game parties. Your party."

She shook her head, and her shoulders slumped. "No, they found me on January 1, at the police station with a note that said 'Savannah, age seven, birthday in May.' When Mama Hazel and Dad adopted me, they put the first down as my birthday because that's how they looked at it. The officers who found me on the first gave me a new life."

Collin's hands gripped the steering wheel tighter. He'd known Savannah was adopted, it was no secret in town, but he'd never had reason to ask anyone about how she had come to be on the Walters Ranch.

"I always assumed you were adopted through some program, like for orphaned children or something."

"I was technically a foster child, although Mama and Dad were my only placement. They'd signed up to be foster-to-adopt parents, and because I'd been abandoned, I went to a home with permanency in mind instead of a stopgap to fix a drug problem or homelessness or abuse. Most fosters are taken from their families. Mine left me on the steps of a police station." She scooted farther away from him on the bench seat. "I don't remember much about my life before I came here."

"Maybe that life doesn't matter," he said. The words sounded lame to his ears. Of course her life before Slippery Rock mattered. His certainly did. Taking care of his sisters when his parents didn't come home for days on end had made him who he was. A provider. A person who always needed to know there was enough money and food and shelter to keep the people he loved safe.

"Yeah," Savannah said, but the word had an ugly sound. "It will matter to the tabloids. They live to make celebrities larger than life, and they laugh as they try to destroy the icons they've created."

"So you don't want to sing because you're afraid they'll turn on you eventually?"

They crossed the western limits of the town, and Collin made the turn onto the two-lane road that led to Walters Ranch.

"No. I mean, I don't want all that splashed around the media, but I entered that first contest so I wouldn't just be Levi's sister or Bennett's daughter. I wanted to have something to offer the family. I certainly blew off any help I could be at the dairy as a kid." She twisted her hands in her lap again. "I'm not sure a singing career is worth the sacrifice of them giving up their privacy, getting dragged into some salacious gossip piece about the biracial country music singer they adopted who doesn't know her own birthday. I sound pathetic."

"You sound like someone who has a choice

to make. If you want to be a singer, Van, be a singer. It's not a crime to have had crappy biological parents. You might even inspire other foster children."

"I'm no role model," she said, and there was a tense finality to her voice.

Collin made the turn into the ranch drive.

"Sure you are. You're a woman from a town of fewer than ten thousand people who placed third in a national singing competition. Who scored a big record deal and went on a spring tour with Genevieve Anderson. You could be the poster child for role models."

Collin parked the truck beneath a tree and turned to look at her. Rain streaked the windows of the truck and sadness shone in her big brown eyes.

"Can I ask you something?" she asked, her voice quiet. Rain tapped at the windshield.

He ran his fingertips over her hair, and Savannah turned her cheek into his palm. "Yes, I want to come in. And, no, I won't."

"Not that. We already talked about the defiling of my childhood bedroom. What are we doing, Collin? You're driving me home, and we're meeting at the lake and at the cabin for sex, and I have about three pages of silly text messages from you. What are we doing?"

He'd been asking himself the same thing and

he had no answers. He wanted to say having fun, but this was more than fun. This conversation meant something, and the something that it meant made him feel twitchy inside. He liked this version of Savannah, but despite sharing her feelings about her life before Slippery Rock, he still didn't really know her.

And she definitely didn't know him. She didn't know that he hated his parents, that he sometimes wished they didn't exist. It was childish, and he knew as an adult he should be over their repeated abandonment, but there it was.

Part of him wanted to shake Savannah until she realized that the people who'd left her on those police station steps had done her a favor. They'd given her a chance at a better life.

His parents had simply ignored him, Mara and Amanda until he'd had to do something about it. And even after their grandparents were caring for them, Samson and Maddie refused to sign away their parental rights. He'd begged Granddad and Gran to have those parental rights terminated, but his grandparents had refused, believing that if they gave Samson and Maddie enough room, they would come back willingly.

Collin guessed he couldn't blame them for that; they were Samson's parents, after all. Parents, the good kind, didn't turn their backs on their kids. Not even when the kids deserved it.

"I'm not sure what we're doing," he said finally, and then decided to take a chance. The kind of chance he'd taken when he'd dialed his grandparents' phone number, not knowing if they would even care. "I do know I want to see you again. Not just for the lakeside sex," he said, trying for a lighter tone.

Savannah rewarded him with a smile.

"Me too." She pressed a quick kiss to his cheek and then reached for the truck door. "I like the person I am here. It's weird—before I left, I thought I hated this place. Now that I'm here it's like I don't recognize the person who left it. And the person who was living in Los Angeles and then Nashville and then on a tour bus is a complete mystery."

"I like the person you are now," he said, the words feeling tight in his throat.

Savannah opened the door and dashed through the pouring rain. On the porch, she turned and waved before hurrying inside. She switched off the light shining beside the door.

Lightning struck in the distance. Collin decided the four-wheeler would stay with him for the night. Carefully, he turned the truck and started back down the lane.

For better or worse, it seemed as if he was in a relationship with Savannah Walters.

The thought made him smile.

CHAPTER THIRTEEN

"I WANT OUT." Savannah paced the small bedroom she'd dreamed of running away from too many times to count in the past. The place she'd run to when the life she'd thought she'd wanted began crumbling around her.

Scratch that. Her Nashville life hadn't crumbled—she'd imploded it with one stupid, huge, regrettable act. All because she'd felt uncomfortable on the stage she'd pushed to stand on. Now she'd fully realized her life in Nashville wasn't what she'd truly wanted at all.

"It looks as if you're going to get your wish." Guy's voice was heavy through the phone line. "They dropped three of the four acts this morning. You're the only one they're still holding tight to."

Why? Why couldn't they just drop her already? The sooner the record label signed off on her release, the sooner she could breathe. Genevieve would have no reason to spill her dirty little secret if Savannah was no threat.

She'd told Collin a white lie last night in the

truck. Yes, she'd been uncomfortable on stage and talking to the press, and it was because of her past. Leaving Nashville was only partially about the press hounding her, though. It was also about Genevieve threatening to go public with Savannah's affair—technically, one-night stand—with Genevieve's road manager. And husband. If the press got wind of that…not even the quiet life she was picking up in Slippery Rock would be safe.

God, how could she have been so stupid?

Philip Anderson said all the right things—it was a business marriage, it was an open marriage, and Genevieve had drawn up separation papers.

He'd neglected to tell her the separation papers were more than five years old, had never been filed, and that, while he considered their marriage open, Genevieve didn't.

She stood by her man.

While Savannah had sex with him on a tour bus.

Only Guy, Genevieve and Philip knew what she'd done, and she was more desperate to keep this dirty secret between the four of them now than the day she'd left Nashville. She'd packed her suitcase into the old Honda and gotten out of town as quickly as possible, on Guy's advice.

She'd stayed away from everything music related, as Genevieve had angrily ordered her.

"What are they waiting on?"

"What label heads are thinking never makes sense. Don't worry, though, if Genevieve pushes and they drop you, we'll find a home somewhere else," he said, misreading her anxiety about being dropped. Savannah didn't want a new deal. She wanted to disappear into the sunset.

She wanted more days spent in the sunshine with Collin, in bed with Collin, in a rainy truck with Collin. Away from the press. Away from the spotlight. She just wanted to be the Savannah that she was in Slippery Rock.

"I'm not sure I want that," she said, and waited for Guy to tell her not to worry. She wasn't disappointed.

"Savannah, I know touring with Genevieve was stressful, and I know your life since the reality show has been a whirlwind, but don't let one executive trying to balance his revenue sheets make this decision for you." His deep voice seemed to echo over the phone line. "You have a bright future. We'll find a label that is a good fit—"

"No. I don't— I can't— It isn't what I want." She had to give him a legitimate reason not to return to Nashville, and she didn't think having a crush on a guy from high school was the reason. "I don't like living on tour buses, and being on those stages is… It's almost crippling. The crush of people is too much and the music they pipe into my in-ear monitors is too loud and everything just starts to go hazy."

Guy listened while she told him just how uncomfortable she was in front of the crowds, and how much she feared the media microscope that, to date, had barely existed.

"The media loves you. You never made a big deal of your ethnicity, but you can be that barrier-crossing artist. We can do a big spread 'At Home with Savannah' or something with one of the big magazines. You can control the story. You can be the first woman of color to make it into the top fifteen on the country music charts—"

"Only because of the reality show. As soon as I left the show, the song dropped like a rock."

Guy ignored her. "You don't need to worry about finding a new slot, the labels will be fighting for you."

The thought sent a chill up Savannah's spine. It had been a relief when her vote percentage hadn't made the cut into the top three, and when the show single began sinking, the relief was even stronger. She'd felt like she could breathe.

She'd only taken the tour slot because her parents had sounded so disappointed when she hadn't made that final cut. Selfishly, she'd wanted them to be proud of her so she'd ignored the anxiety she had when she performed during the show tapings, signed on to Genevieve's tour, and dreaded every minute of it.

Now that she saw her chance to be free of the circus that went with being in the spotlight, she was desperate to hold on to that freedom. She didn't want record labels fighting over her. She didn't want crowds cheering her name. She hadn't wanted those things *before* the incident with Philip, and she didn't want them now *because* of what had happened with the man. She didn't want her actions to reflect badly on her family.

She didn't want Nearly-a-Boy-Scout Collin to know about any of that.

She wanted to be stronger than the woman who'd run from Slippery Rock two years before, and she wanted to be stronger than the Savannah who, instead of just walking away from a situation she didn't like, imploded her life and hurt another singer, Genevieve, in the process.

"I don't want the labels to fight over me, and you deserve a client who wants to be in that spotlight. Whatever you have to do, just get me out of the contract. I don't want the attention."

"Listen, you'll change your mind in another week or so. I'll call when I know more. You hang in there." Guy hung up before Savannah could say anything.

She sat heavily on the edge of her bed. For the past few days she'd been able to put Nashville out of her mind, and she would be damned if she let it spin out of control again.

The strong woman she wanted to be wouldn't hide in her childhood bedroom all day, Savannah decided. She straightened her shoulders and left her phone on the bed.

Mama Hazel was working in the kitchen. Dirty breakfast dishes were piled in the sink, but she was busy gathering ingredients for the market pies. Savannah put the drain plug in the sink and began filling it with hot, soapy water.

"Hummingbird, I'm just going to make more of a mess," Mama said.

"We clean as we go. Isn't that what you always told me?" Savannah began washing plates, stacking the soapy, clean ones in the other side of the sink for rinsing.

"I think I said that just to give you something to do instead of sitting at the table with those big eyes of yours," Mama Hazel said with a smile. "I never knew what you were thinking."

Savannah began rinsing the clean plates and stacking them on the drainer. "Mostly, I was wondering when I'd have to leave." All the air seemed to be sucked from the room with her words. Mama's hands stilled at the big island. Savannah peeked over her shoulder.

Mama Hazel stood at the big, butcher block island, floured hands covering her mouth, her eyes wide with shock. "Savannah," she whispered.

"I didn't want to leave," Savannah said quickly. "I was afraid I would do something wrong and that you wouldn't want me here." She forced the words out fast, knowing that if she didn't they wouldn't come. The two of them— the four of them, actually, but she would start with her mother—had needed to have this conversation for a long time. She'd started it in the farmers' market, but then backed away from it. She couldn't keep leaving things half said. The woman she wanted to be would have this conversation. So Savannah took a deep breath.

"Oh, baby," Mama said, and wiped her hands on her apron before crossing to the big kitchen sink. She gathered Savannah in her arms, and Savannah thought if she could just stay there everything would be okay. No one would have to know just how royally she'd messed up this time. She wouldn't hurt her family.

She wouldn't have to see that look in Collin's eyes. He'd been sympathetic last night in the truck, but that had been a sanitized version of her life pre-adoption. She hadn't told him about the dirt or the cold or the yelling voices she could sometimes still hear.

She hadn't told him about the fear that maybe it was her fault she'd been left on those steps with a ragged piece of paper pinned to her chest. And she hadn't told him that as a child, every time she started to feel comfortable in this house, she'd lashed out. Disrupted things in any way she could, just to see if they would send her away like the people with the angry voices had done. One of the psychologists Mama Hazel took her to called it Reactive Attachment Disorder. She hated that label. She hated more that the label was right.

"You could never do anything that would make me turn my back on you. Not then. Not now." Mama Hazel stepped back. She pushed a braid behind Savannah's ear. "Nothing."

"I must have done something that made them leave me on a set of steps on a cold January day."

"You don't know that," her mother said, shaking her head.

"You don't know that I didn't."

Anger lit Hazel's brown eyes, bringing out the golden flecks that both Levi and Savannah also had. "Of course I do. You've lived in this house for almost twenty years, and not one time have you done something so egregious that your father or I would turn you out. I can't imagine you or any other child could ever do anything that would warrant that."

"Then why?" Savannah gripped the dish towel in her hands tightly. It was a question she'd asked herself at least a million times, but until today she'd never been brave enough to voice the words aloud.

"I don't know." Hazel put her finger under Savannah's chin, forcing her to look up. "I have to believe, though, that whoever it was had a heart, otherwise they would have left you anywhere except a police station."

"I never moved. I didn't run after her." Savannah was positive the person who'd left her was a woman. She couldn't put a name or a face on her, but she was positive it was a woman. "Why didn't I run after her?"

"I don't know." Hazel was quiet for a moment. "I've always been grateful to whoever left you at that police station, Savannah. Grateful he or she didn't just leave you on the side of a road or alone in an apartment. Grateful because, had they left you anywhere other than that police station, it's likely you'd have died, and I would never have had the chance to be your mother."

She chanced a glance at Mama Hazel, seeing nothing but sincerity in her gaze.

"You're *my* baby, my hummingbird," she said and put her arms around Savannah again.

"I love you, Mama," she said, and realized she had never said those words out loud to anyone before.

Hazel sniffed. "I love you, too, Savannah."

Savannah felt a little piece of her soul heal with the simple words spoken in a kitchen that was so familiar to her. All those nights spent in family counseling, all the days spent angry with her lot in life, all the times she'd been too afraid to ask the hard questions, rolled through her mind.

She'd wasted nearly twenty years of her life being afraid of who she was. Collin was right. She was Savannah Walters. What happened before she was given that last name didn't have to ruin her future.

She was through being afraid.

"I'm not going back to Nashville."

Mama held her at arm's length for a moment, her gaze inspecting Savannah as if she expected her to have sprouted horns or wings or maybe a tail. "Are you feeling all right?"

Savannah wiped at the tears on her cheeks. "Despite the waterworks, yeah, I'm good. Better than I've been, maybe ever."

"But you love singing."

How many people were going to tell her what she loved? She liked singing. She was good at it. Saying that she loved it was an exaggeration.

"I saw singing as a way to do something that was me. Something that would make you all proud of me. Levi was the football star. I wanted to shine for you, too, and I knew I could sing, so that's what I did."

"But you didn't have to do anything to shine. You shine all the time, just by being yourself." Mama poured two mugs of coffee and motioned Savannah to the kitchen table.

"It doesn't matter, it's just what I thought. Still think, maybe. But being on the reality show and then joining the tour—" she shook her head "—made me realize that I like singing for me, not for crowds. The crowds and the noise and everything that goes along with a singing career make me feel like I can't breathe." She sipped her coffee, waiting for Mama to tell her she was wrong.

"Okay."

Savannah blinked. Mama Hazel sipped her coffee and then added another spoonful of sugar from the little bowl on the table. "What? You're an adult, Savannah. If you don't want to be a singer, you don't have to be a singer. What do you want to do?"

The million-dollar question, and one for which her answer was still a little murky. She liked being with Collin, but dating an orchard owner wasn't exactly a career aspiration. She liked

hanging out with Amanda, and she'd liked working with the kids in the Nashville music program.

"Do you remember that camp we went to after
my freshman year?"

"The family camp."

A halfhearted smile crossed Savannah's face.
"Therapy camp, Mama."

Mama Hazel waved her hand. "We were there
as a family—"

"Because I ran away from home and wouldn't
talk about it. We had daily sessions with a therapist, and then there were the horse therapy things
and the bonding exercises." And before she'd
come back to Slippery Rock, it had been one of
the happiest experiences of her life, despite the
fact that she'd pretended she'd hated every minute of it. "Thank you."

"For what?"

"For taking me there. I don't think I ever
thanked you for that." Savannah thought about
the week the four of them had spent at the camp,
and an idea began to form in her head. "There
was a music program I volunteered with in Nashville. It's one of the only things I liked about
being there. It was a mix of kids, some from
rich neighborhoods, some from poorer. I think
I'd like to do something like that."

"Run a music program for kids?" Mama Hazel

seemed to mull the idea over for a long moment. "You could talk to the school, I guess."

"No, I'm thinking more like a camp that is musically based. For foster kids. A place for them to go, to be themselves, to have music. To keep music in my life, but in a way that I'm comfortable with."

Mama reached across the table and put her hand over Savannah's. Her darker skin was soft and smooth, her nails clipped short and painted a light pink. Savannah squeezed her mother's hand in hers.

"I think that is a beautiful idea," Mama Hazel said and patted her hand.

"Yeah?"

She nodded. "Yeah."

Savannah drew in a slow breath. A music program. Her own music program, not for aspiring singers or songwriters or guitarists, but for kids who were just looking for something or some place where they could belong.

It was a scary thought. An exciting and scary and energizing thought. Now she just had to figure out how to make it work.

FOR THE FIRST time since Levi's football injury three years before, Collin skipped out on their dart game at the Slope.

He pulled his old truck into the drive at Walters Ranch just before seven and walked to the door. Levi answered.

"I knew that look at the bar meant something," his friend said, giving him a light shoulder shove. "She's not ready."

"Is this where you give me the big brother talk?" Collin entered the house. Mama Hazel and Bennett sat in their matching rocking chairs. Bennett watched the Kansas City Royals on TV while Mama Hazel worked on some kind of puzzle in a magazine.

"I figure you know the drill on that one, having two sisters of your own." The two of them sat on the sofa facing the big brick fireplace.

"When will your house be finished?" Collin asked.

"Another week or so."

"Then we just have to get Savannah out, and we'll be empty nesters," Bennett added from his chair, his deep baritone filling the room. "We didn't realize we'd raised two kids who couldn't live on their own."

"Hey, I survived two years in Los Angeles and Nashville, thank you very much," Savannah said from the stairs. She wore a short navy dress with thin straps at the shoulders and a skirt that swirled around her thighs. Collin swallowed hard.

"And I did four long years at college and another two and a half in the pros. It's like you don't like us or something," Levi said.

Collin liked the banter in this cozy living room. He missed bantering with Mara and hadn't yet figured out how to banter with Amanda.

"And now you're both back. It's like you two are homing pigeons," Bennett said, laughter in his deep voice.

"You hush, we love having both of our children at home," Mama Hazel said diplomatically.

"You'd just like us better in our own homes, we get it," Levi put in.

The play-by-play was fun to watch and almost familiar to Collin, although his memories were of Bennett, Hazel and Levi teasing like this and Savannah mostly off to the side. Interesting that she was joining in now.

That joining in meant something. He hoped it meant he could start thinking about Savannah in the long-term instead of this open-ended but short-term thinking he'd been doing.

A few minutes later they left the house. Collin handed Savannah into the truck and backed down the lane.

"Nice look. I wondered if you had any pants that reached past your knees," Savannah said.

"Made a special trip to Shanna's Closet. Did you know she carries menswear now, too?"

"Really? I thought those probably came from

the sporting goods store at the marina," she said, gesturing to his khakis.

"Ouch." Collin put his hand to his heart as if he'd been punched, making Savannah laugh. "And here I was going to tell you how nice you look."

"This old thing?" She grinned. "Where are we going?"

"The Overlook," he said, mentioning a restaurant with wide windows and the best views of the lake.

"Nice choice."

"Well, Bud's closes at seven thirty, and Merle gets annoyed if too many people eat the fruit off his drink setups."

They passed the rest of the drive in companionable silence, with Savannah appearing to focus intently on the fields they passed.

Once seated with glasses of wine on the table, she said, "I'm not going back to Nashville."

It was the farthest thing from Collin's mind and he shook his head. "You have to, it's your job." He paused. "Not that I want you to go back. Unless you want to go back."

"I don't, and singing isn't going to be my job much longer, even if I did." She fiddled with her napkin. "The label is cutting new artists, trying to level their revenue lines. Four artists were on the chopping block, and three of them are already gone. I'm the last."

"I'm sorry," he said, but he wasn't. The thought of Savannah staying in town made him happy. He was a jerk.

"I'm not. I told you the other day I didn't like the attention of the media, but it's more than that. I didn't like being on stage at all. All those people watching me, I couldn't relax."

"You might have gotten used to it."

"That's what my manager said, or at least, it's what he implied. He also said there will be a feeding frenzy for me when the label makes the announcement." Savannah kept fiddling with her napkin. "I told him I didn't want to continue on."

"And he said?"

"He said what any good manager would say to a fledging artist who he feels has cold feet— that I don't really know what I want."

Finally she looked at Collin and what he saw in her gaze wasn't fear or uncertainty. There was a bit of what he thought might be discomfort, but mostly her gaze seemed sincere.

"But you know what you want."

"I do. Kind of. I don't want to be in the spotlight, and I'm not a role model, but I do know some people who would make good role models. I want to figure out how I can put those people in touch with foster kids. I might not have gotten bounced around like so many fosters do, but there is still a stigma attached to being in the system. I'm thinking about creating a music camp just for those kids. I want to do something that matters."

Collin didn't really know what to say. "You want to make a difference."

"Apparently, I do." She sounded as shocked as he felt. But having said it, she put the crisp, white napkin in her lap and reached for a piece of bread from the basket the waitress had brought with their wine. "I thought I just wanted to show my parents that I could do something, and maybe that's part of what this is. I just don't want any child to feel the way I felt for so long. Like they don't belong or that they might be sent away again. Kids deserve better than that."

"Savannah," he said, and reached across the table to take her hand.

"Do you know my parents went into family counseling with me four different times? Every single time, I would just sit on the couch and try not to talk because I was afraid of the things I might have said." She bit into the bread.

"You're not afraid now?"

She was quiet for a long moment and some other emotion, something he couldn't put his finger on, crossed her face. "Oh, I'm still afraid, just not of Mama or Dad or Levi." She glanced at him.

"What brought all this on?"

"I had a rooftop talk with Levi a few days ago. I made myself talk to my mother this morning, after my manager called. And when you and I talked last night, it's like something opened up inside me. I think it's been trying to open for a while, but I just kept hiding away from it, letting life happen to me. I still have questions, but I'm making peace with some of the answers."

Collin raised his glass and, when she did the same, he clinked the glasses together. "To facing the music," he said.

THAT NIGHT SAVANNAH lay in Collin's arms in his loft apartment over the barn. She watched the night sky through his bedroom window. A few high clouds skirted in front of the moon and thousands of stars twinkled in the sky. And the man in bed with her wrapped his arms around her waist while she slept.

It was the most protected she had ever allowed herself to feel.

Savannah lifted Collin's hand to her mouth, kissing his fingers. His answer was a light snore at her shoulder.

Between last night in the truck and tonight at the restaurant, she had placed nearly all of her fears at his feet. He hadn't run away. Hadn't told her not to call. Hadn't used the clichéd "it's not you, it's me" excuse and left the restaurant.

He'd toasted her decision.

There was only one secret left and she hoped she would never have to voice it. If she didn't have to talk about it, she could pretend she hadn't fallen that far down the self-destruction rabbit hole.

The truth was, she didn't want to face what she had done in that trailer, not really. She wanted it to just be in the past. To lie there silently until she forgot it. Forgetting had to happen sooner or later. After all, she'd already managed to forget seven years of her life.

CHAPTER FOURTEEN

SAVANNAH GOT HER WISH.

Within a week from the phone call with her manager, the record label dropped her, citing financial difficulties. Guy had been right about one other thing: the other label heads wanted her. She had offers from not one but six different labels, from small startups to New-York-backed labels. Not one of them offered the typical deal that favored the label over the artist.

Guy thought she was nuts to turn every single offer down, but Savannah had never been happier.

She'd had important talks with not only her mother and Levi, but Bennett, too. When she mentioned the music camp, Bennett immediately jumped into action.

Her father had skipped work at the dairy to take her to a small plot of land at the north end of the ranch.

"What do you think?" he'd asked, getting out of the big truck and spreading his arms toward the open area. A few of the familiar oaks and

maples were scattered across the area, along with a set of railroad tracks that had been unused for as long as Savannah could remember.

"It's pretty," she said. "Isn't this where Levi moved the old herd, after you did the switch to an organic operation?"

"For a while, but the cows needed more room. We're renting space over at the Harris farm, so this is just empty land. I thought you might be able to use it."

Savannah shot him a glance. "To start my own dairy operation? Have you forgotten the absurdity of my attempts at milking so soon?"

Bennett put his arm around her shoulders. "For your music program. It could be a school— there are plenty of open storefronts downtown, but if you built something new, it could be more than that."

"Like the therapy camp we attended." Savannah had hoped to turn her program into a camplike program, eventually. She'd never expected her father to hand her several acres of prime ranch land. "I'll buy it from you."

"You'll take it from me," he corrected, squeezing her shoulders. "And you'll do wonderful things here."

Savannah wiped a hand over her eyes. She wasn't going to cry about that afternoon with her father or the gift of the land. She'd cried at the time, and that was enough. It was enough that things with her family were coming together. Her plans for the music program would come, too.

Then there was Collin.

She had spent nearly every night since their date at the Overlook in Collin's arms.

Life was suddenly offering Savannah everything she had always thought she didn't want. It was Memorial Day, and they'd spent the day with Collin's friends. Friends she was beginning to think of as her own. She sat in a lawn chair in Adam's backyard, watching the last rays of sunlight sink into the lake. Despite the pile of fencing in one corner, the yard was lovely, filled with flowers and shrubs, the grass a thick cushion under her feet. Savannah curled her toes against the cool grass and smiled. Their yard was perfect, right down to the little spit of sand at the water's edge that Jenny said Adam had brought in a couple of summers before.

Adam's wife, Jenny, handed Savannah a wine cooler and then took the seat next to her. Jenny's long braid was pulled through her baseball cap, and she wore cut-off jeans and a T-shirt with a flag painted on it. The men were standing around Adam's fire pit, roasting marshmallows and talking about the intricacies of s'mores-making.

"They're still fifteen mentally, I think," Jenny

said, her gaze full of laughter. "So you're Levi's sister and Collin's girlfriend?" At Savannah's nod, she continued. "I'm trying to figure out why I don't remember you from school at all."

"I kept to myself, probably a little too much."

"But you sang the national anthem a few times." She shook her head. "I should have remembered, but until Adam pointed you out on that singing show, I swear I missed everything about you."

Savannah liked the strawberry-blonde. She was warm and funny, and seemed to immediately accept Savannah as part of the group.

"If it's any consolation, I don't remember you, either. Small towns are weird, aren't they? We're all supposed to know one another and yet I swear I still see people at the farmers' market that I've never seen before. And some of the people I do know, I still can't figure out. Like, I've lived here since I was seven, and I still don't understand why Merle and Juanita pretend they aren't an item," Savannah said.

Jenny's eyes widened. "They are? Everyone says it's just work flirtation."

"Believe me, when you work with the two of them, it's evident. They arrive at the same time, leave at the same time. Half the time he offers to drive her home. They should just come out about it already."

"What other unseemly affairs are running around this town?" She leaned on the arm of her chair.

"You mean other than me and Collin?" That made Jenny laugh. "I think the rest of the town is an open book. But I wouldn't be surprised if James has something going on." She pointed a finger at the deputy sheriff, wearing old jeans and a black T-shirt, his aviator sunglasses resting on top of his head. "He is way too relaxed to not be having some kind of sex, but no one in town is connected to him."

"He does volunteer to go to a lot of out-of-town conferences."

"So he probably has a different girl in every town," Savannah said, weaving a story about James's clandestine affairs in her mind. She laughed. "No, him sneaking around a strange city with a Jessica-Rabbit-type isn't his style."

Jenny inspected the man in question for a long moment. "I don't know. I hear still waters run deep."

A few minutes later Collin and the rest of the guys returned to the seating area with charcoaled marshmallows on plates. While they began layering marshmallow, chocolate and graham crackers, the first fireworks rocketed into the sky with a loud boom.

Sparks of purple, red and green lit the night

sky, making it seem like a fairyland. Collin sat beside Savannah and took her hand as the next rockets went up.

"At least the firebugs didn't take a run at the actual display," James said, his tone dry.

"Those jerks couldn't figure out how to rig a firework if I wrote them a manual," Amanda said from her spot near the fire pit. The younger children were gathered around her, eager for more sweets.

Collin squeezed Savannah's hand. She finished the dessert and licked the remnants of a scorched marshmallow from her fingertips. A sudden burst of rockets lit the sky, washing it with a combination of sizzling white, orange, blue and purple displays. When the last of the fireworks sank toward the lake, Jenny yawned.

Savannah settled against the back of her chair, content to watch the fire and feel the warmth of Collin next to her. Before she knew it, he was shaking her shoulder.

"Come on, milkmaid, time to go home," he said.

Savannah shook her head. "The fireworks just ended."

"An hour ago. You fell asleep." He helped her to her feet and put an arm around her shoulder. Savannah felt off center, as if she'd lost her balance during her nap.

The backyard was mostly empty. James and Levi had gone, so had her parents, and Collin's sister and grandmother. Adam and Jenny were gathering the empty chairs and their two kids were sleeping soundly on chaise lounges near the deck.

"We should help them clean up," she said.

Adam waved a hand. "We're leaving the big work until tomorrow, just putting the chairs in the shed. Go," he said.

At his truck, Collin opened her door, and Savannah climbed into the truck. It seemed like it only took a couple of minutes to reach the orchard. He cut the engine and was around the truck before Savannah could climb down. Collin lifted her in his arms and carried her inside and up the stairs to the apartment.

He'd left a light on in the window, and it gleamed against the honeyed hardwood floors and leather furnishings in the living area. Collin pressed a kiss to her forehead and pushed the light sweater she'd put on at sunset off her shoulders.

His lips tasted like heaven when he pressed them to hers, and Savannah wound her arms around his neck. He pressed little kisses to her jaw and down her neck, and when he found the madly beating pulse in her neck a wave of heat rushed to her core. Collin reached one arm under her knees and supported her back with the other. His lips were hot on her own until she felt the soft comforter of his bed against her back.

Like the rest of the apartment, the space was all Collin, from the navy-striped comforter to the antique dresser and bed frame. Because the loft was mostly an open space, he'd put a clothing wardrobe along one wall. He toed off his shoes, kicking them in the general vicinity of the over-size wardrobe. Savannah kicked off her sandals and they clattered to the floor.

His hands were sure against her body, his mouth knowing exactly where to kiss, where to nip. When to take time and when to skim over. Savannah measured time through the loss of her clothing, and it wasn't taking long enough. She didn't want fast or hard, she wanted him and she wanted the night. All of it.

He unzipped her dress and helped her wriggle from it, leaving her clad in only a pair of lacy boy briefs.

She pulled his shirt from his body, dropping it to the floor before pushing her hands past the waistband of his shorts to take him in her hands. Collin shoved his cargos and boxers off and reached into the nightstand drawer. The foil packet rustled in the darkness. Savannah took it from him, so that she could roll it over his length. Collin groaned.

Then he was inside her, filling all of her empty spaces, until she felt as if she might combust from his nearness. They reached orgasm nearly in tandem, and Collin collapsed on top of her, holding most of his weight off her by resting on his elbows. His forehead met hers and she offered her lips for another long kiss.

God, she loved him.

Savannah froze.

Collin moved to the side, wrapping his arms around her from behind and burying his face in her neck. The same thing he'd done countless times over the past couple of weeks.

She loved him.

His breathing regulated, his arms loosened around her, and Savannah weighed the words in her mind. Before finally talking through some of her childhood issues with Mama Hazel, she'd never admitted to loving anything. Now she realized she could love in more than one way.

A deep, certain love for the family that had chosen her.

And a hot, scary, uncertain love for the man she had targeted that first night at the bar.

A man who liked her well enough to sleep with her, who took the nagging of his friends when he skipped out on darts night in stride, and who had never said a single thing about love.

Or even strong like.

They'd never truly discussed what was happening between them other than to agree that they both wanted it to continue. The "it" could be anything from more sex to more berry planting, Savannah had no idea.

And now she was in love with him.

Panic pricked at her consciousness.

Wait, this didn't have to be a bad thing. Not talking about what this relationship was didn't mean it wasn't anything. They enjoyed one another, were compatible in bed, and laughed at a lot of the same things. She ran her hands lightly over the arms still locked around her middle.

A man didn't hold a woman the way Collin held her without feeling something. He didn't have to know that she'd bypassed higher levels of like and gone straight to love. She could prove to him that she was worthy of a man like him, given the time.

GRAN WAVED AT Collin as she motored her scooter past the truck and onto the street leading toward the dock. She'd been coming to the farmers' market for a month now, and although she continued to walk better every day, Collin made her promise to use the scooter.

Slippery Rock was small town, but most of it showed up for the farmers' market, and crowds could be dangerous for her.

He spotted Savannah through the plate-glass window and couldn't stop the smile that spread over his face. Today she wore a long striped skirt in shades of purple and lavender with a jewel-toned tank top and leather sandals. She'd pulled her hair back, but several coils had escaped and fell around her face in crazy patterns.

"You're going to make her fall in love with you, ya know," Levi said, his voice quiet. Collin hadn't heard him walk between their two booths.

"It isn't that serious," he said, and caught the slight stiffening of Levi's frame. Collin immediately regretted the lie. Or maybe it was the truth. He had no clue how Savannah felt, and he wasn't ready to put words to what he felt for her. Mostly because he didn't know what he felt for her.

She made him laugh. She made him want her. She made him think about a future that included more than the orchard, more than Gran and Amanda and Mara. She made him feel as if he wasn't alone, and he'd been alone in the sea of people he knew for a long time.

None of those things meant she was in love with him, though, and none of them meant he was in love with her. What they meant, exactly, he was still trying to figure out.

She could tell him she didn't want to be a singer and that she didn't want Nashville until she was blue in the face, but that didn't change the fact that she'd chosen the singing competition when she'd left town before. There had to be more to her sudden unwillingness to go back than stage fright and the overzealous paparazzi.

That part didn't make sense to Collin, anyway. From what he'd been able to glean, the media—both legitimate and gossip—had been nothing but excited about her performances on the reality show and the subsequent tour. Surely, if one of them was out for blood, there would be hints of it in the earlier pieces.

What did he know, though? He was an orchardist from a small town on a Missouri lake. A man who had two more days to make a decision about the future of his business but who kept delaying the inevitable.

His counter-presentation had fallen by the wayside over the past couple of weeks with Savannah. At this point, he would have to either accept their offer or turn it down. Collin didn't want to do either.

Before he could deal with that, though, he needed to deal with Levi.

"I didn't mean that," he said and shrugged in apology. "We haven't talked about what this is between us."

"I love my sister, but she has a habit of not talking about the important things. Mama Hazel says it goes back to her being abandoned the way she was. Even if she's not talking, I can guarantee you she's feeling, so—"

A flurry of activity near the entrance to the farmers' market caught Levi's attention and he stopped talking. Collin looked in that direction.

He saw a small orange flag tilting wildly left and right, and the murmuring got louder. He couldn't make out the words, but a few of the people nearer the tumult waved him over.

Gran stood over a young boy who looked to be about Amanda's age. Her scooter was precariously parked with its front wheel atop the curb and its back wheels on the street. She held on to the boy's shirt with one hand and waved the orange scooter flag with the other.

"Citizen's arrest!" she yelled as the crowd parted to let Collin through. "I caught him. I caught the paint vandal. Citizen's arrest," she hollered again, and then released the flag. She reached into her backpack, and pulled out a brilliant yellow whistle and blew.

The crowd put their hands over their ears at the shrill sound. Collin winced, but kept moving forward until he could reach Gran. He put his hand over hers, ceasing the whistle.

"Gran, what are you doing?"

Gran straightened and looped the whistle

around her neck. She didn't release the shirttail of the young man in question.

"I didn't do anything," the kid said.

Gran shook her head. She reached into her backpack again and pulled out a can of blue spray paint. "I found him with this—" she held the can up as if it were a prize "—in the alley behind the market. He's the paint vandal."

A police cruiser chirped its sirens behind the crowd, but they only moved far enough for the officer to open his door. James exited the car, aviator sunglasses over his eyes. He wore the sheriff's department uniform.

"Hey, Mrs. Tyler. Bud called in about your arrest. What happened?"

Gran recounted her story to James, who made notes in a small notepad he pulled from one of the tabs on his utility belt. He took the can of spray paint, careful to only touch the edges of the lid, inspecting it closely.

"Book him," Gran said, as if she were a character from some old television cop show.

James grinned. "Nice line, but I can't."

"I caught him red-handed."

"He may have been up to some mischief, and I'll check out the alley before I release him. This—" he gently waved the can of paint "—isn't the same kind of paint the street vandal used. It washes off with water. Harmless. This stuff doesn't."

"Oh," Gran said, and frowned.

"I told you I didn't do nothin', lady," the kid said.

"I'll be the judge of that," James said and handed the kid into the backseat of the police cruiser. He went into the alley behind the market.

"Gran, what are you doing?" Collin put her gently back on her scooter and walked beside her to the truck. "You could have been hurt."

Gran harrumphed. "By a kid with a can of paint? Not hardly."

"How did this get started?"

"A few of us were talking over at Bud's over coffee. That paint vandal has been making all kinds of statements in their murals in town. Painting over the storm drains, writing on the sidewalks. Good use of color, by the way, although a very poor choice in placement. Vandalizing a street isn't the same as painting an environmental warning on canvas for a museum. When I was coming back, I saw him—" she pointed her thumb over her shoulder "—in the alley with the same blue paint."

"It isn't the same paint. You heard James."

"What kid carries around paint for no reason?"

"School project?"

"It's summer break, try again," Gran said.

"Repainting yard furniture? Getting a soapbox car ready for the Fourth of July race?"

"Well, sure, there are other reasons. Doesn't mean any of them are true."

Collin sighed.

James returned a few minutes later. "No sign of fresh paint in the alley or within the surrounding block." He focused on Gran. "Thank you for your diligent pursuit of justice," he said. Gran blushed.

"Don't encourage her," Collin said.

"I'm going to go release the suspect. See ya." He cut through the crowd to the squad car.

Collin turned to Gran. "You heard James. I'm a diligent pursuer of justice."

"What justice?" Amanda joined them, an empty cardboard box in her hands. "We sold out of berries just a couple of minutes ago. What do you mean, justice?"

"Gran thought she was arresting the downtown paint vandal. Turns out she was just harassing one of your classmates."

Amanda's expression was troubled.

"Don't worry, I'm sure by the time school starts in the fall he'll have forgotten all about Gran's attempted citizen's arrest."

Amanda shook her head. "I don't care about that, it's just… I know who made those paintings."

Collin's eyes widened. "You do? Why didn't you tell James?"

"Because it's me."

Collin's jaw dropped and his stomach turned. "You're the paint vandal?"

"No, I'm the sidewalk artist trying to get people to stop throwing trash into the streets."

Sweet Lord, not another crusade. In the span of a few weeks Amanda had gone from duct taping streets to vandalizing public property.

"Amanda—"

"I'm not wrong this time. I didn't disrupt the city or the traffic. It's a few paintings to remind people to put their trash in the proper receptacles so plastic straws and foam cups stop polluting the lake."

Collin sighed. "You hang up a flyer or write an editorial, then. You don't deface sidewalks and storm sewers."

Amanda rolled her eyes. "I didn't deface anything. The paint washes off with the next rain, and it isn't harmful to the water, but in the meantime, it's a reminder."

"A reminder of what?"

"To be responsible."

Somehow, Collin didn't think the mayor, the city council or the sheriff's department would see Amanda's sidewalk paintings as responsible.

"See, she's got the right idea. We all have to work together to be responsible citizens." Gran chose that moment to rejoin the conversation.

"Ten minutes ago, you were citizen's-arresting the paint vandal."

"And now I see her side of the story. She's showing her purpose," Gran said. She hugged Amanda's shoulder.

"Exactly. Like Savannah told me. 'You have to have a purpose.' This is mine."

Collin turned toward the window into the storefront of the market. Savannah.

Damn it.

COLLIN DIDN'T SPEAK to Savannah from the moment she got into his truck until he parked beneath the big maple tree at the side of the house. Amanda and his grandmother pulled in behind them.

"Is something wrong?" she asked, trying to figure out what had happened to turn Collin from the funny man she'd driven into town with four hours earlier to the almost angry man she saw now. His shoulders were rigid, his mouth set in a firm line.

"Just trying to find a *purpose*," he said, jumping out of the truck and stomping onto the porch.

Savannah stood beside the truck for a moment, watching him. Collin slammed through the front door and returned a moment later with a beer. He popped the top and drank.

"Are you mad about something?" she asked

when she reached the porch. Collin sat on the porch swing, sending it rocking crazily. Savannah stayed in the yard with her arms resting against the porch railing.

"Me," Amanda said from behind her. "Gran tried to arrest the paint vandal today, only she got the wrong person. The paint vandal is me."

Savannah was shocked. The town had been talking nonstop about the paint vandal since the first Keep Waterways Clear message had been painted on the sidewalk outside Bud's on the dock.

"Why?"

"Because you told her to find a purpose," Collin said, flinging his free arm out.

"I already knew my purpose, I just found another way to make myself heard. My purpose is to save the environment. I don't have a way to clean up the air or the atmosphere, but I can protect the water. People need to know that when they drop a cup in the drain it goes straight to the lake."

"Yes, your purpose is to save the environment by vandalizing the sidewalks and roads in town. Speaking of, how did you get into town? I never reinstated your car privileges."

Amanda crossed her arms over her chest. "I drove the four-wheeler over the back roads. Add it to my list of crimes."

"Collin," Gran said, her voice calm. "She was coming from a good place."

"Of course she was. Just like she was trying to shrink the carbon emissions by rerouting traffic. It doesn't matter why she does this stuff, she's a nuisance."

Savannah watched as Amanda's face went from angry and sullen to shocked and hurt in an instant. She put her arm around the girl's shoulders, but Amanda shook her off.

"That's right. I'm a nuisance to the town because I'm trying to protect the environment. I'm a nuisance to our parents—that's why they keep leaving. And I'm a nuisance to you because I'm one more thing you have to look after." Her voice broke. "It doesn't matter why I did it. It matters that it isn't what *he* would have done." Amanda's voice was filled with anger and hurt, but before Savannah or Gran could take her inside she turned and ran, disappearing behind the barn.

"Amanda, honey," Gran called after her, but she was too far gone.

Savannah's heart twisted painfully. She knew those tears—she'd cried plenty when she was Amanda's age, had let the sadness turn into anger and let the anger feed the distance between her and her family.

Amanda didn't deserve that.

"Collin, she had the right idea," Savannah began.

"Collin." Gran shook her head. "She didn't deserve that." The older woman limped inside.

Savannah wasn't sure whether she should go or stay, but the mutinous look in Collin's eyes convinced her to stay. To fight. Because wherever Amanda had run off to, she'd eventually be back, and Savannah didn't want the teenager to face the wrath still evident on Collin from the set of his stiff shoulders to the staccato taps of his feet against the porch.

"Having a purpose in life is a good thing. An empowering thing," Savannah said after a moment. "I wasn't even sure she was listening that day."

"When was it that you turned my sweet little sister into a vandal?" Collin put the beer down on the little table beside the swing. "Just how much of this mess do I have to clean up?"

And that was just about enough. Savannah hadn't done anything wrong. Yes, Amanda was wrong to paint her save-the-world messages on the sidewalks and streets without permission, but at least she hadn't done permanent damage.

"I don't know, Collin, do you want to pin the painting on me or are we going back in time to the duct taping? Or was it the fire starting? Technically that happened before I met her, but I was in town so she might have sensed a rebellious ripple in the atmosphere."

Collin gritted his teeth. "You knew she was impressionable, and you knew she was struggling."

"Every teenager is impressionable and struggling on some level. Pretending they aren't—that you never did—isn't helpful."

"Says the woman who ran away from home not only as a teenager but as an adult."

"Now you're reaching." Savannah wanted to march up the porch steps and slap that angry look off Collin's face. "And you're starting to tick me off. I didn't tell your sister to paint murals on the sidewalks. I listened to a young girl talk about feeling powerless and invisible, and I know how that feels."

"You like being invisible."

"To the general public, to people I don't know, yeah. Invisibility is great. But invisibility to people I know? To people who come to my house? That isn't so great. My God, you don't even realize it, do you? You, Levi, Aidan, James, Adam. When we were growing up, you were the stars of this town. You're still the stars of this town. And I was the invisible girl hanging out on the fringes. That isn't your fault. The five of you were football gods, and you were teenagers, and you expected people to fall at your feet. My being invisible back then *was* my fault because I didn't think I was worth the attention.

"But Amanda…she's not me. She shouldn't be faulted because she has a passion, and she shouldn't be treated as invisible because she doesn't have a football résumé like her older brother."

"I should have seen it, but I didn't because I've been…" He trailed off.

"Busy with me," Savannah realized. Suddenly she understood where this was coming from. Collin wasn't angry with her because of Amanda's actions, he was angry with himself for not putting his sister before his own needs. "Well, here's one more thing you didn't see. I love you." His gaze struck hers. "And I'm leaving."

"Savannah," he said, coming down the porch steps.

She held her hand out to stop him. "I'm not the one you need to fix things with right now. I'm just annoyed enough that any fixing you might try will only make things worse. I'll take the four-wheeler," she said and marched to the barn.

STORM CLOUDS ROLLED in quickly from the west, and Collin cursed. He'd searched the barn, but hadn't found Amanda. Savannah had been gone about fifteen minutes—there was time enough to catch her and make her talk to him. She couldn't just drop an "I love you" on him and storm off. Thunder cracked in the distance, shaking the ground. It was going to be a bad one. Savannah would have to wait; he needed to find his sister to apologize.

A flash of red caught his eye and Collin turned to see Amanda, ponytail bouncing, run into the house. Well, one mystery solved. Thunder cracked again and rain began to pour from the sky. Collin sprinted for shelter of the screened porch. He shook off the rainwater as he continued into the house.

Amanda sat at the kitchen table but when he came in the door, she got up.

"Don't. Don't run to your room and slam the door. Why did you do it?" he asked.

"I thought I was pretty clear," Amanda said as she crossed her arms over her chest.

"You were clear on the environmental cause. You weren't clear on why you thought vandalism was an answer to that."

Amanda pushed her brows together and bit her lower lip. Gran got up from the table.

"I'm going to go lie down. Citizen's arresting takes it out of an old lady like me," she said. She patted Amanda's arm as she left the kitchen. "Talk to him, jellybean," she said, and then Collin was alone with his baby sister, feeling completely unprepared for whatever was about to happen.

"Well?" he asked when it became apparent that Amanda wasn't going to answer his question.

"Because no one would listen to me," she said finally. "After that assembly, I asked about starting a recycling drive, and when I had permission, we set up the bins. But the kids at school are incapable of reading those signs and just kept throwing trash wherever. So I thought maybe a city-wide drive would get more attention. I had a whole presentation ready for the city council a few weeks ago, but they said presenters have to be eighteen and wouldn't let me talk."

"So you duct taped the streets."

"At least then they could see how much better traffic would be without the stupid one-ways. I figured if they saw one better way of doing things, they might be open to hearing about another."

"And when that didn't work you came up with another idea."

"Getting the lake cleaned up is important, and I thought with the Bass Nationals people still considering us, a cleanup drive would get their attention. A lot of people don't realize what goes into the waterways from the storm sewers."

Another roll of thunder cracked, shaking the house. Amanda flinched.

"Just a storm, no weather radios or alerts," Collin reassured her.

"I didn't mean to be a nuisance." Her voice was barely a whisper, but Collin heard her clearly.

"Kiddo, you aren't a nuisance. I didn't mean that. I was just angry."

"Because of me, you had to go down to the police station twice. Had to make excuses for me to James."

"James is like family, no excuses needed. And he likes a good prank." Collin tried to make light of the situation.

"If I wasn't here, you could focus on the orchard more."

"If you weren't here, we wouldn't have the new garden planted and it wouldn't be flourishing."

"I didn't mean to make things harder for you."

"And I didn't mean to make things harder for you." He waited a moment and then put his hand on Amanda's arm. She turned her face into his sleeve, holding on to him as if he were a life ring. "I didn't realize how much you needed me to be more than your brother." Her shoulders shook against him.

"Mom and Dad…they don't think of you as a nuisance." He considered his next words carefully, trying to find the words that would soothe his sister, not make her feel worse. But there were very few kind words that could be used in association with their parents. "The truth is that they don't think of any of us at all. That is their weakness, their problem. It isn't a reflection of you or me or Mara. It just is."

"They just suck," Amanda said after a long moment.

"Yeah, they kind of do." Collin patted her shoulders as her sobs eased. "The thing is, though, because they suck, we get Gran and we had Granddad. You've always got me, and Mara, even though she stays busy with her work."

"And you've got me," Amanda said between sobs. She released her grip on Collin's shirt and stepped back. "I'll apologize to—"

Collin shook his head. "This one is just between us. As long as you promise no more street art."

Slowly, she nodded her head.

When Amanda went upstairs, Collin sat by the window and watched the storm rage. Wind blew through the treetops violently, whipping limbs in different directions so fast it was like watching a tennis match. The storm had come up more quickly than he'd expected, but Savannah should have had ample time to get home by now. He picked up the phone, just to make sure.

Levi answered.

"I just wanted to make sure Savannah got home okay," he said without preamble. Then paused. "We, uh, had an argument, and she left just before the thunderstorm hit."

Outside, the rain had stopped but the dark gray clouds remained ominous. Wind shifted and began to gust.

"Van isn't here. I haven't seen her since the four of you left the market."

Collin swallowed. "She left here about a half hour ago."

"Plenty of time to get here. I'm calling her on my cell, see if she got bogged down." Levi was quiet for a moment. "Went to voice mail."

"I'll take out a four-wheeler, just to make sure she's okay," Collin said.

He hung up the phone just as the first tornado warning siren rent the heavy air.

CHAPTER FIFTEEN

COLLIN HELD HIS foot firmly on the four-wheeler's accelerator, forcing the vehicle through the shearing wind. The rain held back, but the skies remained gray and angry-looking. The tornado siren stopped, and he breathed easier.

He'd followed the muddy track from the house to the lake, but there was no sign of Savannah. He paused near the dock beside the churning water and checked the weather app on his phone. Another thick line of storms was building to the west. If she had gotten this far, it was only another three miles to the ranch. She could be anywhere between, but he didn't see tracks in the mud. Even with the hard rain, he thought he would see some kind of sign that Savannah had been this direction.

He looked behind him. She might have stopped at the cabin for shelter. It would only take a couple of minutes to check, and if she wasn't there, he would continue toward the ranch.

Collin returned up the muddy track to the ridge, the four-wheeler's wheels slipping a bit in the mud. The cabin was dark, but since it had only rudimentary power, that wasn't surprising. Power was always the first thing to go up there.

He stopped the four-wheeler and went to the porch. The door opened before he could reach for the knob. Savannah, soaking wet and wrapped in the old quilt, stood shivering in the doorway.

"I r-ran out of g-gas," she said and pointed to the side of the cabin. He saw the rear of the four-wheeler peeking around the corner. "City girl sen...sensibility strikes again," she said and smiled.

Collin wrapped his arms around her, not caring that her soaking-wet body was getting him wet, too.

"You can't go running off into a storm like that."

"I didn't know a storm was coming. I was just mad."

"Yeah, well, me, too."

The siren sounded again and Collin pushed Savannah inside. A weather alert scrolled across his phone, warning of a possible tornado. His signal blinked out before Collin could look at impact areas or damage predictions.

"We need to take cover."

"I was hiding under the bed earlier," she said, and Collin couldn't tell if she was joking. He stared at her, heart pounding.

"Seriously, it seemed like the best option with the windows rattling and the walls creaking."

Collin pressed his mouth to hers. "Never, ever, hide under a bed when weather sirens are going off," he said when he released her. Dragging the big table to the wall, he motioned her under it. "Rafters can go right through a mattress. A hard-topped table is sturdier, offers more protection."

"Thanks for the lesson," she said, ducking under the table. "Would you get your butt under here with me now?"

But Collin couldn't stop rambling about tornado protocol. "Of course, storm cellar or a basement is the best option, but we don't have either of those up here."

Savannah grabbed his hand under the table. Collin tried his phone again, but the cell signal was gone. That meant the storm had taken down a tower. And that meant it wasn't just a storm and those sirens weren't just warnings. He pulled Savannah's body more firmly against his.

"Is it a tornado?"

He considered lying. "Yeah, those sirens aren't just warnings, and it's knocked out a tower somewhere," he said, jiggling his phone. Hail began to pound the cabin roof.

Savannah shifted closer to him. "I'm glad you found me."

"Yeah," he said, running a hand over her head.

"Me, too. It isn't every day a beautiful, ticked-off woman tells me she loves me and then rides off into a tornado."

Savannah elbowed him. "In my defense, you were being a jerk, and could you lie and tell me this is only a severe storm? Please?"

"No, I won't lie to you," he said, and he realized he meant more than just lying about a storm. He didn't want to lie to Savannah about anything. He didn't want to leave out anything, and he didn't want to tell any more half-truths. He wanted to share his life with her.

He loved her.

The weather siren faded into nothing. Collin waited a moment and then left the relative safety of the table to look outside.

Large chunks of hail and a few roof shingles littered the yard around the cabin, but there was no major damage that he could see, at least to the clearing around the cabin.

Savannah joined him on the porch.

"Did you push the four-wheeler back here?" She nodded. "I'd have just run for shelter."

"I was trying to be responsible."

"Well, next time ditch the four-wheeler and run for cover, would you? You'll stay drier." And be safer, he thought but didn't say the words.

Savannah looked up at the sky. The thick, gray clouds from earlier had thinned, letting a little blue through. Savannah pointed, the quilt dropping to puddle at her feet.

"That doesn't look good," she said.

Collin looked in the direction she indicated, and it was as if a shutter had been drawn over the sky. The thick clouds were still there, but there was also a green tint. The clouds began to rotate and the wind picked up. No warning sirens sounded, but Collin had no doubt what this was.

"Get inside," he said, pushing Savannah back through the door. She crawled under the table and Collin followed her, putting his arms around her waist as he cradled her body against his.

Wind rushed by the windows, rattling the panes of glass. He couldn't hear anything but the wind, couldn't feel anything but Savannah's ragged breathing.

Savannah held tightly to his hand and yelled, "Is it on us?"

"No," he yelled back. "Close, but it's not here."

"What do we do?"

"We wait," he said as the wind continued to howl around the cabin.

SAVANNAH THOUGHT THE howling wind and shaking windows would never stop. She sat under the kitchen table, praying the thick oak would hold the roof of the house off them if the tornado came, holding Collin's hand.

She didn't want to die, not when she'd made an idiot of herself by getting mad and admitting she was in love with him. She should have told him in a more romantic setting—maybe after they'd made love—not in the middle of an argument involving his sister and street art.

He squeezed her hand as a particularly strong gust of wind hit the house. It sounded angry to her, almost like the roaring of an airplane engine on take-off.

And then everything went quiet. The wind dissipated, rain stopped lashing at the windows and the eerie gray-green light outside seemed to lift.

She looked at Collin but he didn't move for a long moment. Finally he hit a button to activate his phone. He tapped a few buttons but nothing worked and he put it back in his pocket.

Together, they crawled out from under the table and went to the porch. Big limbs from the cucumber magnolia crisscrossed the yard, along with bits of shingles and chunks of hail, already starting to melt in the steaming heat. She saw a few of the orchard trees bent at odd angles.

"Oh, God," she said, her voice quiet in the stillness surrounding the cabin.

"It missed us," Collin said, looking up at the sky.

"This is a miss?"

He nodded. "It's a miss. Straight-line winds, maybe, but that's the worst of it."

"Farmer's intuition?"

"Something like that," he said and smiled. He put his arms around her, pulling her body against his. "I'm glad I found you."

"Me, too."

"I'm sorry I yelled at you. And Amanda. But mostly you."

"Sometimes I bring the yelling out in people."

"Don't do that."

"Do what?" she asked.

"Don't be self-deprecating about the woman I love," he said.

Warmth filled her heart. "You don't have to say that just because I got mad and yelled it at you back at the house." She wanted to believe he meant it, but something held her back.

"I'm not saying it because you yelled it at me first. I'm saying it because I mean it. I love you, Van."

Savannah looked up at him and she knew she had tears in her eyes. "I'm not yelling it now, either, and I'm not angry, and I am glad we survived whatever this was," she said, gesturing at the mess surrounding them. "And I love you."

Collin pressed his lips to hers, and Savannah thought it was the sweetest kiss she had ever experienced.

"Let's go see how the rest of the orchard fared.

And if the landlines are working, I'd better call your family to let them know you're okay."

Savannah climbed onto the four-wheeler behind Collin, and he drove slowly over the muddy lane back to the orchard. More shingles littered the yard from the barn and from the house, and the towering oak he usually parked the truck under had lost a big branch. But at first glance, everything looked fine.

"Gran, they're here," Amanda yelled, coming out to the porch. She jumped off the steps and hugged Collin. Gran limped to the porch.

"Thank God," she said, clasping her hands to her chest.

"We're okay," Collin said. "Everything okay inside?"

"A few knickknacks knocked off the shelves, but nothing major," Gran reassured him from the porch. Savannah breathed easier. "Phones are out, though."

"So is my cell." He looked around as if assessing where to start. "I'll start cleaning up. Do you have a radio on?"

Gran nodded. "It's all static, but it's on. Amanda, you can help me get the mess inside cleaned up."

"Should I collect shingles with you?" Savannah asked, unsure what her job was right now. She wanted to contact her family to let them know she was okay, and she wanted to know they were okay, but with the phones out of order she couldn't call.

"No, go inside with Gran and Amanda. I'll get the worst of this picked up."

She pressed a kiss to his lips. "I know how to pick up shingles," she said.

"There could be nails and staples. I'll deal with it."

It took nearly two hours to set the inside of the house to rights, and another forty-five minutes for Collin to collect the roof shingles and secure them in one of the oversize cardboard boxes they used to transport things to the farmers' market. When he finished, he told Gran and Amanda to stay at the house while he took Savannah home.

She gasped when they reached the end of the lane. The little farm stand had been flattened by the wind. Destroyed fruit had rolled across the road and into the ditches on either side. The folding chair Amanda usually sat in was twisted around the base of a tree and the mailbox was nowhere to be seen.

"Holy cow," Savannah said. "Your stand."

"I guess it's good I have that grocer contract coming up, huh?"

"Don't even joke about that."

"It's joke or lose my mind with the what-ifs. Amanda could have been in that stand."

"She wasn't."

"She would have been if we hadn't been fighting."

Pain struck Savannah in the chest. "But she's fine."

Collin got out of the truck and moved the worst of the debris off the road. It took them nearly thirty minutes to drive the ten miles to town, and with every minute they were in the truck Savannah's anxiety level rose.

There was debris everywhere. Power poles were strewed across the fields like a child's forgotten Lincoln Logs. A cell phone tower had snapped in two and lay in another field.

"That explains the cell coverage," Collin said as they passed. He squeezed her hand in his.

A couple of cars had been flung into the ditch at the side of the road; when Collin stopped to check, no one was inside. Savannah wasn't sure if that was good or bad. Mailboxes lay across the blacktop; a few had been flung into the branches of nearby trees. Branches and roof shingles were everywhere. At the city limits, the welcome sign had been ripped to shreds.

In town, the damage was worse. Collin drove slowly down the street. Power and phone lines lay across several yards, roofs had been ripped from houses, and a few boats could be seen floating out in the middle of the lake, along with their moorings and portions of the wrecked docks.

"This isn't straight-line winds."

Collin shook his head. "This is a tornado." He slammed his foot against the brake. The farmers' market was a pile of rubble, cement blocks lay haphazardly around, and the plate-glass window shattered. Cars were stacked atop one another and sitting at odd angles in the street. A police cruiser rested under a downed power line.

People were everywhere, looking shocked. A few picked up random pieces of debris, but most couldn't seem to comprehend what they were seeing.

Everywhere she looked, there was carnage. Savannah bit back the urge to tell Collin to go faster. She needed to get home. She needed to make sure her family was okay. Needing his support, she squeezed his hand.

"I know." He looked at the ruined market for a long moment, then put the truck in gear and swerved to avoid another big tree branch. "I'll get you there as soon as I can."

Savannah's heartbeat pounded and it was as if she couldn't get any air into her lungs.

Collin put his hand at the nape of her neck and pushed her head down between her knees. "Breathe," he ordered her, "just breathe."

Savannah gulped in one and then two breaths

of air, and when the truck floor stopped spinning beneath her, she sat up.

They'd cleared the city limits, and Collin turned onto the highway that would take them to the ranch. The worst of the damage seemed to be behind them.

The farther they got from town, the less destruction she saw. Tree branches and shingles still littered the fields and yards, but there were no more mailboxes wrapped around power poles and no cars flung into ditches like discarded toys.

A few minutes later Collin stopped the truck behind Mama Hazel's sedan. The ranch seemed to be fine. No shingles in the yard. She could hear the cows mooing in the pastures.

"This is weird," she said. "It's like nothing happened here."

"Probably nothing did. Tornados are weird that way. One street is destroyed, the next untouched."

Collin took her hand and together they climbed the porch steps and went inside.

Mama Hazel sat in her rocking chair, puzzle book in hand, but staring straight ahead. When she saw Savannah, she made the sign of the cross over her chest and closed her eyes.

"Levi and your father just left to go find you." She bustled to Savannah and drew her into a bear hug. "I told them to wait, but after you called—" She looked at Collin. "I couldn't get them to wait once the storm passed."

"The four-wheeler ran out of gas," Savannah started to explain.

"We took shelter at Granddad's cabin on the ridge."

"I'm just glad you're both okay. What about your family?"

Collin told her his family was fine. When he recounted the damage in town, Hazel's expression clouded.

"It sounds devastating."

Savannah wanted to go after her father and brother, but Collin convinced her to stay put. It seemed like a year had passed before she heard four-wheelers in the distance. The three of them hurried to the porch.

Bennett and Levi came around the side of the house and when they saw Collin's truck, both seemed to relax.

"We tried to call. Phones are down," Collin said, and then told them about the devastation they'd seen on the way to the ranch.

"We should go into town, see what we can do to help," Bennett said. Levi and Collin agreed.

Savannah and Hazel stayed at the ranch, and as Savannah watched the taillights of Collin's truck disappear down the road, she thought the worst had to be over.

COLLIN SURVEYED THE grove of peaches and kicked his booted foot against the four-wheeler's tire. He'd taken to wearing boots instead of his usual tennis shoes because of the debris they continued to find around the orchard. Pieces of drywall, he didn't know from where, and limbs and branches were everywhere. The little fence Granddad had built around the plum trees was completely gone.

"Crap," he said.

Savannah echoed his thoughts. The peach trees had been hit the worst by the straight-line winds that accompanied the tornado on its way to the town. Entire rows had been flattened and on one side the trees were completely bald, all the leaves, blossoms and fruit littering the surrounding area.

"What do we do?" she asked.

Collin sighed. "Wait for the insurance adjuster to get here then replant. I'll use some of the saplings from the greenhouse, but we'll have to buy new stock, too."

"That doesn't sound so bad."

"In three years, when the new trees start producing, it won't be."

In the meantime he was going to have to have a tough conversation with Westfall Foods. No peaches could mean no contract, and he really needed that contract now that the orchard had suffered severe storm damage. He'd also lost about fifty apple trees and at least as many pear.

"Oh, Collin, I'm sorry," she said, and he squeezed her hand.

"The beauty of farming," he said, only half kidding. When things went well, there was nothing better than working his orchard, but when things went badly…there was nothing worse than the sense of dread that accompanied a failed harvest.

Or a ruined orchard.

They returned to the house.

Amanda and Gran were waiting to go into town. Crews were working to get the town cleaned up, and the council had asked as many as could come to be at a meeting that afternoon.

Because of the damage to the city and county buildings, everyone met on the courthouse lawn. Someone had lined up folding chairs, but no one sat. People milled around, talking to friends and neighbors, but most still appeared to be shell-shocked.

Collin couldn't blame anyone. The tornado had flattened three buildings: a day-care center set up inside an old church, an empty warehouse and the Slippery Rock Grill. Several other buildings and homes had lost roofs or windows.

Adam had run into the day-care where his kids were thought to be, trying to get them into the safe basement of the cabinetry business he ran with his father, but had gotten caught in the collapse of the building. The day-care workers had already taken the kids to the storm shelter in the basement of the sheriff's office, but Adam hadn't known that. He was in a coma in a Springfield hospital.

James's father, Sheriff Jonathan Calhoun, had been caught in the storm, and was also in the Springfield hospital with a badly broken leg and a fractured wrist. They'd found him pinned under the police car Collin and Savannah had seen just after the storm, and Collin couldn't stop blaming himself. If he'd just gotten out of the truck, he might have found Sheriff Calhoun. Might have gotten help sooner.

Thom Hall, the mayor, stepped to the front of the crowd and motioned at them with his hands.

"We just received word that the governor has declared Slippery Rock a disaster area. We'll have help with the cleanup here within the next day," he said, and it was as if the town breathed a sigh of relief. It was barely thirty-six hours since the tornado had struck, and a disaster declaration would go a long way toward putting Slippery Rock back together.

"We've received word that Sheriff Calhoun is recovering well, and we're hoping for good news about Adam Buchanan soon, too." Thom wiped at his brow. "In the meanwhile, I know the newspaper ran a few articles about the Bass Nationals hosting an event here in the fall—the tornado has put that on hold. They aren't convinced we can get the marina and the outlying areas cleaned up in time."

"We need that tourist money," someone said from behind Collin. Several others joined in. Collin couldn't have cared less about the fishing tournament. What was two days of tourism compared with all the disaster cleanup still to be done?

"Don't worry, we're still negotiating. What they've said is that if we can get a staging area set up, we could still be in the running. Originally, that area would have been at the fairgrounds, but the grounds were among those hit the hardest by the tornado. We need a vote on whether or not to proceed with the staging area."

Collin stepped forward. "I think our time and money is best spent on businesses and homes and families that will be in Slippery Rock longer than a weekend."

"Agreed," said a voice behind him. He didn't bother to look back. He didn't care who agreed with him; it was obvious Slippery Rock needed to focus on rebuilding, not new building.

"Well, now, the thing is this tournament wouldn't just be two days of tourism. We've done the research. The tournament spans two weekends, but the traffic leading up to the event is significant, and the increased traffic could last up to a year. That is nothing we can ignore."

"We need all the bodies and money we can get working on businesses," Collin said, "not some fishing expo that will be gone in two weeks."

"What about a benefit?" Savannah said from beside him, and Collin looked at her as if she had grown horns.

"Benefit?" Thom asked.

"Something that will raise money for disaster relief while still providing the staging area the Bass Nationals needs to move forward." She released Collin's hand and moved to the front of the crowd. "Nashville is full of charitably minded people, both in the entertainment industry and out of it. With the right incentives, we could get a strong lineup of entertainment, and could probably get volunteers to work on the staging area. All those set designers and stage crews could probably come up with a strong design."

"Savannah," Collin whispered, but she didn't hear him. Or she ignored him.

The townspeople began talking among themselves. Savannah spoke directly to Thom, and Collin's eyes nearly bugged out of his head when she said she would make a few calls.

Calls to whom? She had no record label, no record deal, and she'd fired her manager just before the tornado. As the meeting broke up, he followed Savannah to the truck.

"What was that about?"

"A solution to the problem. The town possibly gets the staging area and Nashville artists get a project."

"You're not part of Nashville any longer."

"True, but I know Nashville people. My not wanting to sing doesn't preclude me from knowing people who do," she said reasonably.

Collin couldn't wrap his mind around the fact that Savannah's big solution to the town's problem was to go back to people she no longer wanted to work with. Savannah volunteering for anything left him curious, and he knew that was just the annoyance talking. She wasn't the self-absorbed person he had always assumed.

She was kind and warm and had a big heart.

He just wished in this case, she'd kept her kind, warm heart to herself.

CHAPTER SIXTEEN

SAVANNAH WAVED TO Collin from the porch as he drove away. What had she just gotten herself into? The last thing she wanted to do was call anyone in Nashville for help. She had just felt so lost. Her family was going about their usual business, with Levi spending a lot of time with the rebuilding efforts. Collin was busy getting the orchard back up and running.

She had nothing to offer, and it left her feeling sickly.

She didn't like that feeling.

Maybe a benefit concert wasn't the best idea in the world, but it was an idea she was fairly certain she could pull off.

In her bedroom, she called three other singers who had been dropped by the label. All three of the new artists seemed enthusiastic about the plan. Then, she called Guy.

"Does this mean you're reconsidering my firing and your disappearance from town?"

"No," Savannah answered quickly. She didn't want Nashville, but she was willing to use it if it would help Slippery Rock. "It means my home-town is in shambles and I'm trying to help them pick up the pieces."

"I'll make a few more calls," Guy promised and hung up.

That night Savannah met Collin, Levi and James at the Slope. The neon sign had been destroyed by the tornado, but the rest of the building was intact.

Adam's wife, Jenny, had called that afternoon to report he had fluttered his eyelids. It was progress.

The four of them sat around one of the round tables while Juanita and Merle flirted across the bar. Since the tornado, their covert relationship had come out into the open. Savannah thought the two of them were cute together.

She popped a peanut in her mouth and chewed. Levi finished his beer, and James ordered another round. Collin was quiet, as if he were still upset about the concert benefit idea. Savannah didn't understand why he would be upset. The concert wouldn't affect him at all.

"Is everything okay?" she asked.

Collin nodded. "Just thinking about my meeting tomorrow with Westfall. I'm going to have to turn down their offer."

"But you could still supply the apples," she began.

Collin shook his head. "I don't want to be focused on a contract with them when the orchard is still in disarray. I wasn't all that hyped about their offer, anyway. I liked the money aspect, but taking everything away from the market, the local businesses, that wasn't a good feeling."

Savannah squeezed his hand. "I'm sorry."

"There will be other contracts."

James tore the wrapper of his straw into shreds. He'd been pulling double shifts since the tornado, acting as the interim sheriff as well as a patrol officer.

"You should contract with yourself," he said.

"I'm pretty sure that's what I'm already doing."

"I mean like those companies you see on TV. They ship a box of food each week with recipes inside. People pay a boatload for fresh foods like that. You'd make a killing."

Collin shook his head. "Those programs provide vegetables and meats, too. I'm a fruit guy."

"Definitely a fruit," Levi said and chucked Collin on the shoulder.

"With the market down for the season, though, some of the vegetable growers will be looking for another outlet. Might be worth a talk," James said.

The idea was interesting, Savannah thought, but Collin remained focused on the bowl of peanuts and his beer.

"Hey, Savannah, your old touring partner's on

TV," Merle called out across the bar. He turned up the volume on the small screen hanging on the back wall. Savannah's heart fell when she read the headline: Country Superstar Files for Divorce.

Video images showed Genevieve Anderson rushing from a courthouse with her head down as if to avoid the glare of the rapidly flashing camera bulbs. The reporter began talking.

"Citing irreconcilable differences, country music superstar Genevieve Anderson filed divorce proceedings against her husband and manager, Philip Anderson, Monday afternoon. The Andersons have been one of Music Row's power couples for nearly a decade, but rumors have been rampant that the marriage hit a rough patch earlier this year."

Savannah wanted to snort. Obviously, Genevieve's people had reached out to the reporter to ensure a favorable story. Savannah had no evidence, but she was positive she wasn't the first person to be taken in by Philip Anderson; his moves were too practiced for that.

"I was able to sit down with Genevieve earlier this afternoon to talk about this terrible time." The reporter smiled happily into the camera while delivering that last line, and Savannah's stomach twisted. It was as if the reporter's predatory eyes looked directly into hers.

"Should we go?" she asked, but all three of the men seemed intent on the television.

The image on the screen switched from the reporter to Genevieve, looking pale and withdrawn. She wore a pair of black pants and a black button-down blouse with a pale gray cardigan over her shoulders. She looked like a cross between a funeral mourner and a preacher's wife, Savannah thought, and then admonished herself. Genevieve had every right to mourn her husband's infidelities.

"What happened, Genevieve?" the reporter asked with a grave look on her face.

Genevieve brushed a tissue under her eyes. "I think it's always hard on a couple when one spouse is more accomplished than the other. Hard feelings develop and then distance." She dabbed at her eyes again. "It's like a damn country song," she said, deadpan.

Collin snorted. "As if she knows anything about living a country music song."

"She's been the top female artist five years running," James pointed out.

Savannah slunk back against her chair. She didn't want to be part of this. Not the conversation, not the television-watching. She wanted to be out of this bar, and she wanted Collin to come with her.

"Doesn't mean she knows real country," Collin said stubbornly.

"We hear the 'irreconcilable differences' excuse all the time, though—what made you say enough is enough?" The reporter cocked her head to the side, offering a supportive smile to the singer.

The camera switched back to Genevieve, who appeared to think hard about her answer. The tissue disappeared into her clutched hands and she drew a breath.

Savannah wanted to run.

"I think, when your husband refuses to stay out of the bed of your opening act, that's enough," Genevieve said. She put her hand to her heart and made her voice soft. "I'm sorry, I really don't want to talk about this any longer," she said. But there was a look of malice in her eyes that Savannah had seen once before. That night on the tour bus.

Genevieve wasn't heartbroken at the infidelity. She was glad to finally have a reason to kick her man—and Savannah—to the curb.

Collin didn't even look at her. He simply stood and walked out of the Slope.

Savannah watched him go, feeling as if she'd been punched in the stomach. She hurried after him, getting to his truck just as he started the engine. She heard the car doors click locked and she knocked on the window.

"Collin, I can explain," she said, but he wouldn't look at her.

Collin revved the engine, drowning out her words, and then put the truck in gear, making it jump backward. Savannah staggered back, putting as much distance as she could between her and the truck. He kept his gaze focused on the parking space in front of him as he backed into the street. Once clear, he sped away, his tires squealing a bit as he rounded the corner.

"I can explain," she said again, but he was gone.

THE NEXT DAY, COLLIN, dressed in his funeral suit again, sat in the marbled foyer leading into the Westfall Foods conference room. He had considered wearing cargos and a T-shirt, but in the end decided to button up what was left of his pride in the freaking uncomfortable suit and tie.

He ran his index finger around his collar but that offered little relief. The room still felt as humid as a July afternoon when a rainstorm was coming.

A buzz sounded and a leggy secretary with red-gold hair led him to the conference room door. "Good luck," she said as she held the door open for him to pass.

Collin sat on one side of the table, wondering again why he'd bothered. A simple phone call and a no would have let him off the hook. Of course, calling in a no was a lot easier than putting on a suit and driving two hours to deliver that same no in person.

But right now, Collin wasn't looking for easy. He was looking for exhausting. Something to take his mind off the ridiculous fool he had been to fall for Savannah's song and dance about stage anxiety and wanting to please her family.

To fall in love with her.

At least now her eagerness to stage a benefit concert made sense. She'd been hedging her bets in case Genevieve spilled her nasty little secret. The small-town girl with the small-town tragedy. People would eat that up, and many would skip right over the affair.

It had all been a lie. The bit about anxiety and parent-pleasing was just a cover for having an affair with her boss's husband. The bit about being in love with him...probably just a mind game.

He was done with mind games. It was time to focus on what mattered: the orchard and the security of his family.

Collin passed the unsigned contract to Jake

Westfall, who glanced at it and then passed it to the other executives.

"I have to say I'm surprised, Collin," Westfall said.

"Until four days ago, I would have been surprised. The tornado that hit Slippery Rock changed everything. I can't, with a clear conscience, commit to being the main provider for your grocery stores when I'm going to have to replant much of my orchard. I might still be able to deliver all the fruit you would need, but that wouldn't leave anything for the people in my community."

"They can still get Tyler Orchards' fruits at our grocery stores," Westfall pointed out.

It was the argument Collin had been having for weeks and he was tired of it.

"Some of them don't have cars anymore, much less the money for organic grocery-store prices." Collin gathered his folder and stood. He didn't want to be in this room, talking to these people. He wanted to be in his orchard, fixing things. "Maybe in another couple of years when our groves are back to one hundred percent, but now isn't the time."

He left the conference room and didn't stop until he was behind the wheel of his truck. Then Collin stripped off the tie and threw it onto the floorboard.

He was done.

SAVANNAH WANTED NOTHING more than to get into her old Honda and disappear down a busy highway. She sat at the kitchen table, watching Mama Hazel roll piecrust at the butcher block. It had been more than a week since Genevieve's not-so-veiled outing of Savannah as the cause of the collapse of her marriage. Collin wouldn't talk to her, and she kept catching strange looks between her parents.

Levi had moved out. Sure, his house had been completed, but the move had seemed almost planned to Savannah, which was silly. Levi wasn't the sort to abandon anyone. He was a grown man who needed his space, that was all.

Still, it left a lot of space to fill in the main house, and Savannah had no idea how to make it feel less empty.

"Thom Hall called. We have three firm yesses for the benefit, and two crews have volunteered to build the staging area as long as the town provides the materials."

Hazel looked up from her crust-rolling. "Oh, hummingbird, do you think that's wise?"

"I made a promise to the council. Besides, it isn't me singing." The thought of even announcing the performances made her feel squidgy, but when the council members had asked her to emcee, she hadn't been able to turn them down. She waited a long moment, but Hazel didn't say anything. "I'm sorry I embarrassed you and Dad."

Hazel's busy hands stopped moving. "You didn't embarrass us."

"Then I'm sorry I hurt you." She wasn't sure how many other ways she could tell them she regretted her actions during the tour. The one thing she didn't regret was not telling them earlier. Because she'd kept it quiet, she'd had nearly a month to repair some of the childhood wounds she'd held on to so tightly. Those repairs were worth the new scars.

"You didn't hurt us. You hurt you. Just like you always hurt you." Hazel came around the butcher block and sat beside Savannah at the table. "That isn't a condemnation, baby. You've been reacting to situations since we brought you home. Pretending everything was fine and then lashing out, or ignoring what was happening around you until it all came crashing down. I thought you'd finally come to terms with your past, and I don't know what more I can do to walk you through it, but I'm here. I'm right beside you."

Sharp little knives of pain stabbed Savannah's chest. "I did come to terms with it. Getting off that bus with Philip Anderson made me confront all the different ways I've sabotaged my life since those police officers found me on the steps. I don't want to be that scared little girl anymore. I was just hoping that was one implosion I could keep secret from everyone."

She took a deep breath. "I knew almost from the moment that I set foot on that first LA stage that I didn't want to be a star, but I wasn't sure how to stop the madness once it started. The longer I was on that stage, the harder it got to be there. When Philip Anderson invited me onto that bus… I can't explain it, not really. I didn't want to be there, not with him. I wanted a reason to not be in Nashville or on the tour at all."

Savannah picked at a corner of her nail polish. "I think I thought that would give me a reason to leave, to stop the craziness of the tour and singing. But I never meant to hurt you or Dad. I didn't mean to hurt Genevieve. I'm so sorry."

Hazel squeezed Savannah's hand. "I wish I could go back to the day you were left so I could tell you it wasn't your fault."

"I think that part of me was broken before they put me on those steps. I think, if that part of me had been whole, I wouldn't have waited on those steps. I'd have run after them or at least knocked on the door behind me."

Hazel wrapped Savannah in a hug. "I never thought you were waiting to die. I always thought you were waiting to be rescued. There is a difference, you know. The person waiting to die thinks she has no value. The one waiting to be rescued knows she has value, even if she doesn't understand it."

"What value did I have?"

"You've always had value, Savannah. Always. You're a kindhearted, lovable woman."

If she was so lovable, if she had value, why had Collin walked out on her after that interview? She wondered. Why hadn't he stood beside her or at least let her explain? She knew the questions weren't fair to Collin; after all, she was the one who'd gotten on that bus, and she was the one who kept that action a secret. That knowledge didn't change the fact that those questions kept ricocheting around her mind.

He'd walked out without letting her explain, and he kept distancing himself from her.

The man she loved saw no value in her now, and it hurt more than she ever thought anything possibly could.

CHAPTER SEVENTEEN

TWO WEEKS AFTER the tornado, country music stars, professional fishermen and tourists crowded the downtown area of Slippery Rock.

Collin sat off to the side, watching people traipse around what used to be the abandoned warehouse but was now a staging area. He still didn't understand how dropping everything to build a staging area for a fishing competition that was still months away was a better bet for Slippery Rock than rebuilding their existing businesses. He also didn't buy the town council's explanations about future tourism, bigger events and community theater. Frankly, Collin was tired of thinking about it.

If Amanda hadn't wanted to come, he would be at the orchard today, watching the new saplings take root.

As it was, he sat in a folding chair between James, who was considering running for sheriff during the fall election cycle, and Levi, who was considering all the pretty, nonlocal girls wandering around the event area.

Collin tried to get interested in the girls, but none of them appealed. Their skin was too pale or their tans too fake, their hair too straight, their legs too short.

The truth was none of them was Savannah, and that annoyed the crap out of him.

What kind of fool was he that he was still hung up on a woman who had never been fully truthful with him?

You weren't exactly truthful with her, either. The voice in his head was angry. Annoyed. Sexually deprived. *You didn't tell her everything about your past, so why hold her to a higher standard?*

Because his past didn't include an affair with a married man.

The crowd began to settle, and Savannah came onto the stage. She wore that blue dress she'd worn when he'd taken her to the restaurant overlooking the lake, but instead of strappy sandals, she'd paired the dress with cowboy boots. His heart caught in his chest. She looked pale. Sad. Nervous.

Beautiful.

He wanted to go up on stage and tell her everything would be okay. Add another layer of stupid to his hormones.

"Welcome to Slippery Rock, everyone," she said, her voice booming through the speaker system. "I'm Savannah Walters, and my family owns a dairy farm just outside town called Walters Ranch." The crowd applauded, and Savannah waited for them to calm down. A light breeze swept her hair to the side. "Some of you might also recognize me from a reality show competition, but today I am just here as a resident of Slippery Rock. I'd like to thank everyone who is helping us to rebuild our town."

A stage worker brought a guitar on stage and Savannah slipped the shoulder strap over her head. Collin blinked. She was performing? He stood to go but Levi put his big hand on Collin's arm, stopping him.

"You're going to want to hear this," he said, and as he had always followed Levi's instructions since their football days, Collin sat.

"Before the real acts come out to entertain you, I'd like to ask a favor. My parents never got to see me perform in person on that reality show, and I'd like to remedy that now." She strummed her hand over the strings and a light melody drifted into the night air.

Collin found himself transfixed. He'd heard Savannah sing several times on TV, and a few times in person when she didn't realize she was singing. Like that day they'd planted the berry garden. He'd never once seen her use an instrument, though.

Her thin fingers worked the strings and, although her playing was tentative, it was as if she became part of the guitar, part of the stage.

He swallowed.

Savannah sang about a lost girl, unsure which direction to turn. "All this time, I was waiting for a rescue. I didn't realize the rescuer was you." Her fingers strummed, filling the air with her melody. "I didn't realize I could rescue you, too."

Collin searched out Mama Hazel in the crowd and saw tears tracking down her face. She was Savannah's rescuer. Her mother had finally made Savannah see that she was worth saving, and it must have worked. If it hadn't, she wouldn't be on that stage, wouldn't still be in Slippery Rock.

He drew in a breath. Loving Savannah wasn't the problem. Allowing her to love herself? That was the problem. He'd wanted her to be like him, but she was a different person. Stronger maybe, because she had every reason in the world to leave this town and yet she had stayed.

"I'll be back," he said and left the table.

"Told him he'd want to stick around for this," he heard Levi tell James before he was out of earshot.

Collin made his way around the staging area. Thunderous applause shook the ground when Savannah finished singing.

"Okay, okay, thanks for bearing with me.

Now, give it up for Twila Jones," she said, and the crowd went wild.

"Is that an amazing song or what? You better give me first crack at it for recording, girl," Twila said, and then the music went hot as she started her set.

Collin didn't know why he was back there, other than to make a fool of himself again. He needed to apologize to her. Needed to see for himself that Savannah was okay after that performance.

He crossed behind an extra set of stage lights and stopped short. Savannah sat atop an old wooden spool the builders must have left behind when they'd finished construction earlier that day. Her feet tapped along with the music and she swayed side to side.

He couldn't see her face, but she seemed happy.

Collin sucked in a breath and started forward.

"Van," he said, using her family's nickname for her. She stiffened in her seat and then slowly turned to face him.

"Collin," she said. Her voice was flat.

"Could we go somewhere to talk?"

She pointed to the main stage. "I'm kind of on the job," she said, raising her voice to be heard over the music.

"This won't take long."

She considered him for a long moment and Collin couldn't help the feeling that she might somehow find him lacking. Too late now, he was here, and this needed to be said.

They left the area and crossed the street, passing by Bud's and continuing along the new dock that had already been built to replace the one destroyed by the tornado. At the end, Collin gestured for Savannah to sit beside him.

Side by side, they stared at the middle of the lake for a long while. Twila's set raced on behind them, the crowd hooting and hollering along with her songs about breakups and girls' nights.

Finally, Savannah said, "Well, this was enlightening, Collin, thank you."

She stood to go.

"I'm sorry." He forced the words past his lips. These two, he knew, would be the hardest. He'd never liked admitting he was wrong and "I'm sorry" meant exactly that.

"For walking out on me? For repeatedly ignoring my calls and texts? For that day at the lake? Or the afternoon at the cabin or any of the days or nights we spent in the loft?"

He stood and turned to face her. "All of it," he said, and when her face paled, he wanted to take the words back. He couldn't take them back, though, because they were the truth. "I'm sorry that I walked out and for everything after. I'm sorry for starting all of this on a lie." Savannah blinked. "I'm not who you think I am."

"You're Collin Tyler, Orchardist, Plum Tree Planter."

He smiled and shook his head. "I'm all of those things. But I'm also an idiot who has a problem seeing any viewpoint that is different from his own.

"My father wasn't a traveling salesman, and we didn't come to live here because he was gone too often. Samson and Maddie Tyler weren't cut out for parenting. They didn't like the structure or the responsibility. From the time I was small, I can remember them leaving the three of us home alone. I was the oldest and so I was expected to care for Mara, and when Amanda came along, her, too. That way they could… I don't know, go to Las Vegas or Mexico or whatever places sounded better then Kansas City or Tulsa or Little Rock or whatever town they decided to move us to."

"How could they…how were they not reported?"

The smile he offered her was sad. "How could your biological parents get to the point they left you on the steps of a building? People abandon their children every day in a hundred different ways."

"What happened?"

"I was ten. Maddie told me Samson had a job interview, but she had to drive him. I knew what that meant. They needed a break. She left two twenties on the table, told me to make sure we all got to school and to order pizza for dinner.

"When I woke up the next morning, Amanda had a fever, so I knew she couldn't go to the babysitter's. I told Mara we had a free day, and she hated school so she didn't complain. What I didn't account for were the ten days we'd already missed that year. The truancy officers banged on the door and they had a woman from children's services with them. She slid her business card under the door."

Savannah sat back down at the edge of the dock.

"We avoided the truancy officers and the aid worker, but the money Maddie left only lasted three days. By the fourth, it was impossible to keep the girls from crying, and I knew if anyone found us, we'd be taken and maybe separated. I knew if we weren't together I couldn't protect them."

"My God, Collin, you were just a baby."

"I'd seen Maddie pack this red book with us every time we moved, and I figured it had to be important. I thought maybe there was money hidden inside or something. There wasn't. It was an address book. I called five numbers before

I found anyone who admitted to knowing us. It was Gran and Granddad. They came to get us the next day and we've been here ever since."

"But I've met your parents. Maddie and Samson."

Collin nodded. "They come here from time to time, usually when they need money. Sometimes when they're feeling nostalgic for family. Every time, they leave as suddenly as they came."

Savannah didn't say anything for a long moment. Collin gripped the dock tightly, his legs swinging a bit over the water.

"I know what it is to be abandoned, to not know why the people who are supposed to love you don't. What I didn't understand, not until tonight, was that I never allowed myself to truly feel that void. I had to be strong for my sisters, and then I wanted to make sure Granddad knew I was a good worker so he wouldn't send us away."

"I felt the void."

"I know. And I should have realized it when we talked about it that night, but I couldn't wrap my head around why you would blame yourself."

"And now you do?"

He nodded. "Because I finally felt the void. Without you."

SAVANNAH DIDN'T WANT to hear any more. Not about Collin's parents, who had abandoned him not once but several times. Not about his determination to be strong for his sisters.

Definitely not the part about her being the cause of his void.

God, if he said that again she was going to crumble. She was going to fall into his arms and pretend he hadn't shattered her when he'd walked out of the Slope that night. And when something happened that he didn't like, he would leave and she would be shattered again. Only she wasn't sure she could pick up those pieces again. Savannah wasn't completely sure she'd picked them all up this time. There were still some jagged edges she kept scraping up against.

Edges like the way he looked sitting beside her. There was a vulnerability in his gaze she hadn't seen before, and she thought she'd never seen anything sexier. And sexy was definitely not where she wanted this conversation to go.

"Don't say that," she said. "We were barely dating—"

"'All this time, I was waiting for a rescue. I didn't realize the rescuer was you. I didn't realize I could rescue you, too'."

"Don't quote my song lyrics to me." *Don't, Collin, please.*

"You wrote that." She could only nod. "You wrote it for your mom." Savannah nodded again, wishing she could stand and walk away.

Why was it the guys who always did the walking? She wanted to be the one to walk. And yet, she stayed.

"I think it's about you. I think you wrote it not about a mother who saves an unwanted child, but about the unwanted child finding worth in herself."

"Stop." Savannah couldn't do this, not with Collin. Not when he was sitting there telling her what she was feeling after he'd walked out on her.

"You were always worthy, Van. It was the people around you who weren't. I wasn't." He paused. "I didn't want to admit that I needed anyone. I wanted to be that solo person, free from baggage and responsibilities, at least on a personal level. Turns out, I'd filled my life with responsibilities so that people would need me. So that I couldn't be left behind. Gran and Granddad. My sisters.

"You didn't need anything from me, so I pushed you away, and when I didn't want to push you away anymore I convinced myself that I was what you needed. My solid, straightforward, Boy-Scout-wannabe persona would solve the problems of the wannabe country girl singer with anxiety."

"You're pretty good with that Boy-Scout thing."

"I've practiced it nearly my entire life, I should be. I never admitted to myself that I needed you. I admired your spark and fire. Your willingness to change your life. I admitted that I love you, but I still didn't want to need you."

He said *love*. Savannah tried not to read anything into the word, but it roared through her veins like the winds that battered the cabin. Love was present tense. Love was possibility.

"I need you, Savannah Walters."

Her hands trembled in her lap. She drew in a long breath. "I'm not the woman you need, Collin," she said.

Savannah stood and walked off the dock.

When she crossed the street, Savannah ducked inside an open door leading into what used to be part of the farmers' market. She leaned against the cool wall and tried to breathe.

Collin might think he needed her, but he was wrong. And she was too scared to take a chance on his being right. He couldn't need her. No one needed the lost little seven-year-old with the dirty clothes.

"You can walk away a million times and I'll come after you a million and one," Collin said from behind her. He'd followed her into the cavernous room. "You don't have to love me back, and you don't have to need me the way I need you, but I want you to hear me. I need you, Savannah Walters. Not for sex, and not to volunteer in the orchard and not to give my baby sister advice on finding her purpose—"

"Technically, I was advising myself. She took it to mean her. I'm not sorry she took it as advice for herself, though, because every human being needs purpose." She bit her lip. "I want you to know that."

"Then I know it."

His expression was earnest, his hands hanging loosely at his sides.

"How do I know you won't just walk out again?"

"How do I know you won't?" Collin reached across the space between them and took her hand.

The touch sent a jolt of awareness through her that settled into a warm buzz.

"What I know about you is that you are strong. You were left alone in the cold when you were seven. It cracked you, but it didn't break you. When my parents walked out, it broke me. Every single time. And until I walked out of the Slope the other night, I didn't realize how badly. Because what you did before we were together, it's the past. We all have regrets, Van, and I don't want us to be a regret."

Savanna looked up, focused on him for a long moment. "You don't mean that. What I did—"

He cut her off. "The baggage we carry shapes us, but it doesn't have to define us. I don't want mine to define me, not any longer. I want to define myself. With you."

His hand was gentle along her jaw and Savannah leaned into the soft caress.

"I can't change the past or how it affected me." She swallowed. "Walking onto that stage this afternoon took every ounce of courage I have. I don't have any left to walk away from you."

"Then have the courage to just stand," he said. "I can promise you, I'll stand right here with you."

Savannah looked into his eyes. And though her impulse was to run, she stood still.

CHAPTER EIGHTEEN

COLLIN TURNED OFF the truck lights as he pulled to a stop near the newly constructed grandstand. The construction took up most of the area where the old warehouse had stood, but there was a section off to the side that remained empty. The work crews had hauled off the last of the debris just before the benefit concert.

"It's after midnight. Do you really think anyone is going to notice we're out here?" Savannah asked, whispering even though they were in the truck with the windows rolled up. No one could hear them.

"It only takes one busybody to ruin the moment," he said. He opened his door and then said quietly, "Let's get this in the ground before one of James's deputies comes out on patrol."

Savannah stepped out and joined him at the back of the truck. "I still say we could have just told them we were planting a tree."

Collin shook his head. "Savannah. Dear, sweet, over-fifty Savannah. Have you never done anything illegal in your life?"

"Well, (a) I'm under thirty. And (b) planting a tree isn't illegal." She reached for the tailgate latch and it banged open.

Collin winced.

"Sorry, forgot how heavy that thing is. You should really spring for one of those new trucks with the self-releasing gates."

"I like this truck, just like you like your Honda." He reached into the bed and pulled a sapling from it.

Savannah grabbed the shovels and followed him. "I heard they're thinking of making this part of the grandstand area a park."

"Good thing we're going to give the park some shade, then." He set the tree to the side and began digging a hole.

Savannah kept her flashlight trained on the soft earth, making it easier for him to see what he was doing. "I can't believe I let you talk me into this. I'm changing my reputation, you know."

"In case you hadn't already noticed, people here don't care about what happened in Nashville. Some of them didn't even connect you leaving the tour with Genevieve's claims." He shot her a glance. "Also, and I can't stress this enough, I'll like you even if your new reputation becomes tarnished."

"You'll love me," she said, and there was laughter in her voice and a softness in her eyes.

At least, he thought he could see softness, it was hard to tell in the dim light of the stars and the flashlight.

"Forever," he said, and finished digging the hole. "Start the water," he instructed, and Savannah climbed into the truck bed. She inserted the hose into the water tanks he used during the driest of summers to nourish the trees. The tanks had gotten a lot of use over the past couple of weeks with the new plantings. Water began to drip from the hose, and Collin took it.

He let the water flow over the tree roots for several minutes, making sure to soak the ground so that the sapling wouldn't die.

Savannah slid her arm around his waist and clicked off the flashlight. Moonlight glistened on the lake and a few cicadas buzzed in the grass.

"How about the sign?"

"Behind the seat."

Collin turned off the water and grabbed the wooden sign, made from the same oak as the sapling they'd just planted, and began to work it into the soil.

When it was placed, Savannah took his hand and read, "'The strength to rebuild is one of the finest acts of courage,'" along with the date of the tornado. "Fitting, since the oak symbolizes courage, I think."

"You looked it up?" he asked, though he didn't

know why he was surprised. The quiet girl he'd thought Savannah was all those years would have looked up the meaning of the tree they were planting as a memorial. It stood to reason that the strong woman he knew her to be now would look it up.

"As soon as Amanda said live oaks were what she would want if she ever got trees of her own." She'd looked up other trees, too, but since the planting of them seemed to be a Tyler thing, she hadn't brought up trees of her own. Although, if she could get the music program idea off the ground, she would definitely look into specific trees for that.

"I'm going to have to remedy that situation, and soon," he said.

"She has a birthday coming up. Her eighteenth."

"An important birthday, for sure." He squeezed his arm around her waist. "Thanks for coming with me tonight."

"Thanks for inviting me to commit a random act of tree planting that neither of us is sure is entirely legal." It was the first time she'd been invited to tag along on a mission that, to her, seemed like something her brother and their friends would have done as kids. It made her feel as if she was part of their group. Part of him. She liked that.

"Speaking of legal, we're probably really pushing our luck that no one has come by yet." Collin wrapped the hose and stowed it, along with the other tools, in the back of the truck.

Savannah wasn't ready to leave just yet. She stood near the tree, arms folded over her chest, just watching it. Collin came back, put his arms around her middle and pulled her against him in the darkness.

Savannah leaned against him for a long moment, content. "There's something I need to tell you." Something she'd wanted to tell him since the night of the benefit, but there had been too much to do. She'd needed to get back to the staging area, then everyone had been celebrating, and although the benefit was less than a week in the past, she'd found a million more reasons to keep this to herself. She didn't want to keep it to herself anymore, though. She wanted him to know just how important his love was to her.

"Anything."

"The song I wrote for the benefit?" She drew in a slow breath, wrapping her arms around his. "I didn't only write that song about Mama Hazel or Dad or Levi. I wrote it about you."

Collin pressed his lips to the crown of her head and then turned her in his arms to kiss her mouth. "I'm honored."

"Twila wants to record it, but I'm going to keep it. It's ours, nobody else's."

"Thank you. I can't write you a song, but I could plant a tree for you. What kind would you want?"

"Any tree?"

"Any."

She was quiet for a long moment. "Well, the cherry tree symbolizes love and the wisteria is planted for romance."

"You've done your homework."

"When you're in love with an orchardist, you start thinking about tree-type things," she said. "Redwoods are for wisdom. There are a lot of choices. Elders symbolize fairylands."

"I could surprise you—plant one of each at the cabin."

"I don't want them all." She knew exactly what she wanted and she didn't care that it was probably cliché. "The wisteria is the prettiest."

"Then wisteria is what you'll get. How about at the cabin?"

"A lifelong symbol of our love...where it all started. I like it."

"Technically, it started at the Slope."

"I don't think Merle would like a wisteria tree planted in the middle of his dance floor."

"Good point." Collin threaded their fingers together. "I love you," he said.

Savannah relaxed in his embrace, wanting to hold on to the moment as long as possible.

"I love you," she said after a long moment and pressed her lips to his. The kiss was sweeter than any she'd tasted and Savannah realized it was because she was home.

Home was the sweetest feeling she'd ever felt.

* * * * *